The Second Chance
Shoe Shop

MEL SHERRATT WRITING AS

MARCIE STEELE

The Second Chance
Shoe Shop

bookouture

Published by Bookouture

An imprint of StoryFire Ltd.
23 Sussex Road, Ickenham, UB10 8PN
United Kingdom

www.bookouture.com

ISBN: 978-1-78681-004-5
eBook ISBN: 978-1-78681-003-8

All you need is #shoelove

PROLOGUE

Last Christmas

Riley glanced over her list, all of its items crossed through with a black line. It was Christmas Eve and even if she had forgotten to buy anything – which she was certain she hadn't – there was no way she was going out again. The fridge was crammed full of festive food. Champagne was chilling. The table was laid for two, crackers on the plates, candles waiting to be lit, the scent of mulled wine still heavy in the air from the ones she'd lit earlier. All she was waiting for now was Nicholas to arrive before she could relax and enjoy herself. She checked her watch – 5:30 p.m. Only two hours to go.

Underneath the Christmas tree, several presents of all shapes and sizes were wrapped in shiny paper, with tinsel bows and curled silver ribbon. Riley had agonised for ages over what to buy Nicholas, alongside stocking-fillers of DVD box sets, after-shave, a large chocolate selection box and the obligatory cheesy Santa socks. In the end, she'd chosen a watch, not too expensive but costing enough that he would know how much she cared.

Already having taken a long and luxurious bath, she smiled fondly as she looked at the new clothes she had laid out on her bed. As a child it had been a Christmas tradition to have new clothes to wear on Christmas Day, something that both she and her sister, Evie, had continued. Once Christmas dinner was over, there had been Christmas pyjamas to slob out in. She'd bought Nicholas pyjamas, knowing she would have great fun removing them before they went to bed.

She did indeed feel as excited as a child at Christmas. This would be the first time Nicholas had stayed over at the flat. He lived in Newcastle-Upon-Tyne, visiting Hedworth for work once or twice a week. They'd met after he'd rushed into the shoe shop she managed, complaining that the sole had come off his shoe and he needed to buy another pair immediately. Only a few minutes after leaving the shop, he'd come back and handed her a business card. She hadn't called him but he had called the shop, several times, until she'd agreed to go out with him. They'd been dating for four months now.

Yet as Christmas came upon them, she'd found herself wanting to spend more time with Nicholas. A few hours here and there during the week wasn't enough for her any more. She'd wanted to bring up the subject of whether they would share Christmas Day in Newcastle or Hedworth for quite some time. She hadn't been to his house yet. It was awkward with her working across six days a week, and more convenient for him to come visit her. But Christmas was different. She only had a couple of days off before the post-Christmas sales started, and she wanted to spend them with him.

When Riley had broached the subject, Nicholas's face had been comical to say the least, and she thought she'd somehow misread the situation. But he'd laughed when she'd suggested that, saying that she had only taken him by surprise. He'd been planning to take her up to Newcastle, but he'd fallen behind in decorating his living room and it wouldn't be finished in time for Christmas. It suited Riley more for him to come to her flat. And she knew he'd be impressed with her organisational skills in ensuring that they had the perfect first Christmas together.

A text message alert pinged and Riley reached for her phone. It was from her friend Ash. She was going into Hedworth that evening and had sent a photo of the dress she had bought that afternoon in the December sales. Riley quickly texted a message back and then shimmied into her woollen dress. Grabbing her heels from inside the wardrobe, she slipped them on and gave herself a once over in the mirror. Brown hair straightened to perfection: check. Dress fitting snugly: check. Make-up accentuating her brown eyes, slimming down her chubby cheeks and plumping up her lips: check.

Her phone rang. Her heart did an involuntary flip when she saw it was Nicholas. She answered the call as she walked through to the living room.

'Where are you?' she asked, not giving him time to speak. 'How much longer before you'll be here?'

There was silence down the line.

'Nicholas?' Still silence. 'Nicholas? Hello? Are you there?' She took the phone away from her ear to see the time ticking on the screen. The call was still connected.

Finally he spoke. 'Yes, I'm here.'

'Oh!' Relief flooded through her, then a second of panic. 'You're not driving, are you?'

'No, I— I—'

His pause was long enough for her to pick up on his anxiety. 'What is it?' she asked.

'I'm a bastard. I'm a coward. A liar. A snake.'

'What do you mean? Nicholas, have you been drinking?'

'I've never been more sober in my life. That's why this hurts so much.'

'What does? You're not making sense to—'

'I'm— I'm married.'

'Yes, I know you're married. You told me you were going through a divorce and—' She stopped.

'I'm still with my wife. I lied about us splitting up.'

And then Riley began to understand.

'You're not coming, are you?'

'I'm sorry. I've wanted to tell you the truth for some time now but I—'

'*You* told me I would have you to myself for two days. I have presents, food, champagne!'

'I just couldn't. I wanted to stay with you but it's impossible to leave my wife and kids.'

Riley squeezed the bridge of her nose and closed her eyes momentarily. She remembered the hurt in her mother's eyes when Riley had told her she wouldn't be spending Christmas Day with the family. That was a tradition too.

'How old are they?' He'd told her that Bethany and Callum were grown up, Bethany at university and Callum at college. But then again, Riley was beginning to see that anything he had told her may have been a lie.

'Five and three.'

She gasped. 'You bastard!'

'I'm sorry!'

'Why didn't you tell me?' she yelled. 'Instead of letting me down right at the last minute.'

'I couldn't find the words. I want to be with you, Riley. But it's impossible.'

As he continued to apologise, she glanced around the room, through blurry eyes, at the lights twinkling on the Christmas tree, at the carrot and the empty glass she had left on a plate to fill with sherry at midnight as a bit of fun, the presents under the tree that would never be opened. It couldn't be more perfect.

Now, it couldn't be more pathetic.

She disconnected the phone and sat down with a thump.

'Merry Christmas, Riley,' she said before bursting into tears.

CHAPTER ONE

Riley Flynn stared out of the window as the bus moved slowly along in the rush-hour traffic. It was a cold March morning, with not even a hint of the promise of spring. Rain poured down, the dreary weather matching her mood. She was only minutes away from work, and the thought didn't thrill her in the slightest. In fact, nothing could make Riley smile at the moment.

Life had changed dramatically over the past few months. On Christmas Eve she had been full of festive spirit, hoping to spend the following day with the man of her dreams. Only, he'd turned out to be her worst nightmare because when he'd told her about himself he had left out one important, one *crucial,* detail. He was married. Not married in the 'I love her but we have children and I can't leave her yet' sense, but married in a 'I love her to bits and I love my family as much as I love having a bit on the side' sort of way.

A bit on the side. Had she seen the signs? Had the truth been lit up in flashing pink neon lights and she had ignored it? Looking back – because she had analysed *everything* since she'd found out the truth – she might have had an inkling, but he'd told her he worked away from home, that he couldn't see her as often as he would have liked. Long-distance had suited her at first, as she was still getting over the break up of a previous long-term relationship. But had it really suited her? Or had she only made herself believe that it had? She knew she'd been getting anxious, wanting more from Nicholas. But to ring her on Christmas Eve and do that to her? She'd never forgive him for lying and cheating.

She wiped a hand across the steamy window, staring out at the street as the bus inched along. People rushing past, umbrellas up, or diving into one of the row of shops just outside the town. They came to a halt again a few seconds later, but at least they had nearly reached the High Street now. The main bus station in the centre of Hedworth was only a few minutes away, and once she got off the bus another week of shoes, shoes and more shoes at Chandler's would begin.

Even though the shop was closed on Sundays, the email she'd received on Saturday was still on her mind. The owner, Suzanne, was coming in to see the staff. She and her husband, Max, hardly ever called in. The last time had been in January when Suzanne had told them that sales needed to improve. From the tone of this last email, it was clear to Riley that she was going to bring bad news.

There wasn't much competition for shoes in Hedworth, apart from the larger Debenhams store and the odd corner displays in some of the high street chain stores. Even though sales had been slow, Riley had thought things would pick up again, and that Chandler's was well known enough to weather the economic storm.

Dan and Sadie had been on her mind constantly on Sunday. She had sat on the information from the email for the rest of the weekend, choosing not to tell her work colleagues and spoil the one day a week they had off. Dan Charles and Sadie Stewart worked full-time as shop assistants. Like her, they had worked at Chandler's for years. What would happen to them all if the shop closed down? Being such a close team, Sadie and Dan had been there to see Riley through her last break up, with Tom, two years back. More recently, Riley and Dan had both been there to support Sadie when her husband, Ross, who they had all known for many years, died of cancer nine months ago.

'So, do you fancy a pizza at mine this evening?' a voice said.

Riley had almost forgotten that her friend, Ashleigh Whittaker, was sitting beside her on the bus. She and Ash lived in the same new-build block of flats, two flats on each of its three floors. For twelve months they had shared one of the flats, but when another one became available to rent, Ash moved out. The flats were fairly small for two people, despite the appeal of sharing the rent. Now, Riley lived at number four and Ash below her at number two. Most mornings they caught the bus together.

Riley turned sharply, cricking her neck. 'It's eight thirty in the morning, Ash.' She rubbed at her neck to ease the pain. 'You're always thinking about food!'

Ash pulled out her earphones, wrapped the cord around her fingers and then shoved them into her pocket. She pushed her blonde fringe out of her eyes and grinned. 'I love my food more than life itself.'

'Yes, you eat like a pig but you stay as thin as a rake, even if they are the worst clichés to use,' Riley muttered, but her tone was friendly. When she had turned up at Ash's flat at Christmas, sobbing uncontrollably, like the good friend she was Ash had comforted Riley as best she could. The words 'sneaky bastard' and 'two-timing lowlife' had peppered the air for quite some time. Since then, Riley hadn't told anyone else what had happened. Humiliated by it all, she'd thought it best to say that she'd cooled things down with Nicholas of her own accord.

The bus pulled into Hedworth bus station. Ash sighed as she got to her feet. Riley shuffled along the seat before following her down the aisle. They joined the throng of people on the short walk into the town centre.

'Nicholas was an idiot.' Ash put an arm around Riley's shoulder and brought her close for a hug. 'You can do much better than him.'

'I'm thirty-two and haven't even been engaged once, never mind six times like a lot of women my age before they settle down,' she joked. 'I don't think I'm marriage material.'

'You don't need a man to live a fulfilled life!'

'Says the woman who slept with a twenty-three-year-old on Saturday night!'

'Ah, yes.' Ash grinned. 'Still reliving the memory.'

Noticing her cheeks reddening, Riley pushed Ash playfully as they walked up the stone steps towards the upper level of the High Street. A few minutes later, they said their goodbyes. Ash worked in Hedworth Shopping Centre, on the first floor, in a clothes shop called Jazz. Between the two of them, Riley and Ash could kit themselves out quite cheaply with staff discounts on fashion and shoes. Although Riley often bought clothes from Jazz, it was a rare occasion that a pair of shoes would come into her own shop that she or Ash would ever buy. Chandler's sold sensible shoes – lace-ups for school children, boots for workmen, comfortable flats for women.

Catching a glimpse of her reflection in the window of the chemist's, Riley sighed. The razor-sharp hairdo she had started out with that morning after straightening it had transformed into a dark, wavy mess. Her coat almost hung off her small frame with the amount of weight she'd lost recently. Unlike Ash, who always tried to feed her up, Riley wasn't into comfort eating. If anything upset her, she went off food altogether.

She pulled back her shoulders and quickened her step. It was time she pushed Nicholas to the back of her mind, focused on work and began to think about herself for a change.

Hedworth was a small market town, close to neighbouring Somerley. Sampson Street was the main shopping street, well known for its bars and restaurants. In the middle was Hedworth Shopping Centre, set over two floors. The indoor market had been relocated and was now on the ground floor, and was a good place to find fresh and locally produced food, and stalls that sold crafts supplies, T-shirt printing services, carpets and flowers, as well as a cafe.

Most of the streets had been pedestrianised three years back, with seating areas put in and stone pots filled with flowers.

Chandler's Shoe Shop was in one of the oldest rows of buildings in Hedworth. The shop front gleamed with welcoming, freshly-painted woodwork and large windows to let in the light, as well as showcase their stock. But that hadn't always been the case.

A year earlier, a team of builders had been hired to modernise the shop, put in the windows at either side of the door, install easy-clean laminate flooring and paint the walls a bright cream. The floor space had been cleared as much as was possible, with white shelving replacing the dark wood, and four leather-look cubes had been pushed together in the middle of the shop for customers to sit on whilst they tried the shoes.

Up ahead, Dan and Sadie were waiting for her.

'I hate drizzly rain,' she told them.

'Ah, that rain that gets you wet,' Sadie muttered. 'Where did that silly saying come from? All rain will get you wet if you're out in it.'

'I look like a drowned rat.'

'You look as gorgeous as ever,' said Dan, waving Riley's comment away before rubbing the palm of his hand over his head. 'And at least you have hair. I'd kill not to be losing mine.'

Riley located her keys and unlocked the front door. Sadie switched on the main lights and shrugged off her coat, brown curls cascading down her back as she pulled off her woollen hat.

'I can't wait for the summer,' she said. 'I hate winter with a passion.'

'Sea, sand and plenty of the other. Give me some of that right now.' Dan handed his coat to Sadie. 'Your turn,' he smiled sweetly.

Riley grinned and passed her coat to Sadie too. The shop had been refitted to a high and modern standard upstairs, but behind the scenes it left a lot to be desired. The basement where their staffroom was located wasn't a nice place to be, so they avoided it as much as possible.

'How was your weekend?' Riley asked Dan as she made her way to the till.

'So-so.' Dan flicked on several switches as he followed her.

'Daaaan,' she said.

'Yeeesss?' he replied.

'You said you had a big date on Saturday.' Riley raised her eyebrows inquisitively.

'It didn't turn out to be a big date. The woman I met was about five foot two.' Dan pointed to his head. 'She was so tiny, I could have eaten her and I wouldn't have been full.'

Riley laughed. At six foot two, Dan towered over most people. He had joined a dating agency in January and the stories of his escapades and near misses had become the highlight of each morning for Riley and Sadie in the few minutes before they opened the shop.

Sadie joined them. 'What are you two talking about?' she asked.

'Dan's latest date.'

'Ah. So this one wasn't a match either?'

'Definitely not.' Dan shook his head. 'Setting aside the fact that I turned into the hunchback of Notre Dame every time I spoke to her, she was not on my wavelength. I mean, she enjoys watching *The Sopranos* and *Breaking Bad* over TOWIE and Corrie.'

Riley caught Sadie glancing at her and rolled her eyes to the ceiling. There was something wrong with every woman Dan dated. She wondered if he ever wanted to settle down or if the dating game kept him on the market, open to relationships but not exactly interested in having one. More likely he was still nursing his broken heart after splitting up with his partner, Sarah. Riley tried not to laugh out loud. With the two of them unlucky in love, Chandler's was like a lonely hearts club at the moment.

'I love *The Sopranos*,' Sadie teased. 'Do you not like me?'

'I *love* you, you daft mare,' Dan teased. 'But you're my friend anyway. I want a woman to fall for, not another BFF.'

Riley flounced off then, mildly irritated by Dan's banter. Why did everyone think that having someone to love was the be-all and end-all? It wasn't.

'*Get a grip, Riley Flynn,*' she spoke in a hushed tone.

'What was that?' Dan turned towards her.

'Oh, nothing.' Riley shrugged. 'I'm just deciding what exciting task to tackle first today.'

Riley booted up the computer and scanned through her emails while Sadie and Dan opened up the shop. Dan turned the radio on, and almost immediately a Pharrell Williams song began playing. Riley dipped her head quickly behind the computer screen.

'Riley, they're playing our song!' Dan cried out, making the one person who had come into the shop jump in the process. 'Sadie!'

'I'm not in the mood.' Sadie marched past him quickly. 'You'll have to do it by yourself today.'

'But,' Dan grabbed her arm and pulled her back, 'you know the rules. Whenever it comes on, we dance. No matter how we

are feeling, no matter what we are doing. It's our thing! Come
on, Riley!'

But Riley wasn't listening. As Dan and Sadie stood side by
side in the middle of the shop floor, clapping and dancing to
'Happy', she re-read the email she had received on Saturday, her
shoulders drooping more with each line.

As she was still the shop manager for now, Riley decided to
leave her staff dancing to the remainder of the record. Let them
have a bit of fun while she worked out what the long-term ef-
fects of the email would be.

She went downstairs to the staffroom and made coffee for
them all. Then, adding a packet of biscuits to the tray, she went
back up to the shop floor.

It was time to break the news.

CHAPTER TWO

After handing out cups of coffee, Riley sipped from hers as she watched Sadie finish off a sale to a young woman with a toddler. The little girl had tried everyone's patience for the last ten minutes, screaming as Sadie and her mum tried to put a shoe on her tiny foot. She was safely tucked away in her pushchair now, still sniffling, her eyes red from crying.

Sadie was a natural with the younger customers. She helped out with the children when they came into the shop with their parents and was always ready to reward them with a sticker once a sale had been made. She had a 'yummy mummy' look to her, and dressed to highlight her pear-shaped figure. Delicate curls framed her round face, her smile creating dimples at each side of her mouth. Shiny brown eyes held her grief over the death of her husband far more than she'd ever realise.

'There you go, Lacey.' Sadie pressed a smiley face sticker onto the little girl's coat. 'That's for being such a good girl for me and Mummy.'

Riley glanced at Dan, who was rearranging the shoes in the window yet again. They were trying to sell the overstock of the boots after a mild winter had let them down. Even though he was over six feet tall, Dan was slightly overweight for his frame. He had a small beer belly and a double chin, though it wasn't as bad as Dan made out when he was poking fun at himself. He called himself Fat Dan, just in case anyone beat him to it, he said. His lack of hair made his face appear rounder than it was, but he had smiling eyes and a positive disposition that had instant appeal.

Riley watched as he picked up a red Dr. Martens shoe and put it next to a pair of purple Ugg-lookalike boots. Then he picked it up and put it next to another pair of shoes. In the end, he sighed loudly before putting it back where it had been to begin with and coming out of the window display with a look of resignation. He tutted, brushing dust off his jumper.

Each of them wore the shop uniform of black trousers and a red sweatshirt with the shop's name embroidered on it. The sweaters were new, and a bit of a luxury as far as Riley was concerned. Suzanne said the team needed to present a united image. Branding was important, she had chanted at them, as if they didn't know this. But didn't Suzanne realise that there was more to branding than the shop's name? Chandler's couldn't make up its mind about what it wanted to be.

Riley had fond memories of Albert Chandler. He was a gentleman in every sense of the word. Women had flocked to his shop to buy their shoes because they loved to be served by him. She smiled to herself as she recalled how women would practically gasp as he slipped a shoe on their stockinged feet, talking persuasively to them the whole time. His sales technique was brilliant, if a little lewd.

The last time both Max and Suzanne had come to see the staff they had been all airs and graces, nice as pie, before hitting them with the bombshell that the shop was under threat of closure. There had been no thought for the feelings of the staff, who had worked there for many years; just the relentless noise coming from Max as he bleated on about drops in revenue, increasing competition and 'building a viable business model'. Riley had wanted to shout out, to let everyone know that she knew why the shop was losing money, yet she kept the truth to herself. If it became detrimental to the shop's future, however, she would tell Dan and Sadie what had been going on.

'What's up, Riley?' asked Dan as he helped himself to a biscuit. 'You look a million miles away.'

Riley looked from Dan to Sadie and back again. She couldn't put it off any longer.

'I have bad news,' she said.

'Please don't say what I'm thinking,' Dan pouted. 'I can't bear to see Dumb and Dumber again after the last time.' When Riley didn't say anything, Dan froze. 'They *are* coming?'

'Suzanne is coming. Not Max.'

'But that can only mean one thing, can't it? They're going to close the shop.'

'No, they're not.' Riley shook her head. 'We won't let them.'

'We won't have any choice after what they said in January!'

'When is she coming?' asked Sadie.

'Tomorrow evening,' Riley replied. 'Once we close, she wants to speak to us.'

'Sounds about right, give us a rollicking on our own time,' Dan tutted.

'I'm not sure I can stay too long,' said Sadie.

'Don't worry, I'll keep them in touch with the time,' said Riley.

A silence fell.

'What are we going to do if they say we're going to close?' Sadie asked, her voice quiet.

'We're not closing,' Riley repeated with determination. 'We know this shop better than anyone. We can see its potential, even if they can't.'

'They're just money-grabbing bastards,' cried Dan. 'They come in here swanning around as if they run the place, when we all know it's down to you that the shop has survived for this long.'

Riley shook her head, although she knew it was partly true. She often wondered what would happen if she were to move on.

No one was indispensable, but being left to her own devices for so long meant that she could run the shop with minimal supervision. Take her out of the equation, and it might take the shop a while to recover.

'We'll just have to get on with it until tomorrow,' she replied. 'In the meantime, we'll keep an open mind.' She raised her hands in the air. 'You never know – they might be calling to give us a bonus.'

'Riley, you are too funny.' Dan shook his head in despair.

'What we need is to be one step ahead, so to speak,' said Sadie.

'That's good.' Dan nudged her. 'One step ahead.'

'If only we *were* one step ahead,' Riley sighed. 'I'd be lost if the shop closes. I don't know what I'd do.'

'It won't close,' said Sadie firmly. 'We won't let it.'

'Let's see what Suzanne has to say first.' Riley got to her feet as an elderly lady shuffled in, pushing a tartan shopper in front of her. 'It might not be as bad as it seems.'

'You're right,' agreed Dan. 'We won't let them grind us down until we know what we're dealing with.'

Riley tried to make her smile seem real. Deep down, she knew more than any of them that if things didn't pick up soon, they would indeed be doomed. Chandler's might very well close. And then they would all be walking the streets, looking for jobs.

Riley was still awake just after midnight. She flicked on the lamp next to her bed, knowing that she wasn't going to settle any time soon. She couldn't get the impending meeting with Suzanne out of her mind.

Riley had been the manager at Chandler's for eight years. After a long illness, during which she had managed the store single-handedly, the original owner, Albert Chandler, had passed away. For the staff, things had gone downhill from there. All of a sudden the jobs they loved had become more about sales targets, weekly meetings and appraisals – words that none of them had known much about until Suzanne and Max Woodward had marched in and announced that they wanted to compete with every other shop on the High Street, and become *the* shop to go to for shoes. Riley had known instantly that they would fail. She bought most of her shoes from Jazz. They were much more fashionable and often half the price.

It had been so much harder to work for Suzanne than Albert, despite the fact that she and Max still left everything to Riley. All the ideas she put forward had been tossed to one side. Suzanne knew best, it seemed. No matter how persuasively Riley argued that the shop should stock a shoe she had seen in a fashion magazine, there was always confrontation. And Suzanne would constantly tell Riley that she wasn't managing the staff effectively, because their targets weren't being met. The targets Suzanne had given them would never be met in London, never mind Hedworth, with its population of less than 200,000. Targets were all well and good, if they could be achieved realistically. Riley knew all about S.M.A.R.T. and *Getting Things Done*. Goals were one thing, targets were another. Sales were slipping, that was a fact, and just like everything in her life they had spiraled down the drain since New Year.

Riley picked up her Kindle and opened up the book she was reading. So far *Chasing Pavements* had been all about a woman falling in love. Every time she started to read a new scene, something would remind her of how lonely she felt. After what happened with Nicholas her heart hadn't had time to mend. On top of that, splitting up with her first love, Tom, had made Riley very wary of getting into a long-term relationship again.

She and Tom had been together for eight years. They'd met in their early twenties, after he had been travelling for a year and come back home to settle in Hedworth. He was so worldly wise, fascinating her from the offset with his adventurous spirit, and she fell for him immediately. They bought a house together, planned to marry and start a family, but that had never happened. After six years he upped and left, saying he felt stifled by their relationship. Riley found out much later that he'd been more interested in a woman he worked with. The last she'd heard was that they'd moved to Australia to start up a new business.

It hadn't meant that she wasn't at fault too. Riley thought that affairs usually started because one person wasn't happy in the relationship. If they were happy, they wouldn't stray. They wouldn't feel trapped. But it had hurt that all her plans had been stopped in their tracks. It was the reason she had fallen for Nicholas and his charms. Usually she had a good radar for idiots but this time it had failed her.

With that last sorrowful thought, she scrolled through her reading list. There was bound to be a crime novel or psychological thriller that would be far better suited to her mood.

CHAPTER THREE

Sadie had been up for over an hour and it was still only six thirty. She relished the peace and quiet of the morning, knowing it would be shattered when her daughter, Esther, woke up. Esther was six years old, and a whirlwind at the best of times, but until the mornings started to get that little bit lighter Sadie would be safe for a few minutes longer.

Luckily for her, when she went to work Sadie could drop Esther off at her mother-in-law's, safe in the knowledge that she would be well looked after. While Paul Stewart, Sadie's father-in-law, worked full-time, his wife, Christine, took Esther to and from school as well as watching her during the holidays and when Sadie was at work. Sadie couldn't even begin to think about the possibility of the shop closing. Her wages were her only source of income now and she wouldn't be able to cope without them.

Christine and Paul were always making reference to Ross being 'up in Heaven', so Esther hardly ever got too upset. It took the burden from Sadie, meaning she could grieve alone when she needed to, not worrying about her grief rubbing off on her daughter if she overheard. It wouldn't be easy for a child so young to lose her dad and then have a mum who wasn't capable of putting on a brave face.

After making another cup of tea, Sadie sat down at the kitchen table. Her journal was still there from last night. She opened it up and read through the words she'd written:

It's been nearly a year since Ross died, yet every morning I still feel like it was yesterday. I still feel his presence around the house - is that mad? I often hear a noise and think it's *him, maybe in the living room when I'm in the kitchen, and I rush in half expecting him to be watching a football match. I see him everywhere I go. I'll see a dark-haired man on the street and want to touch him so he'll turn around and I can be sure it isn't Ross. So I hurry to catch him up, wanting to see his face, then feel disappointed once I know it's someone else.*

Esther has been my world since Ross left us. In a way, she's had to grow up a lot quicker than I would have liked, and I blame myself for that. Those first few months were bad. But now we are more than over the worst - we are a team of two. I feel blessed to have her.

Sadie paused for a moment, remembering when Ross had died. For a long while, she didn't know if he would be coming home again, and whether it might be the last time she would see him at the hospice. She'd been on constant alert, waiting for the call. She didn't want him to pass away without her having the chance to say goodbye.

She'd needed Esther to be there too. Both sets of parents thought she was too young but Sadie was adamant that she stayed until the end. Esther had been only five but Sadie had needed her there. She knew she was being selfish, but she hoped one day that their daughter would take comfort from it, that she was with her daddy when he died.

Her shoulders drooped. Everyone said it would get easier with time. It hadn't, but to the outside world she *was* getting over it. People were even asking her when she was going to find someone new. As if that would help erase her pain.

She continued to read the words she had written the night before:

I'm dreading the anniversary of his death - what do other people do on those days? Do I take Esther out, maybe somewhere Ross and I used to go? Share memories of the past? Or do I make new memories for her? Or get photos of Ross out and create a collage, or something? What do I do?

Somehow it helped Sadie to cope if she wrote down her feelings. It was better than spilling it all on the Grieve Together website that she had joined. She'd been a member of the site for a few months now, anonymously, of course, going by the name of Clara Goodwin. She never mentioned any personal details and no one knew Esther's name either, just that 'Clara' had a young daughter.

After a few more minutes she decided to log on to the site to see if her friend Tanya had replied to the last private message she'd sent her. Yes, there it was:

Tanya: *I think it's best that we grieve for however long we need to, don't you? We are over it when we are over it, and if that is never, then that is fine too. Maybe we will move on, but for now, being in limbo is okay.*

Sadie found herself nodding to the empty room. Tanya was a widow too, and they'd formed a bond, often chatting in private rather than for everyone else to see.

Hearing footsteps above her, she closed down her laptop as Esther thundered down the stairs.

'Mummy!' Esther ran towards her with her arms outstretched.

'Morning, poppet.' Sadie gave her a hug and picked her up to sit on her knee. 'What would you like for breakfast today?'

'Toast and strawberry jam.'

'Toast and strawberry jam . . . ?'

Esther nodded vehemently, her brown curly hair, like her mum's, bobbing up and down. Long lashes framed wide brown eyes that reminded Sadie of Ross every time she looked into them. She was a happy child, despite losing one parent at such a young age.

Sadie looked at her but didn't speak.

'Oh!' cried Esther. 'Toast and strawberry jam, please!'

'Good girl.' Sadie put her down on the floor again. 'Right, let's get you dressed, fed and watered and then we're out of here.'

'Morning, Daddy.' Esther waved at the urn which took pride of place on the hearth.

Sadie wrinkled her nose. Talking to the urn was a habit that Esther had developed and, although it made Sadie feel uncomfortable, she was hoping Esther would just grow out of it. Christine thought Sadie was mad to leave the urn on display, but it had been something that Ross had asked. 'Burn me up and keep me on the hearth,' he'd told Sadie when she'd been on one of her regular hospital visits. She remembered batting away his comment, saying that he would have to live forever because he couldn't leave them to fend for themselves. He'd left them barely six months later – a very painful six months for Ross. Sadie had suffered a different kind of pain ever since.

Dan woke to the sound of his phone. Eyes still closed, he reached across to the side of the bed and fumbled about, trying to switch it off. The phone dropped to the floor, still bleeping at him.

He glanced around the bedroom, which was decorated in pale creams and lilacs. It was as homely as a guest bedroom but Dan preferred to remember it as his childhood hovel. He could still picture the numerous posters of Ducati and Kawasaki motorbikes on the walls, socks and trainers piled up in the corner, and the dartboard on the back of the door – the holes were still there, to prove how much he'd practised. For years as a teenager he'd wanted to be a professional darts player, practising at every spare moment until he'd worn the carpet threadbare. But then he'd found girls and his career plan had faltered.

There was a knock on the door.

'Morning, love.' Mary, his mum, came in. She popped a large mug of coffee on his bedside table. 'It's nearly seven, don't go back to sleep.'

'I won't, Mum.' Dan wanted to cover his head with the duvet and do just that, but instead he turned to his side and hoisted himself up onto his elbow. 'Thanks.'

'The weather is still mucky out there, so I'd take the bus rather than your bike, if I were you.' When Dan didn't reply, Mary left the room. She knew better than to try to have a longer conversation at that time of the morning, so all she ever mentioned was the weather. 'Looks like a hot one today,' she'd say. 'It's a bit nippy out there,' she'd tell him. 'It's snowing!' she would exclaim in an excited childish tone.

Rubbing a hand over his head, the blond hair almost the same length as the stubble on his chin, Dan sat up in bed, trying to waken himself and muster enthusiasm for the day ahead. Not for the first time did he wish he had been sleeping next to a woman who was in love with him. Instead, he was back at home with his parents after splitting up with his long-term girlfriend, Sarah, a year ago. Sarah had stayed in the flat they had rented and he had come back to his old room, because he couldn't afford to rent alone. Although it wasn't anything to be ashamed of, given rent and property prices had risen far more than the average salary in Hedworth, Dan felt as if he'd taken a step backwards, and was saving money so that he could move out again. Living at home allowed him to do that, so even though Mary smothered him at times, he'd learned to cope. As mums go, he could have done far worse.

Dan yawned before taking a slurp of his coffee and running a hand over his protruding stomach. Despite his job keeping him on his feet all day, he just didn't seem able to shift the extra kilos. The weight wasn't the reason he and Sarah had split up. Complacency had ruled for the last year of their four-year relationship, ending with Sarah having a one-night stand. It had hurt him deeply, though at first he had tried to forgive her, to forget about it and keep the relationship going.

Sarah had slept with a man after staying somewhere overnight for a two-day conference. She'd told him it had been a long day, she'd had one drink too many at the bar, and when the guy had helped her into his room . . .

Dan turned onto his back and put a hand behind his head. Sarah hadn't seen the man again. It wasn't as if the night had turned into an affair, but she had been mortified at what she had done, enough to tell him and beg for his forgiveness.

It was something he could never have done. He'd never strayed, even though their sex life had been practically non-existent for a few months. He would have had the decency to finish the relationship first. But Sarah sleeping with someone else had made him realise that they were both still in the relationship because they didn't want to admit to each other that it wasn't working.

'Are you out of bed yet?' Mary shouted up the stairs.

'I'm coming!' With an exaggerated sigh, Dan got up, wishing that he actually was coming. He hadn't had sex in four months – and his last escapade hadn't been much to be happy about. He was desperate for a woman to wrap her arms around his chubby waist and say that she loved him.

Stretching as he looked out of the window, he sighed when he saw it was still pouring down. Even so, he decided he would take his bike after all. As well as the exercise, he needed to clear his head. He had more important things to think about right now than his long-dead relationship. Like what Suzanne the dragon would have to say to them all that afternoon . . .

CHAPTER FOUR

Even though she had been up extra-early that morning, Riley only just managed to get to work on time. She and Ash had been walking to the bus stop when their bus had driven past them, several minutes early, and there hadn't been another one for thirty minutes. It was at times like these that she missed her car. Her last one had died when she had taken it for its MOT. She'd toyed with getting another one but wanted to save some money first.

During the rest of the day, a sense of dread crept in as she worried about the meeting. After watching a woman walk around the shop in ten seconds flat and then back out onto the High Street, Riley wandered over to Sadie. She looked as worried as Riley felt.

'They won't close the shop, will they?' Sadie asked, unable to mask the concern in her voice.

'I don't know,' said Riley, truthfully. 'I really hope they don't.'

'So do I,' Dan shouted from the other end of the shop.

Riley nodded, knowing they would have no choice in the matter if it was what Suzanne was coming to talk to them about.

Suzanne hadn't got a clue how to run Chandler's. Unlike her father, she had never wanted to be in the shoe business and had chosen to be a housewife, living the life of luxury as Max climbed the corporate ladder. Max hardly ever visited the shop and hadn't been near since Christmas, thank goodness. Riley hadn't been too happy with him after the last few times he'd visited.

Riley had always had an interest in fashion and had worked in retail since she left college. She was always looking online for the latest trends and the next big thing in shoes, despite not being allowed to stock anything even if she spotted it. She drove Ash mad with her chatter about Twitter and Facebook accounts where she followed lots of the fashionistas. She spent hours on their websites, checking out the latest trends, longing to be able to bring them to Hedworth. Some of the designers loved interacting through social media and she felt as though she knew a few personally.

At 5:00 p.m., Suzanne waltzed in. Chandler's closed at 5:30 p.m., giving her ample time to strut around the shop, checking things out, straightening a shoe here, moving a pair of boots there. Honestly, Riley felt like she was watching a game of chess.

'This display needs a good clean, Riley.' Suzanne wrinkled her nose as she ran a finger over a shelf.

'They were all cleaned this morning,' Riley explained, not wanting her to get the upper hand. 'We have a daily cleaning rota.'

Suzanne raised her perfectly arched eyebrows in answer and glared at her for a moment. Riley couldn't help wondering what Max had ever seen in her. Everything about her was snippy, from the way she held her head to the rough-cut hairstyle which Riley knew must have cost a small fortune to make that messy. Blonde streaks made her look trashy rather than chic for her age of fifty-three, and her expensive, old-fashioned and sensible clothes were an odd combination. But her brusque tone was the worst thing about Suzanne. How she put on an air of authority, thinking she was better than the staff who worked for her.

Suzanne and Max lived in Cheshire, about forty miles north of Hedworth. It was good in one sense, as it had made visits to the shop a rare occurrence. Suzanne liked to keep in touch mostly via stroppy emails, lots of them, several times a week.

Albert had shown Riley photos of his daughter's house once – a five-bedroom palatial villa, with electric gates, a sweeping drive and the best of everything inside. At first Riley had been envious, but the more she'd got to know Suzanne, the more obvious it became that although she had the house and the husband, she wasn't necessarily happy behind closed doors. Riley wondered if that was the reason why she had kept an interest in the shop rather than sell it immediately after Albert died. Perhaps it was her piece of independence.

As Suzanne disappeared into the staffroom, everyone breathed a collective sigh of relief.

'I could drag my nails down a blackboard and the noise wouldn't irritate me as much as hearing her voice,' said Dan, shuddering as he folded his arms.

'Let's just hear what she has to say first,' said Riley, trying to keep her spirits up even though she couldn't have felt less cheerful.

When the shop closed half an hour later, Suzanne reappeared. She was holding a clipboard and tapping on it with a pen.

Riley, Dan and Sadie stood in a line in front of the till, reminding Riley of being at school waiting to go back inside after break.

Suzanne cleared her throat, even though she knew she already had their attention.

'I'm on my own today because Max is working overseas at the moment. But I want you to know that he is as concerned as I am that the shop hasn't been doing well lately,' she told them. 'Well, that's an understatement really. We're losing money.' She looked at each one of them in turn. 'And as we said earlier in the year, things needed to improve. But they haven't.'

'We've had lots of ideas—' Riley started.

'I've already thought of something to spur you on.' Suzanne held up her hand. 'We're going to have a sales competition between you all!'

Riley glanced at Dan and Sadie in turn before staring at Suzanne. 'Is this a joke?' she asked, her brow furrowed.

'No, it isn't,' Suzanne pouted. 'It's something to get you motivated.'

'We don't need motivating!' Riley fumed. 'We're dedicated staff and we want to keep this shop afloat just as much as you do. There's no need to put us into competition with each other. We're a team.'

'A bit of healthy competition never did any harm.'

'It does when it comes with a threat,' said Sadie.

Suzanne turned her head sharply towards her. 'No one is being threatened, Sadie,' she snapped. 'All we are trying to do is instil a bit of—'

'Fear?' Dan joined in. 'You think we'll be prepared to work to make the shop a success while we're not even sure our jobs will still be there at the end of it?'

'How dare you question my integrity,' Suzanne retorted. 'Don't forget that I own this shop, and I have the last say on everything. Whoever brings in the least amount of money during the next three months' – she looked at them all in turn again – 'might need to find somewhere else to work.'

Riley, Dan and Sadie all began to speak at once.

'You can't do this!' cried Dan.

'We've been loyal to this shop for years,' said Sadie.

'We're not just a number on a sheet,' said Riley. 'We've helped build this business up too.'

'You did a great job of that, didn't you?' Suzanne pointed to the shop floor. 'The shop was empty when I arrived and I assume it stayed the same way until you closed the doors?'

Riley's eyes dipped to the floor. Suzanne was right: no one had come in, not even just to have a look before heading home.

'*We* did what we could,' she defended them all, 'and what Albert would let us do. It wasn't easy to move forward with someone who wanted his business to stay the same.'

'You're blaming my dead father?' Suzanne raged.

Riley shook her head. 'Of course I'm not. But you have to admit, the business was failing because he wouldn't move with the times.' She pointed to the electronic till. 'It took us about three years to get that. And the computer is falling apart. If you want us to do a proper job, then you need to give us the tools to do it. And we need to order new ranges of stock, too.'

'We haven't got cash to flash around,' said Suzanne, 'as I'm sure you're well aware.'

Riley opened her mouth to speak but decided against it. If she said what she thought, that Suzanne and Max were both selfish and irresponsible, that Suzanne's car was worth more than her annual salary, and that they were only trying to close the shop so that they could sell on the assets and pocket everything, she would be dismissed on the spot.

'So, on to the competition.' Suzanne tapped her pen on the clipboard again. 'I've made you a chart to put up in the staffroom. You can each record your sales on there. It will spur you on.'

Riley clamped her teeth together again and stayed quiet until Suzanne left and she could speak to Dan and Sadie alone.

'She is *not* taking our shop away from us,' she said as soon as she knew Suzanne was out of earshot. 'We'll just have to come up with some way of bringing in more sales – and splitting them evenly between us so that they either have to choose all of us, or none of us, to leave.'

'Like that's going to happen,' said Sadie. 'Everything you've suggested has been turned down.'

'Maybe.' Riley gnawed on her bottom lip. 'Forget the competition, but if we have to turn this shop around in three months, then we should have free rein to do whatever we see fit. Am I right?'

'Hell, yeah!' Dan whooped.

Sadie smiled. 'I like your style.'

'I think it's high time we had some fun,' said Riley. 'Somehow, we're going to make Chandler's Shoe Shop the talk of Hedworth.'

Riley's flat was identical in layout to Ash's, but it was decorated completely differently. Where Ash's place was full of blacks, whites and chromes, Riley's rooms were full of colour. The living room and kitchen were combined, and she had pale wooden flooring and a floor-to-ceiling window which made the room light and airy.

The kitchen was made up of a row of white units with a black marble-effect worktop. The tiles above created a flash of magenta to match a small settee and armchair. The flat's one bedroom had been decorated in pale lemon with deep purple and grey accessories.

Riley loved that Ash still lived so close. She'd known her since school, and at times like these she missed having her as a flatmate to talk to. Still, at least they had more room to move around, now they had separate flats.

Riley adored the whole feel of her flat, and loved to come home and relax. That evening, after she had been to the gym, she sat watching television. But her mind wasn't on the programme. The meeting with Suzanne had unnerved her more than she'd thought. No wonder she, Dan and Sadie had all been so sharp and snappy. It wasn't like any of them to be rude, overreact or to speak as if they could say whatever they liked.

Riley knew her staff far better than Suzanne ever would. They wouldn't want to compete against one another, no matter what they were threatened with.

For now, if they had no choice but to take part in this competition, for three months they would just add a tick to each of their sales charts in turn, regardless of who made the sale. There could be no overall winner that way. Riley wasn't going to make it easier for one of them to be fired. It didn't bear thinking about.

Riley had never been out of work. At college, she'd opted to study for three A levels, hoping to make up her mind about what she wanted to do as she studied. She'd taken Sociology, Business Studies and Law, passing each one with good grades. But once they were out of the way, still undecided, she'd taken a part-time job as an assistant in a post office. From there, she'd gone to work in Dorothy Perkins as an assistant manager and then she'd been offered the job at Chandler's. And she'd stayed because she enjoyed it. It wasn't a taxing job, unless you had a customer, or a child, from hell. It was a laugh, and she had met two best friends for life in Sadie and Dan. It was cruel for Suzanne to pit them against each other that way. Unless Riley found that Sadie and Dan's friendship over the years counted for nothing now that their livelihoods were on the line, they would all be in this together. One for all, and all that musketeer nonsense!

Since Suzanne's visit, she'd been thinking of ways they could improve their sales. They'd not long ago had the January sale, and now the new summer footwear was about to come in, there was no way there could be any reductions for a while. Despite their complaints about sales being down, neither Suzanne nor Max had ever been keen to reduce prices, or try out any new lines.

Riley was determined to figure something out. She hadn't let her staff down yet and she wasn't about to start.

There was a knock on her door.

'Ash!' she smiled. They hadn't caught the bus together that evening as Ash was working later than usual.

'I thought I'd call to see you before I head out.'

'You look lovely.' Riley checked out her outfit of knee-length black boots and a navy wrap dress underneath a pale blue jacket with a fur collar. Ash's make-up was a little softer than usual, a neutral tone of eyeshadow showing off her blue eyes beneath the choppy fringe of her urchin hairstyle.

'Do you have time for a coffee?' Riley asked, as she held open the door.

'Just a quick one.'

Ash was going out with the twenty-three-year-old 'wonder boy' she'd met on Saturday evening. The text message he'd sent had surprised her – Ash had been convinced he was a one-night stand. But he was taking her out for dinner.

'How did the meeting with Suzanne go?' Ash asked.

'Not too good.' Riley brought the drinks over and sat down, then told Ash about the competition Suzanne suggested and the consequences if things didn't improve.

'What do you think it means?' Ash queried. 'They won't close, will they?'

'They can do what they like. But I'll be so mad if they don't give us an opportunity to do things our way. Between me, Sadie and Dan, we've been in that shop for nineteen years. We know the customers, what they like, what they don't like. I'll try any-thing once but if Suzanne comes in with ideas that won't work, I'm going to have to say something. I can't stand by and watch her ruin Chandler's.'

'You'll be fine.' Ash sounded confident. 'You have been for this long. Don't forget it's down to you that the shop hasn't closed before now.'

'I wish you were right, but I'm nothing special.'

'You're the glue on their heels!' Ash came out in her defence. 'You made that shop what it is today. It might not be what you intended, but it survived because you motivated the staff.'

It was kind of Ash to say that, as well as Dan earlier that day, but Riley disagreed. They worked as a team and she hardly had to keep them under control. Occasionally there was a need to give them a telling off when they weren't pulling their weight, or when Dan fooled around too much, but most of the time everything ran smoothly.

'If we could stock more fashionable items, and at decent prices, we might survive another summer, but even with that I don't think we'll be able to handle another Christmas. At this rate, I'm going to be out of a job come autumn.'

'No, you won't, Riles. You'll work something out. You always do.' Ash glanced at her watch before jumping to her feet. 'I have to go. See you tomorrow.'

Riley nodded. 'Enjoy your date. I want to hear all about it in the morning.'

'I don't have to tell you everything, Riley Flynn,' Ash remarked, her cheeks reddening even more.

'Yes, you do!'

Once Ash had gone, Riley was left with the night stretching out in front of her. Still, she didn't mind so much. It would give her time to do some surfing, catch up with some of the crowd on Twitter. Mind-numbing stuff that might stop her thinking about work.

After the week they'd had, Sunday couldn't come round quick enough. It was just after half past twelve when Sadie opened her front door to find Riley, Dan and Ash standing on her doorstep.

Cooper, who had been Ross's best friend, had arrived earlier and, although the weather had been quite overcast, he'd started tidying the garden for spring. It had only begun to rain during the last hour.

'Christ on a bike, it's lashing down out there,' Ash exclaimed, shaking her head. Droplets of water ran off the hood of her coat.

Riley gave Sadie two bottles of wine. 'We'll be needing a hot toddy instead of these!' she cried.

'What about me?' Dan ran a hand over his head, his tone teasing as he looked at Riley pointedly. 'My hair is such a mess.'

Riley pushed him playfully into the hall.

Sadie grinned as she closed the door behind them, watching them troop through to the tiny kitchen at the back of the house. They made more noise than Esther when her friends were visiting.

'Cooper!' cried Ash as she spotted him drying off his hands. She draped her arms around his neck. 'How are you, me old devil? I haven't seen you in, oh, let's see, a week maybe?'

Cooper blushed as she hugged him. 'Hey, Ash.'

Although his first name was David, Cooper had been known by his surname at school and it had stuck with him throughout his life, so much so that he always introduced himself as that. Sadie couldn't remember the last time anyone had called him David.

Along with his cheeky grin, Cooper had dazzling blue eyes underneath thick eyebrows. His skin darkened at the sight of sun, and his business as a handyman, being outdoors often, meant that he had a permanent T-shirt tan during the summer months. There wasn't an ounce of fat on his frame, his skinny jeans fitting perfectly. A tribal tattoo peeping over the top of his pale blue shirt collar was the only thing that might make him seem a little menacing.

'Where's Christine?' Riley turned around in a full circle. 'Is she upstairs playing with Esther?'

'She's not coming,' said Sadie. 'Paul isn't working so they're going out for lunch on their own. Kind of glad, really.' She looked a bit sheepish as she popped the wine on the side and busied herself getting out glasses. 'It's been quite full-on with her this week.'

Riley grimaced. 'It doesn't get any easier for her, does it? How are you?' She rubbed gently at Sadie's arm.

An uncomfortable silence dropped on the room, as if suddenly it struck everyone that Ross had been gone for a nearly a year. They had been a tight group of friends for years. Ross, Dan and Cooper. Sadie, Riley and Ash. They'd had some great late nights – a little less often since Esther was born – and they had been planning on catching up on a child-less weekend away when Ross had been diagnosed with cancer.

Sadie looked away for a moment, concentrating on getting the wine in the glasses before it went all over the table as her hands shook.

Esther broke up the sombre atmosphere as she came thundering down the stairs. Arriving in the doorway wearing a pink dress and navy woollen tights, her hair in bunches, she threw herself at Dan and wrapped her arms around his thighs.

'Dan, I can do a handstand!' she said. 'Shall I show you?'

'But you have a skirt on, missy,' Sadie reminded her. 'You don't want everyone to see your drawers?'

'What are drawers?' Esther looked up at Dan, a face full of innocence.

Sadie giggled as everyone turned to see what Dan would say.

He bent down and whispered into Esther's ear.

Esther gasped, her hand covered her mouth and then she laughed loudly. 'My knickers!'

Sadie shooed them all out of the kitchen. 'Leave me to the dinner and I'll shout you when it's ready. Cooper, there's beer in the fridge for you and Dan.'

Minutes later, as she warmed up the gravy, Sadie heard peals of laughter coming from the living room. Her shoulders drooped. As much as she enjoyed having everyone round, sometimes it made her think too much. Ross used to love their monthly Sunday lunch gatherings, and they'd carried on the tradition as much as possible after his death. Sundays were family days, he'd always told her.

Her parents lived in Dorset now, so she only saw them when she went on longer breaks during the school holidays. They kept in touch online or on the phone. Only that morning, she'd been speaking to her mum on Skype, planning when they would next go for a visit. It would soon be Easter, so if she could take some time off from Chandler's, she'd book train tickets. Esther loved going by train.

Riley came back into the kitchen. 'Need a hand?'

Sadie wiped away a rogue tear that had fallen and smiled at her. 'Yes, thanks!'

'Are you okay?' Riley asked, a concerned look crossing her face.

'I'm fine,' Sadie sniffed, not wanting to meet Riley's eyes.

'No, you're not.' Riley gave her a hug. 'And it's okay if you're not.'

'Just having an off day, that's all.' Sadie clenched her eyes shut, tears stinging. Luckily, she pushed them back.

'Anything in particular brought this on?'

'Just all of us being together sometimes reminds me that Ross isn't here.' Sadie swallowed. 'I don't want to cry in front of Esther.'

'I know.' Riley grabbed a serving spoon. 'Come on, I'll help you to dish the food out before it goes cold.'

Once they had devoured their dinner, followed by apple crumble and custard, Dan sat back and rubbed his stomach. 'I am definitely Fat Dan now,' he grinned. 'But a very happy one. Hey, Cooper, you got any good jokes lined up?' It was as much of a tradition as their Sunday roast for Dan and Cooper to tell a joke or two. Each month they competed for the corniest.

'Always got to get one up on you, my son.' Cooper dropped his spoon into his bowl with a clatter and an appreciative look at Sadie. 'You want to hear a pizza joke?'

'I do!' Esther clapped her hands.

Cooper glanced at them all through narrowed eyes and shook his head. 'Never mind, it's pretty cheesy.'

Everyone groaned as Esther looked up at Cooper in confusion.

'That's not funny.' Then she laughed anyway.

'Okay, here we go.' Dan rubbed his hands together excitedly. 'A farmer in the field with his cows counted one hundred and ninety-six of them, but when he rounded them up he had two hundred.'

'That is so lame!' cried Riley as everyone laughed. 'Surely you boys can do better than that, otherwise we might have to start finding jokes too.'

'Okay, okay.' Cooper held up his hand for silence. 'A pirate walks into a bar with a steering wheel stuck in his pants.'

The room dropped into silence as they waited for the punchline. Cooper drew it out as long as he could.

'And?' asked Sadie.

'The bartender asks, "Doesn't that bother you?" The pirate says, "Oh ahh, it's driving me nuts!"'

'The old ones are the good ones.' Dan held his hand across the table for Cooper to high-five.

'What are nuts, Mum?' asked Esther.

'Cooper!' Ash swiped at his arm but he moved it in time.

'I am the devil.' Cooper gave an evil cackle. 'Well, that's what the women tell me.' He raised his eyebrows. 'Apparently in the sack, I'm hot stuff.'

'In your dreams,' Ash smirked.

'How would you know unless you'd been in my bed?' Cooper squared up to her playfully. 'You'll never be able to share those details with anyone, so my secret is safe.'

'Secret?' scoffed Dan. 'You think you're God's gift to women?'

'It's better than having to rely on a dating website,' Cooper teased Dan. 'You been getting any loving lately?'

'Don't remind me!' Dan held his head in his hands, pretending to sob. 'My latest one was another disaster.'

'Have you seen anything of Sarah, lately?' asked Sadie, knowing that she was okay to bring up her name. Even though the break up had been Sarah's fault, Dan knew that his friends had thought a lot of his ex, before she slept with someone else. 'I still can't believe you two split up.'

'It wasn't meant to be,' Dan sighed dramatically. 'I haven't seen her in a while, to be honest. And we stopped texting shortly after I wouldn't go back to her. I do miss her every now and then, though.'

'She was a laugh,' admitted Ash, 'but I couldn't believe she would do that to you. And you don't have anyone else lined up to bring for lunch yet?'

Dan shook his head. 'I'm doomed, I tell you. Doomed!'

'Our future looks doomed at the moment,' Riley commented.

'I suppose, if Suzanne has her way,' said Dan. 'But then again, we're not going to be taking part in any competition, are we?'

'Good!' Sadie pointed at Dan. 'You're a master salesman – how can I sell shoes like you do?'

'You've either got it or you haven't,' said Dan. Over the years he'd worked at Chandler's, he'd become known for finding the right shoe for absolutely everyone. He had the gift of the gab, if nothing else.

'I was wondering whether to approach the *Hedworth News*,' said Riley. 'I saw an article in the week about a local woman running her business. Perhaps they'd do a write-up on us? What do you think?'

'Maybe we could do a sale and incorporate that into the article?' suggested Sadie.

'You should do something in the shop window,' said Ash. 'People can't help but look when something is different. Get a crowd, take some photos – and sell some shoes!'

'That sounds a great idea.' Cooper glanced at Ash. 'You do have them every now and again.'

Ash punched him and Cooper tried to look hurt.

'It's definitely worth a try,' Dan added. 'As long as we can all be in the photo.'

Riley nodded. 'I'll give them a call tomorrow.'

On the bus to work the next morning, Riley tried to come up with a different angle for a story that the *Hedworth News* might be interested in. She had read the newspaper since she was a teenager. They covered local things with a sense of pride.

Perhaps the fact that Chandler's was still on the High Street after its owner's death could be enough. They had kept it going, despite not being able to do anything they had wanted to make it modern and competitive.

What could she mention that would grab their attention? Should it be about how long they had survived? Or maybe just the fact that they were a local shop would be enough.

Once at the shop, she began going through the outstanding invoices which needed to be paid that week. Dan came straight over to her as soon as he arrived. It seemed she wasn't the only one who had been thinking about things.

He dropped down on the seat next to her in the staffroom. 'Do you think we should get in touch with the *Hedworth News*? Ash is right. We could do something really silly—'

'Or we could come across as professional,' Riley cut in. 'We want to attract customers to the shop, not clowns who won't spend their money.'

'Of course,' Dan grinned.

'Let's see if we can get anyone interested first. You never know, we might not even be worthy of a slot.'

'How come?'

'It's hardly news around these parts, is it? Yet another shop on the High Street with the threat of closure.'

'It *could* be news if we try to *stop* yet another shop on the High Street from closing,' said Dan.

'We'll make it work somehow,' said Riley.

Dan stood up. 'Better go and help Sadie to open up. Shall I take the banner over to the square again?'

'No.' Riley shook her head. 'I'll do it.'

Just ten minutes later, she went back upstairs with the banner underneath her arm. She'd thought it best to run the idea of a feature past Suzanne first but as there was no answer when she called, she left a voicemail on her phone.

'There's a reporter coming later this morning,' she told Dan and Sadie.

'Ooh, we're going to be in the paper,' Dan cried excitedly. 'Do we know when it will run?'

'Later this week, hopefully,' said Riley.

Sadie gave her a huge grin. 'You're a star.'

Riley tried to put on a brave face as she walked across the High Street in the direction of the town square. Situated outside the shopping centre and the indoor market, there would be lots of passing trade to see the banner. The trouble was, Riley wasn't sure anyone would see the banner who hadn't already seen it for years. They needed something new.

'Another sale?' someone shouted to her.

Riley turned to see a woman with dark hair tied back in a ponytail and wearing a polo shirt with a logo on it. It was Nicci Worthington. She worked on the fruit stall in the market.

'Hi, Nicci, how's married life treating you?' she asked.

'It's nearly a year, can you believe it?'

Nicci's grin told Riley all she needed to know. 'Yes, and I suppose everyone is asking you about the patter of tiny feet,' Riley laughed. She'd been asked all the time when she had been with Tom. People were so predictable.

Nicci rolled her eyes. 'I'm happy enough being an aunty for now. Our Amy is seven months old. I can't believe that, either.'

'How is Jess doing?' Jess was Nicci's sister-in-law and worked at the family sweet stall.

'She's fine. They're both fine,' said Nicci. 'I must admit, the baby certainly calmed Jess down. It's brought the family together too, as well as my sister's wedding. I guess the men will be heading your way to buy formal shoes soon. Only two months to go!'

'You're going to be a bridesmaid for Louise and Mark, I hear?'

'Yes, and my sister had better not dress me up in anything too pink, either!'

Riley laughed as Nicci waved and went on her way. She attached the final loop of the banner in place, checked to see it was level and swiped her hands together. Perfect.

She made her way back to the shop, her thoughts returning to the newspaper journalist who was calling that morning.

Although she was looking forward to seeing Chandler's in the paper, she knew an article might only increase sales in the short term, if at all. It wouldn't be enough to keep the shop afloat. Still, anything was worth a shot to get the message to the people of Hedworth that the shop needed their help.

Half an hour later, Riley looked up from the till as a woman came into the shop. She strode across the floor towards her with purpose, long red hair flying behind her. She wore a grey trouser suit, a white shirt and black heels. Before reaching the till, she pushed black, designer, thick-rimmed glasses back up her nose. Green eyes shone from behind the lenses.

'Hi, I'm Kim Nash,' she said, holding out her hand. 'We spoke on the phone.'

'Hi, yes. I'm Riley Flynn, the manager. Thank you for coming to see us.'

Kim glanced around. 'Do you have an office or do you want to sit here?'

'Here will be just fine.' Riley pointed to the leather cubes at the back of the shop. 'I doubt we'll be busy enough to get moved from these by people trying on shoes, but if we do, we can go and grab a coffee at Ray's Cafe down the street.'

'I thought business was good?' Kim's ears pricked up.

'It is!' Riley cursed inwardly. She'd better be careful what she said or else it might get printed. The last thing she wanted was to give the impression that the shop wasn't doing well. She wanted this feature to celebrate Chandler's having been on the High Street for over eighty years, the business having been passed down to Albert by his father, and then by Albert to his daughter, Suzanne. There was to be no mention of the fact that they were struggling. 'It gets busy later. I chose the right moment for you to call,' she sidelined. 'Now, what is it that you want to know?'

After a few minutes of chatting to Kim, Riley's nerves began to disappear. The journalist was personable, charming, and she only wanted to know about the business. She didn't seem as if she was going to twist Riley's every word or make her out to be a demon.

'We'll do a half-page piece,' Kim told her. 'We'll get most of the facts and figures down, say how welcoming the shop is and how it is keen to stay local and proud. We can mention the sale this coming weekend, and then we can include a photo of you and the staff. That okay with you?'

Riley nodded. 'That would be great, thanks.'

'I was thinking . . .' Kim stood up and pointed to the shop window. 'How about if you set up a chair in the window and try on a shoe?'

Riley's heart sank at the thought. But Dan had overheard, hovering around in the background as he had been ever since Kim had arrived.

'Ooh, that's what we suggested,' he cried. 'I could pretend to be slipping on the shoe, a bit like Cinderella!'

'I don't think that's a good idea,' Riley started.

'I do.' Kim looked at Dan purposely. 'Would it take you long to set up?'

'No, we could have it done in about' – he glanced at his watch – 'ten minutes?'

'Great, let's do it.' Kim turned to Riley. 'Anything to catch a reader's eye. Ah, here's Ethan now.'

Riley glanced towards the door to see a man who looked to be in his mid-thirties. His smile was as welcoming as his colleague's. He popped the black case he was carrying on the floor as Kim approached him. She pointed to the window and told him her plan. He nodded, watching as Dan removed shoes from the display. He caught Riley's eye over Kim's shoulder.

Riley found herself smiling at him. He was a few inches taller than her, with brown hair and a flopping fringe which he swept out of his face so often that she assumed he didn't even notice the habit. The navy suit he wore seemed slick enough to mark him out as the posing type, yet his mannerisms made him seem far friendlier. She imagined image was everything in his profession.

She ran a hand through her own hair, glad that she'd at least found time to freshen her lipstick, and walked towards them both.

'This is Ethan, our brilliant photographer,' Kim introduced. 'He can make anyone look wonderful, can't you, Ethan?'

'Only when I feel the need to,' Ethan replied pointedly.

It surprised Riley that his tone was quiet and assured, not cocky and loud as, for some reason, she had expected. As a photographer, she'd imagined he would be used to bossing people around all day. She felt her skin flush a little.

'Once the window is set up, we'll get you in there and have some fun.' He grinned this time. 'Best shoe forward.'

'That's what I said,' Sadie nodded. 'It's a good headline, isn't it?'

'It is.' Ethan looked around. 'Do you have anything in your size?' he asked Riley. 'We want as bright a colour as possible. And, maybe' – he turned to look towards the door – 'I can take a photo from outside looking in, and inside looking out. We might get a crowd to stop on the pavement while we are doing it.'

Riley sighed inwardly. She was going to be on display in the shop window. Oh, how she was looking forward to that.

'Can't you do it instead?' she asked Dan.

Dan shook his head. 'It has to be you, Riley. You run the joint.'

'No, I don't! It's a team effort.'

'But we won't all fit in the window.' Dan laughed at Riley's face as she protested. 'It has to be you!'

'In that case,' she said, pulling a pair of red heels from a bag, 'it's a good thing I brought these with me!'

CHAPTER FIVE

Once all the shoes and display racks had been removed from the window, the chair was covered in red crepe paper, bought from the stationers' two doors down, and a few silver stars were stapled onto it, to make it resemble a throne. A piece of paper with the words 'Are you one step ahead?' written in black marker pen in large capital letters was taped to the wall by Riley's side.

'I can't believe you have me doing this,' Riley whispered to Dan as she sat on the chair. 'It looks like a set from a pantomime!'

'All in the name of business, darling!' Dan whispered back.

'It's a good job I had a pedicure last weekend,' Riley pouted as she removed her socks and shoes. 'I wouldn't want anyone to see my feet at the best of times.'

'Riley, can you look this way?' asked Ethan. 'I'll just take a few photos to get the angle right and then we'll get going. Okay?'

Riley nodded, her smile stiff.

'Stop squabbling,' cried Sadie, from where she was serving an elderly gentleman. 'You're like a pair of five-year-olds!'

'If you can just sit still a minute, Riley,' Ethan encouraged as he snapped away. 'And smile.'

'I *am* smiling,' she grimaced. 'My face is hurting I've been smiling so much.'

'Dan, can you just slide on the slipper?'

'Slipper? It's a bloody great big heel!'

'Shall I do it like Albert used to?' Dan whispered to Riley, running his hand up her calf.

'Don't you bloody dare!' She slapped his hand away. 'I don't know how he got away with touching so many women's legs without getting accused of sexual harassment.'

'Don't speak ill of the dead.'

'You do!' Riley protested.

'If we can have just you on the chair, Riley,' said Ethan. 'And perhaps you can hold up the sign.'

Dan took it down from the wall.

'You could use it as a hashtag,' Ethan continued. 'Is the shop on Twitter?'

Riley snorted. 'No. Mr Chandler refused to get on with these new-fangled ideas of ours.' She smiled fondly. 'He was a fuddy-duddy.'

'Look.' Sadie pointed outside. 'We have an audience!'

Riley turned around. Three teenaged girls were holding up their phones and taking photos. Joanne and Brittany, who worked in the café, stood having a chat. Two workmen behind them, who were filling the planters with flowers, were leaning on their shovels. An elderly couple stopped to see what was going on and a woman tutted at them as she tried to get past.

'I don't mind photos of the shop,' Riley said, 'but please don't say I'm going to be all over social media looking like a fairy queen!'

Everyone laughed, except Ethan.

'You're doing fine,' he reassured. 'But if you can just sit still for a while—'

'How long?' she spoke through a forced smile.

'A couple of minutes. I just want to make sure I get you in the right light.'

'The right light!'

'Stay still, Riley!'

Riley gritted her teeth as she sat like a statue. 'This is ridiculous. I can't sit here like a waxwork dummy. I have work to do.'

Ethan grinned. 'Okay, Cinderella, I'm done. You can get off your high horse now, before it turns into a pumpkin.'

'Oh, ha ha,' Riley responded, but she was smiling as he helped her get down from the window. 'Did you get what you were hoping for?'

Ethan nodded. 'I think so. I'll email over some photos later, if you like? Can't promise which one will get used, though.'

'It will be the one that makes me look the oldest, the ugliest and the fattest, I expect.'

'Oh, I don't think I have a photo like that.' Ethan stared at her for a moment, eyes twinkling, before looking away.

Riley felt her skin burning up and rushed over to the safety of the till. When she turned back she realised Ethan had followed her.

'If there isn't anything else,' he said as he picked up his case, 'I'll be on my way.'

'When will we be able to see it?' asked Dan.

'Tomorrow or the night after, I expect. Kim will write it up, get it online and in print. I'll bring you a few print copies when it's out, too.' Ethan smiled again. 'Thanks a million. You all did a great job.'

Riley watched as he left the shop, finding herself disappointed that he was leaving so quickly. She should have offered him another coffee but, then again, he'd probably be off to his next job so wouldn't be able to spare the time.

'Be still, your beating heart,' said Dan, as he waltzed past her with three mugs to wash and fill. 'I can feel the tension from here.'

'What do you mean?' said Riley.

'I can tell you like him. It's written all over your face.'

'It isn't!' Riley almost shouted. She lowered her voice. 'It isn't, is it?'

'So you do like him!'

'She'd be mad not to like him,' Sadie joined them. 'He's quite dishy and' – she paused for added effect – 'no wedding ring.'

'That doesn't mean anything nowadays,' said Riley. 'Some men don't wear rings, and he might be in a relationship but not married. I've—' She stopped short, remembering they didn't know what had happened with Nicholas.

'He's single,' said Dan. 'I asked him.'

Riley frowned. 'When?'

'When I'd seen you eyeing him up a few times. I thought it was my duty.'

'I was not eyeing him up!'

Riley felt her skin flush again and gave up trying to protest. While Dan went off to serve a man with a teenaged boy who looked like his double, and Sadie made a start on putting the window back to normal, Riley pondered their words. Sadie was right, plus Ethan seemed nice.

But for now, she didn't think her heart would take another battering. And she had far more important things on her mind, like how to keep Chandler's open and her friends together.

A glutton for punishment, Dan had arranged another date. He met Lorraine in the foyer of Cineworld. It was obvious from the start she was older than she had admitted on her profile – he reckoned she was pushing forty rather than thirty. Riley would say she was mutton dressed as lamb: black leggings and stacked ankle boots, leather jacket over a tight, clingy and low-cut red top. Her skin had an orange tint to it and her make-up was a little on the brash side. Long blonde hair finished off a complete stereotype.

'What do you fancy seeing?' Dan asked after they had introduced themselves.

'*Star Wars*?' Lorraine questioned.

'Fine.' Dan could think of nothing worse. He'd never been a fan.

He tried to make small talk before the film started, but had only been met with one-word answers and the occasional forced smile. Glad when the lights went down, he relaxed into his seat. At least he could stop trying for a while.

'That was great, don't you think?' he fibbed as they joined the throng of people in the aisle on the way out. He hadn't enjoyed it one bit and had nodded off for a time somewhere in the middle. Lorraine didn't seem to have noticed.

'It was okay,' she shrugged. 'Not my thing, really.'

'But I assumed you liked *Star Wars*, seeing as it was your choice.'

Lorraine shook her head as they came out into the brightly-lit foyer. 'It was my ex-husband. He enjoyed *Star Wars* films.'

Dan frowned. 'So you don't like them?'

Another shake of her head.

Dan held in a sigh. He'd just sat through a film that neither of them wanted to see.

They stood in silence in the foyer as people moved around them, some heading out of the building, some gathering tickets and refreshments to take into the next showing.

'Would you like to go for a drink?' Dan asked. Really, he only wanted to be polite, but he also didn't want to go home just yet.

Lorraine nodded. 'Why not?'

In a line outside were several familiar eateries – Coast to Coast, Nando's, Pizza Hut and Gourmet Burger. Dotted here and there were a few independent bars. People rushed inside them all like ants.

Dan pointed ahead to Harley's Bar. 'Shall we try here?'

Lorraine nodded again.

He sighed openly this time. This was too much like hard work. Why hadn't he just called it a night?

Harley's Bar had a 1960s theme, with red leather-seated booths around its edges, and walls covered in mirrors and metal plates with images of long-forgotten singers. In the middle of the room, scatterings of high stools and tables were full of people chatting, some animatedly, after the film. They waited to be served at the bar. Luckily, The Beatles played softly in the background to fill the silence between Dan and Lorraine.

Once they had their drinks, they found a table that they could stand at. Lorraine gazed around the room, still not talking.

'How long have you lived in Hedworth?' he asked, for want of something more interesting to say.

'All my life,' she replied. 'I did think of moving out of the area when Damien and I split up, but I couldn't. You know, in case he changed his mind.'

Dan frowned. Changed his mind? Did people often do that after they divorced?

'How long were you married?' he asked next.

'Ten years. Ten wonderful years.'

Another silence.

'We divorced seven years ago,' Lorraine told him as he moved aside to allow a glass-collector to pass.

'Seven years?' At Dan's calculations that would make Lorraine twelve when she and good old Damien were married.

Lorraine didn't look fazed as she nodded her head. He wondered if she'd even realised that he now knew she'd been lying about her age.

'We have a daughter too,' she added. 'She's fifteen.'

Dan checked his watch after he couldn't think of anything else to say. He wasn't one to make excuses and leave because things weren't working out. After all, he had invited her for a drink, so he needed to see it through to the end. He didn't have to see her again after that but he was too much of a softie to hurt her feelings now.

He glanced around the room, checking out the paraphernalia from the golden years. As his eyes came back to Lorraine, they widened. She was fighting back emotion.

She caught him looking and burst into tears.

'I'm sorry,' she said. 'You're the first man I've been on a date with and I—I just want to forget Damien, move on and start my life again. But being with you reminds me that I miss him so much . . . I still love him, you see.'

'Hey, come on now.' Dan didn't know where to look when she then began to sob loudly. People were looking over at them, at *him*. Some were even frowning. He froze with embarrassment. Did they think he'd said something to upset her? Oh, this was turning out to be the worst date yet.

'I never should have introduced him to my friend,' she stressed, suddenly knocking her drink back in one go. She banged down the glass. 'I would still be with him if I hadn't. She was my best friend too, the bitch. They live together now.'

Dan made a big deal of checking his watch. 'Is that the time? I have to go soon. I have an early start in the morning.'

It was the oldest trick in the book, but he couldn't handle any more.

Lorraine had other ideas. She grabbed his arm and clung onto him. 'You can't leave me,' she said. 'That's what he did. It would be cruel of you to leave me, too.'

Dan tried to release her grip on his arm. More people were beginning to look their way.

'Please, stay and finish your drink,' she said. 'I'm sorry, sometimes I come on a little strong. It's only because I'm so lonely. You must be lonely, too?'

'Excuse me,' said Dan. 'I need to use the bathroom.'

As he quickly walked off, he wondered if he should go. But he couldn't leave her there on her own. She'd be mortified if he didn't return. Instead he passed the exit and went into the gents'.

Pacing the men's toilets for what must have been minutes, he tried to pluck up the courage to go back to her. But he couldn't do it.

He stared at himself in the mirror. 'You can do this,' he spoke to his reflection. 'It's only an hour, and the poor woman will be wretched if you leave before.'

By the time he finally emerged from the bathroom, he peered through the crowd to see someone else standing where he had left Lorraine. Glancing around, Dan realised she had ditched him.

Almost laughing with hysteria at the absurdness of her leaving him in the lurch while he battled with his conscience, Dan dived for the exit and raced out of the pub.

CHAPTER SIX

'She left me,' Dan told Riley and Sadie the next morning as soon as he got to work. 'Can you believe it? I was trying hard not to hurt her feelings by walking away and she just upped and left regardless!'

Riley wiped away tears of laughter as she emptied the float into the till. 'I'm sorry, Dan, but that's the funniest one yet!'

'It wasn't funny at all,' he shuddered involuntarily. 'It was embarrassing. And I had to leave a pint behind because I didn't want to stand on my own when everyone knew I'd come in with her.'

'I mean, the way you describe it all. You're a comic genius! You really should write all this down and turn it into a "dating disasters" book. It would earn you a fortune.'

'I'll have you know that I will not be sharing my woes with anyone other than you two. I tell you because you will make me see the funny side of things. But really, I don't think this dating lark is all it's cracked up to be.' He dropped onto a leather cube and gave a huge sigh. 'At this rate, I'm never going to meet anyone worthy of a second date.'

'Don't be put off by one funny woman,' Riley said. She sat down beside him and put an arm round his shoulders. 'There is another someone out there for you. You just need to find her.'

'I'm trying my best!' Dan sniggered.

'You are indeed.' Riley stood up. 'Now, as it's my turn to fetch the milk, how about I treat us all to something chocolatey? I'm off to the newsagent's to pick up a copy of the *Hedworth News*, to see if we're in there.'

Despite Riley calling and leaving a message, Suzanne had been annoyed that she hadn't been around to be photographed for the feature. At least she had agreed when Riley mentioned holding a one-day sale that Saturday, though her idea of what constituted a sale left a lot to be desired. A pound or two off here and there was hardly going to cause a stampede in the morning.

Stefan, the newsagent, greeted Riley with a huge grin as she pushed open the door. Stefan and his family had run the business for over forty years.

'Riley, you're in the paper today!'

'Is it awful?' she asked, dreading his reply.

He flicked a copy of the *Hedworth News* open at page seventeen and pointed. 'See for yourself, Cinderella.'

When Riley got back to the shop, she had three copies of the paper under her arm. She handed one each to Dan and Sadie.

'What's it like?' Dan flicked through impatiently, scanning the photos.

'It's on page seventeen,' Riley told him as she stepped behind the till. 'I was right. I do look like a fairy queen.'

'With me as Prince Charming at your feet,' Dan laughed as he caught the image.

'Don't you dare call me Cinderella,' she pointed at him. 'Stefan beat you to it.'

Sadie giggled. 'Kim's done a great write-up. They've mentioned the sale on Saturday, too.'

'If it does the job and encourages people to come into the shop, then it's all well and good.'

Her phone beeped and she read the message. It was from Ethan. Over the past couple of days they had exchanged a few emails, then swapped mobile numbers and had sent numerous texts. Just thought I'd let you know the feature is online and in print. Hope it's okay?

Riley typed a message back. Yes, we have copies! It's great, thanks. Even I don't look too bad in the photo! Thanks for doing such a good job.

No problem. I enjoyed it. It was great to meet you.

Likewise.

Riley smiled to herself, remembering Ethan's warm smile.

'Riley, I have an emergency!' A man came rushing into the shop. 'I need shoes for a ball I'm attending this evening.'

Ray owned the café four doors down, was in his early fifties, thick and stocky around the waist with a full head of grey hair. He was still wearing his apron, the café's logo embroidered across the front.

Already standing by the men's section, Sadie pointed to a row of dress shoes. 'Any of these take your fancy, Ray?'

'I don't want to be served by you.' He folded his arms and stared at Riley, before breaking out into a grin. 'I want to be served by Cinderella here.'

'Oh, funny, ha ha!' Riley picked up the newspaper and rolled it up. 'One more wisecrack and I will clout someone with this.'

'But I have to go to the ball!'

'Out! Now!'

Once Dan and Sadie had finished laughing, Riley shook her head.

'It's going to get worse than this, isn't it?'

An hour before the shop was due to close on Friday evening, Riley, Sadie and Dan started to put everything in place in readiness for the sale the next day. Riley found herself despairing as she looked through the stock that Suzanne had said they could reduce. Some of the footwear had been there for years. No one would buy it. With a sigh of resignation, she filled her arms with boxes and took them over to the front window. Dan blew up balloons, Sadie wrote prices on bright purple stars, and they took it in turns to serve anyone that came into the shop. But try as she might, Riley couldn't make the display any more appealing.

When they had done all they could, Riley stretched her aching back and went outside to see how the display looked. It was just as she imagined. Drab and predictable.

She glanced up and down the High Street she loved, spotting the royal blue logo of the chemist, the green of the florist's, the neon sign above the beauty parlour.

Colour.

Once again, she wished Suzanne would listen to some of her suggestions. Only last night she'd seen a new range of sandals, in bright and trendy colours, that would bring the locals flocking. From the buzz already being created online, these were set to be this summer's must-haves, and the best thing about them was that they were a good price to buy in.

She went inside. 'Well, we've done as much as we can,' she said.

'I am knackered!' Dan flopped down on a kiddies' bean bag in dramatic style. He pretended to mop his brow. 'Do you think Suzanne realises just how much work we have to put into a sale that's only going to last one day and hasn't got a cat in hell's chance of gaining us any sales because the price knock-down is only five measly per cent?'

Sadie pulled up a leather cube and sat down next to him. She slipped off her shoe and rubbed at her toes. 'She can't say that we're not making a go of things if we get some sales from this.'

Riley clapped her hands. 'Off home, you two. Get some beauty sleep tonight. I'll lock up and see you tomorrow.'

'I hope Esther doesn't wake me up at the crack of dawn.' Sadie stood up, stretched her hands to the ceiling and yawned.

'I'd love to be woken up by someone as cute as Esther at any time of the day or night,' Dan sighed, then back-pedalled. 'By that I mean a woman. Oh, no. I didn't mean—'

Sadie and Riley grinned at each other. 'I do love it when you put your foot in it,' said Riley. 'We know what you meant. And anyway, haven't you got a date lined up for this weekend?'

Dan shook his head. 'No, I'm going out with the lads. I can't stand any more dating nonsense yet.'

Riley locked the door behind them, relishing the peace and quiet after their hectic day. She checked her watch. Ash was closing up her shop that evening, and was coming across to get her afterwards, so they could go home together. She took a few minutes to check through her Twitter and Facebook feeds, to catch up on anything she had missed. Catching sight of a pair of sandals she'd seen once or twice, she pressed like so she could save them.

Less than two minutes passed before Riley looked up when someone knocked on the door. Expecting to see Ash, she held in her annoyance when she saw it was Suzanne.

'I was just passing,' Suzanne said as Riley let her in, 'and thought I'd see how everything was looking for tomorrow's sale.'

Riley didn't believe her for one minute. Hedworth wasn't a place that you just passed, especially not the High Street where there was nowhere to park.

'It's not looking too bad.' Riley tried to muster enthusiasm as Suzanne surveyed the display.

'I saw your photo in the newspaper, too,' Suzanne snorted. 'You looked like Cinderella.'

Despite her warning to Ray earlier, Riley didn't pick the newspaper up and swipe her boss. 'The write-up is great, don't you think? And they mentioned the sale too.'

'Good. Let's hope it brings people in and they can see you working. We don't want everyone to think all we do is sit around and have silly photos taken.'

We?

'Really, that should have been me in that photo.'

Riley's eyes widened at the thought.

Suzanne's laugh was snide. 'I don't mean sitting in the window making a fool of myself. I would have had one taken by the front door, as the head of the establishment. I don't need to remind you that your job is to sell shoes.'

'Speaking of which, can I show you these, Suzanne?' Riley got out her phone and quickly brought up the website with the images of the new sandals. 'These are set to be a summer sell-out. They're great for the teens of Hedworth, and for the older ladies too. It might be an idea to get some for the shop. What do you think?'

Suzanne peered at the sandals, then shook her head. 'They're too cheap for Chandler's.'

'I'd call five pounds from Primark cheap. These are twenty pounds a pair.'

'Still too cheap. We want to be known for quality, not tat. Quality sells.'

Once Suzanne had left, Riley put her phone away and locked up for the day.

'What's the point of stocking quality, expensive shoes when they aren't selling?' she asked Ash as they made their way to the bus station. 'Honestly, the business is going to be finished by the end of the month at this rate.'

Ash linked her arm through Riley's. 'It will all work out fine, you'll see.'

'If I'm honest, a huge part of me wonders whether I should just chuck the towel in and give up. Find another job rather than waste my time on something that's bound to fail.'

'I can't see you doing that.' Ash shook her head.

'But everything seems to fall on my shoulders regardless of what happens. I don't think I'm ever going to work out what needs to be done. And it isn't my business.'

'You're a fighter. You won't give up until the very end.'

Riley's smile was faint but at least she had one. Ash was right. All she could hope was that the article in the paper did the trick and brought some customers into Chandler's. That, and the sale – it all had to make a difference, surely?

The next morning they were all at the shop early, waiting for the rush that would follow once they opened. Everyone loved to see a sale sign. But they were disappointed when the handful of customers waiting on the pavement spent all of ten minutes trawling the shelves, picking up the shoes and putting them back again just as quickly.

'I thought we might have at least a few sales before ten o'clock,' said Riley, hardly able to contain her disappointment after she had said goodbye to the umpteenth customer who had walked around the shop in a circle and then left empty-handed.

'Still,' said Dan, 'we did as Suzanne asked. It isn't our fault if it didn't work.'

'Maybe not, but I know who'll get the blame,' Riley sighed. 'If we don't sell anything, and that chart in the staffroom doesn't move, then we might all be in trouble.'

Sadie sat down with a thump. 'We're doomed, aren't we?'

Dan sat beside her. 'No, we're going to be fine. We just need to stay positive.'

'Morning.' Riley looked up to see Ethan in the doorway. He was carrying a cake box. 'I thought you might like cupcakes.' He slid the box onto the counter as they gathered around him eagerly. 'No rest for the wicked on sale day.' He glanced around the shop that had only one customer looking at slippers. 'Where are all the people?'

'Indeed,' muttered Dan.

'It's early yet.' Riley threw Dan a warning look as she took a cupcake from Ethan with a smile. Ethan didn't know they were struggling and she didn't want him to find out.

The day wasn't exactly hectic but they were slightly busier than usual. Two women argued over a pair of last year's winter boots, but when it came down to it they fitted only one of them, which was a relief. A group of teenaged boys came in to check out 'the fit bird who sat in the window' and, despite their earlier worries, they did manage to nab a few extra sales. Suzanne would be pleased with that small mercy, at least.

As the doors closed at five thirty, Riley felt glad to be going home. She decided to send Ethan a message. It had been good of him to call and see how they were doing. Thanks for the cakes earlier. They were delicious!

Glad you enjoyed. Do you fancy a bite to eat one night, too? No pressure if you don't!

Riley felt her skin flush a little as she wondered how to reply. 'I think I'd like that,' would probably be much better than 'Yes, right now!'

She settled on: Yes, okay.

Are you free on Tuesday evening?

Riley grinned. He was keen.

Yes. Shall I meet you somewhere?

I could pick you up around seven if you don't mind giving me your address? She texted it to him quickly before she changed her mind.

'What are you grinning at?' asked Dan as he caught her with her head bent over her phone.

'I have a date. Ethan's taking me out on Tuesday.'

'You've pulled?' Dan sounded incredulous. 'I've been trying hard for ages and you haven't been trying at all. It isn't fair.'

Riley smiled. Although nervous, as it had been a long time since she'd been on a date and Nicholas had always come round to her flat for pure convenience, she was looking forward to it already.

CHAPTER SEVEN

Monday morning soon came around. When Riley arrived at the shop, while Sadie and Dan opened up, she checked to see if there were any emails from Suzanne. She was bound to have sent a couple checking up on them, and the sale.

Surprisingly, there were none. But all became clear when, ten minutes later, the woman herself pushed open the door and marched straight over to the till. She was wearing yet another coat, a black and white dogtooth, three-quarter length. Riley sniggered as she thought of Cruella De Vil.

'Morning, Suzanne,' Riley chirped, realising that at least she could be civil to her. 'It's a lovely day out there, isn't it? It was quite warm yesterday, too.'

Suzanne ignored Riley's small talk and flicked a hand around the empty shop.

'Busy, I see?' she said, her eyebrows raised as much as they were capable of.

'It's too early,' Riley explained. 'Most of the customers will be collecting their pensions before coming across if they need anything.'

'Our clientele isn't that old.' Suzanne folded her arms as she glared at Riley, Dan and Sadie. 'I thought the place would be buzzing. What went wrong?'

'I don't think there was enough of a discount,' Riley began. 'I think if we—'

'It has nothing to do with the discount, Riley,' Suzanne interrupted, her tone clipped. 'Sales attract people. Obviously it's your job to make sure those people buy something. I don't know why you find that so hard.' She gestured around the shop. 'Those are good quality shoes.'

'They are,' said Riley, 'but they aren't necessarily fashionable.'

'And how would you know that?'

'I follow the trends. I can definitely tell that those sandals I showed you are going to be popular in summer and—'

'There won't be a shop here in summer at this rate. It's been almost two weeks since I instigated the sales competition.'

'If she listened and stopped interrupting all the time,' Dan spoke under his breath. He looked up to see Suzanne glaring at him.

'Did you say something?' she asked.

'Yes. We worked so hard on Saturday. We can get the people into the shop but we can't close the sales unless we have what they want.'

'Or we reduce the prices enough,' added Sadie.

'Well, if we can't compete by having a sale, then we'll just have to open longer hours.' Suzanne pointed to them each in turn. 'From this weekend, I want the shop opening on Sundays, too.'

'We need more notice than that!' said Riley. Although she'd been expecting this to happen for some time, they'd have to work out either extra wages or new shift rotas so they could take time off during the week in lieu of the extra weekend hours. 'There are only three of us,' she added.

'If the shop closes, you'll have to work Sundays in the shopping centre, no doubt,' said Suzanne. 'So you might as well get used to it. We'll trial it for the next three months.'

'And you're going to pay us for the extra hours *what*, precisely? Double time?' asked Riley, knowing that as well as herself, she had to protect Dan and Sadie.

'Of course you'll be paid for the extra hours, but first we'll have you each on a rota so you won't have to do any. The shop will open on Sundays for four hours, from eleven until three. If that's successful, then we will open from ten until four. You can each have the four hours off during the week to make up for it. The afternoons are dead so the shop can manage with two of you for three days.'

'And have a Sunday off . . . when?' Riley demanded to know.

'For the first three months, there will be no Sundays allowed off work at all. You all want to continue working together, don't you?' Suzanne glared at them. 'I'm sure you'll figure it out between you.'

'She can't do this, can she?' said Sadie once Suzanne had left.

'She can,' said Riley. 'It's a pain, but we knew this might come eventually.'

'Yes, but we expected to be paid for it!'

'I'll sort something out for you,' she replied. 'And if not, we'll just have to stay closed one or two of them.'

'But,' Sadie spoke with tears welling in her eyes, 'you know what our Sundays mean to me.'

'We'll just have to postpone lunch until we've finished,' Riley reassured her. Even so, she was wondering why she herself was trying so hard to please a snotty-nosed cow like Suzanne. 'We mustn't let this get us down. We have to give the shop three months.'

'Don't you find it strange that Max has gone quiet, all of a sudden?' Sadie asked.

'If he has anything about him, he'll stay overseas,' said Dan. 'I wouldn't want to be within ten feet of Suzanne if I didn't have to.'

Riley said nothing. Dan wasn't one to mince his words but this time she had to agree with him.

On Tuesday evening, Riley was just getting home from work as Ash came out of their building. They almost collided in the doorway.

'You're late,' Ash said, giving her a hug.

'I've been stocktaking. It took me a lot longer than I thought it would.' Riley looked her up and down, noticing another new outfit. 'You smell divine. Are you going out with the youngster again?'

Ash's cheeks reddened as she nodded.

'This seems to be getting serious,' Riley teased. 'Are you sure you can handle someone so young long-term? He'll wear you out.'

'I'm getting it while I can,' she grinned. 'You should try it with the dishy Ethan.'

'I might just do that.'

'Ooh, what time is he picking you up?' It was Ash's turn to tease. Riley had texted her earlier to tell her the news.

Riley looked at her watch. 'Just under an hour! Better get a wriggle on.'

'Text me later?' said Ash, as she rushed off.

'Yes, we can compare notes,' Riley said sarcastically.

When she came back out of the building an hour later, Ethan was waiting for her at the door. She smiled, her senses on full alert as he dipped his head to kiss her cheek.

'That's my car.' He pointed to a black Land Rover Discovery. Inside, Riley found it to be immaculate. She breathed in the smell of leather mixed with polish and air freshener.

'It's my one vice,' Ethan said, catching her glancing around in admiration. 'It's the most expensive thing I own but as I do a lot of miles around the town, it's good to travel in style.'

'As long as you don't tell me to listen to the engine purring, we'll be fine,' Riley mocked.

Ethan looked disappointed, then grinned. 'I thought we might go to The Caramel Leaf?'

Riley smiled. 'Perfect.'

The car park at The Caramel Leaf wasn't too busy as Ethan glided into a space. Riley pulled in the collar of her jacket as she rounded a corner and a gust of wind nearly took them off their feet.

'Roll on warmer days,' said Ethan, laughing as he took hold of her hand.

They went inside the restaurant, ordered drinks and sat down at a table in the window.

'I love it in here,' she said. 'Their seats are so comfortable. The thing about being on your feet all day is how much you welcome getting off them at the end of it,' Riley sighed as she settled more.

'Remind me how long you've worked at Chandler's?' Ethan asked as they studied their menus.

'Eight years. It's the first job I've had as a manager.'

'Are you worried about trade?'

'What makes you say that?' Riley wondered if anyone had overheard her talking.

'You seem disappointed about the sale. I'm sorry that the article didn't bring in more customers for you.'

'I'm sure it did! Really, thank you so much for covering it.'

'There seem to be more and more businesses closing down every week, especially on the high streets of small towns like this one. Aren't you worried that yours might not survive?'

'I'm absolutely terrified,' Riley admitted. 'If Chandler's closed, I don't know what else I'd do.' She decided to change the subject. 'How about you? Have you always been a photographer?'

'Yes, since I left school.' Ethan's face broke into a smile. 'If I ever feel the need to move from Hedworth, I know the experience I'm getting by working on the paper will be useful. I'm building up a portfolio.'

'At least there's no backstabbing and bitching at Chandler's, not like there was when I was at school.'

Ethan tipped his head to one side. 'You don't get that?'

'Not at all.'

'Well, you must be one hell of a boss. I've never worked in a place that hasn't had some kind of office politics going on. Don't any of the staff hate your guts and talk about you continually behind your back yet smile sweetly to your face?'

'I hope not!' Riley laughed. 'Actually, I'm sure they don't. I've been very fortunate to have Dan and Sadie on board. Do you live locally, Ethan? Or do you commute to Hedworth?'

'I live in Somerley.'

'Ah, the land of the Coffee Stop.' Riley knew Somerley well. 'That place is a gold mine. I love to visit whenever I have a day off or a free afternoon. They do some fabulous cakes there, too.'

'Yes, it's done remarkably well since reopening.'

'You're very lucky to have it on your doorstep. I'd never be out of there.'

'I hardly ever visit because it's so near. That's the thing, isn't it?'

'Well, the next time you fancy a muffin, I'll come with you.'

Riley blushed as soon as the words came out. It sounded like a double entendre no matter which way she looked at it. She looked down at her menu again quickly.

Ethan laughed. 'I might just take you up on that.'

They placed their orders and waited for their food. The chatter around them was comforting but there was no need for Riley to be nervous as the conversation between them flowed naturally.

'What have you been covering today?' she asked.

'The usual stuff.' Ethan took a sip of his drink. 'I photographed an author visiting a local school to encourage the younger children to read and write. Then I went over to a shop because some woman professes to have found a dead mouse in a bag of crisps.'

'Eww!' Riley grimaced. 'Did she really?'

'I doubt it. I reckon she's after compensation. Or a few free boxes of crisps. The things I've covered . . .'

'So do you only do the happy things or do you cover worse things like . . . oh, I don't know. Accidents, attacks?' She paused. 'Murders?'

'A murder in Hedworth?' Ethan laughed. 'Chance would be a fine thing.'

'I disagree. That thing that people say on the news about not expecting it to happen on their own doorstep isn't true for me,' Riley said. 'Murder can happen anywhere, at any time, to any class of people.'

'You're right,' he nodded, 'but I bet it wouldn't happen on my shift. So instead I'm stuck with the boring jobs such as opening local fetes, fundraising stuff and—'

'Bizarre displays in shop windows,' Riley broke in.

Ethan grinned. 'Well, some are far more boring than others. What about you? Have you never wanted to do anything other than work in the shop?'

'You make it sound so attractive,' she protested.

He held up a hand. 'I meant did you have ambitions when you were younger, something that you'd longed to do but never did?'

'Well, when I was a child I always wanted to be a tennis player and play at Wimbledon.' She hung her head in mock shame. 'Never going to happen, I'm afraid.'

'Pity. I'd quite like to see you in a short white tennis skirt.'

Riley smiled shyly, dipping her eyes for a moment from Ethan's intense gaze.

'Now, though, I wished I'd gone to college to study fashion and design. There's such a variety of things to do these days, plus so many ways of getting noticed with social media. It must be really rewarding to run a business online.'

'It's never too late,' said Ethan. 'Why don't you go to evening classes?'

'I think I'd be too much of a mature student for that now,' Riley laughed.

As the waiter came over with their food, Riley found herself grinning. She was hoping that Ethan hadn't got a wife or girlfriend tucked away at home that would come out of the woodwork at the last minute, because she realised that she really liked him. And the signs were looking good that the feeling was mutual.

'Have you always lived in Hedworth?' he asked.

'Yes. I've been in my flat for two years now. I used to share with my friend, Ash – she's female, by the way. It's short for Ashleigh.' She groaned inwardly – why had she felt the need to tell him that? 'But we have separate flats now, although still in the same building.'

'I don't live alone. I live with Jimmy.'

'Is he your brother?'

Ethan shook his head.

'A lodger?'

'Not exactly.'

'Oh.'

Riley's shoulders wanted to drop but she remained still as Ethan took out his phone. He scrolled through it for a moment and then turned the screen towards her. Staring back at her was the mostly white face of a Jack Russell terrier, with one tan ear and another patch under his chin. Riley had always had a dog at her parents' house but had never had one since. Not with Tom, and sadly not with Ash. They weren't allowed pets in the flats. It was one of the conditions of tenancy.

'Oh, he's so sweet,' she exclaimed, feeling a surge of relief.

Ethan snorted. 'Don't be drawn in by that cute face and the sorrowful eyes. He's a demon.'

'I bet he isn't. He looks a bundle of fun.'

'How about the next time we meet . . .' He looked at her pointedly. 'Will there be a next time?'

She nodded shyly, already looking forward to it.

'We'll take Jimmy for a walk. And maybe, if we can get a bit of time off during the week together, we can visit the Coffee Stop for a muffin?'

Riley beamed, even though she knew he was teasing her. 'Sounds like a plan to me.'

CHAPTER EIGHT

Sadie sat down on the settee. She put her glass of wine down beside her on the coffee table, shifted her feet up to her side and sighed. Losing her job was the last thing she wanted to worry about right now. And then there was working on Sundays.

She couldn't afford to protest, not that Suzanne would even listen. She couldn't bear to think how she would cope if the shop went under.

Sadie loved working with Riley. She combined being a great manager and a great friend perfectly, not like some of the bosses Sadie had worked for. And she had been brilliant during Ross's illness, and far beyond. Sadie often wondered where she would be if it weren't for her close group of friends – Riley, Dan, Ash and Cooper. Although, to be fair, she often wondered whether they'd ever get fed up of her inability to move on, especially as the anniversary of Ross's death loomed.

She picked up her iPad and logged on to Grieve Together to see if Tanya was online or, if not, whether anyone else wanted to chat. Although she relished the silence when Esther was asleep, the loneliness started to creep in.

Tanya wasn't online but she had left her a message. Sadie clicked on the icon.

Tanya: *How has your day been? I haven't been too bad actually. It's been fun at work for a change. How about you?*

Sadie typed a quick message back.

Clara: *Oh, you don't want to know. I may lose my job. If things don't improve in three months, the shop I work in might close :(Glad to see that you've had a good day, though – good days are great!*

She pressed send, hoping that the message wasn't too self-centred. Over the months that she and Tanya had become online friends, she'd given out a little more information than she had on the forum. Tanya had been great to chat to, especially in private. Somehow it had been easier to talk to a person behind a screen. Tanya knew what she was going through. She would sympathise with her when she needed, gently reprimand her when she was feeling too sorry for herself. Tanya could make Sadie smile in an instant with a silly comment.

She took a few sips of her wine while she waited for the message to be answered. When it wasn't, she realised Tanya mustn't be online. She flipped through a few comments and other people's blog posts and then wrote a little in her journal.

The phone rang. It was Cooper.

'Hi, how are my two favourite women?' he asked her.

'One is hopefully asleep and the other is fine, thanks.' Glad of someone to talk to, Sadie took another sip of her wine and relaxed back in the settee. 'Where are you?'

'At the pub having a quick pint. I just wanted to see how you were.'

'Esther wants me to tell you that she got another gold star for her essay on the garden, thanks to you for helping her out.'

'I didn't help her with the essay. I'm useless at storytelling.'

'But you planted the seeds. Literally!'

Last month, Cooper had helped Esther clear a patch at the bottom of the garden to plant some flowers in a spot where mother and daughter could sit and remember Ross. Cooper had

been a great help with the garden. Sadie would never have managed it by herself: she didn't even have an interest in learning
what was a flower and what was a weed. It had been something
that Ross had loved, giving them separate interests. Sadie would
rather bury her nose in a book than in a flower.

They'd been lucky enough to find a semi-detached house that
boasted an extra-long rear garden, backing onto fields. Occasionally, the fields were used by the local school for sports days,
but other than that it was peaceful. It had always been Ross's
dream to have a large garden, and he'd spent hours in it before
he died.

'The lawn needs a good trimming now,' said Cooper. 'Shall I
pop over at the weekend and see to it?'

'Thanks, that would be great. Will Sunday lunch do you as
payment?'

'I'm not sure yet. I might be going to watch the match. Can
I get back to you on it? If not, I could come round early Sunday
morning.'

'Great, see you then. And you might want to make the most
of it as Suzanne says Chandler's needs to open on Sundays now,
to keep up with the times.'

'But I thought most of the shops on the High Street were still
closed on Sundays.'

'They are. In the main, it's just the shopping centre that
opens daily.' Sadie sighed. 'We'll just have to eat later in the day,
if I do a roast.'

'I suppose. Is there anything you need?'

'No, I think we're good.'

After they had said their goodbyes, Sadie switched on the
television to catch up with the news. She smiled to herself,
thinking back over the conversation. It was as if they were a
couple in a long distance relationship and Cooper was phon-

ing after a day at work. She was telling him about her day; he was telling her about his. She found it more comforting than he would ever know, and was dreading the day when another woman would take him away from both her and Esther.

She checked to see if she had any new messages from Tanya but, again, there was nothing. She hoped she was out enjoying herself. That way, at least maybe one of them was doing something exciting.

Footsteps padded down the stairs and a head popped around the door frame.

'What are you doing out of bed again?'

Sadie chose her most stern voice. This was the third night in a row that Esther had crept downstairs after she had been put to bed.

'I need a drink, Mummy,' she said, her voice full of sleep.

'It's too late, poppet.' Sadie got to her feet.

'Can I have a cuddle then, please?'

'Just for a moment and then it's back to bed.'

Sadie tried not to show her smile. There was nothing she liked better than cuddling up to Esther, running a hand over her fine, brown hair and pulling her tiny frame close, even when she was supposed to be fast asleep in bed.

And even if Esther was the only person whom Sadie could cuddle up to right now, she was the ideal solution for comfort anyway.

Riley had gone straight to the gym after she had finished work, and was now at home. Even though she had run five miles on the treadmill, which usually allowed her mind to switch off from anything stressful, she still couldn't relax. She rarely brought work home with her, but tonight was an exception. She grabbed a cushion and hugged it to her chest, hoisting her legs onto the settee.

So far, despite their best intentions, the sale and the feature in the *Hedworth News* hadn't brought in many more customers. There must be something they could do to stall the inevitable?

Ash's words from the night before came back to her. They'd been coming home on the bus together when Ash nudged Riley away from looking at her phone. 'Why don't you start up a campaign online?' she'd suggested.

Riley had frowned.

'Well, we're always on our phones. Twitter this, Facebook that. Why don't you do something that will bring people into the shop?'

'Like what?' Riley looked on in exasperation. 'The only thing I can think of is to walk around naked in the highest of heels.'

'That would bring the wrong audience altogether!' Ash giggled. 'Can you imagine—'

'It was a *joke*!'

Riley picked up her iPad and scrolled through her Twitter feed. Maybe she should open a Twitter account for the shop – a Facebook page too. She'd asked if she could open an account for Chandler's many times, but Suzanne was sceptical about the benefits of social media, especially for a shop such as hers. But now that Suzanne wanted to play games, Riley decided not to wait for her approval. She would use her initiative and gather some followers, maybe tweet some photos of fashionable shoes and then suggest they have nothing similar but people should come down and have a look anyway, in a jokey way. Positive tweets always got retweeted. And funny ones too. She could do funny.

Within a few minutes, she had created an account for Chandler's Shoe Shop and was wondering what to say in the first few tweets. She would have to think about it, but for now, there they were.

She'd wanted to set up a website for the shop for a while, but had always been told that it wasn't necessary. This could be a chance to take the business online. She, Sadie and Dan could all run the account if necessary. Maybe they could get some local celebrities to retweet things for them.

Excitement bubbled up inside her. This could be a great form of advertising. She'd get on to it straight away in the morning after chatting it through with Sadie and Dan. But first she began to add all the fashion designers that she followed. Some of them she was quite friendly with online. Maybe they could help her spread the word a little.

Outside on the High Street, it was still fairly quiet as Riley walked down to the newsagent's. She could feel the sun on her back and looked up for a moment. It was getting warmer day by day. She could definitely feel a change now that March was about to turn into April.

So far, all their hard work hadn't paid off. The Chandler's Twitter feed had gained a few follows and Riley was following people and tweeting photos and witty comments to try to interact with local people. All in all, it ate into her time but as she'd been on Twitter for quite a while she knew how long things could take to build up. Maybe she should look more closely at her own followers and see if she could get any of those people interested in following Chandler's. Or maybe she could tweet about Chandler's from her own account, to see if she could get some retweets.

Her eyes were drawn to a young woman walking past. She wore what looked like painter's dungarees, one strap unfastened, an oversized red T-shirt underneath. Wedge shoes finished the look off, along with a multicoloured tote bag. Riley smiled as she walked past, for a moment remembering a time when she had worn something similar.

She stopped suddenly and hot-footed back over to the young woman.

'Hi,' she said. 'I'm Riley, and I work at Chandler's Shoe Shop. You might have seen me last week in the *Hedworth News*? I was trying shoes on in the window. I felt a bit mad really, but it's because—'

'I remember seeing that,' the young woman interrupted.

'Oh, did you?' Riley was pleased. 'Well, if you ever fancy coming into the shop, I'm sure I can give you a discount.'

'Oh, no,' the woman said, as she began to walk away, 'the shoes are far too expensive and old-fashioned for me.'

'Yes, I can see that.' Riley looked down at her feet. 'Your shoes are amazing!'

'Thanks, I got them in Manchester.'

'I know you might think this is crazy, but could I photograph them to add to our Twitter account? I'm trying to drum up business and what better way than to show off fabulous shoes like those?'

'But I didn't get them from your shop.'

'That doesn't matter. I can think of some way round that.'

The woman turned to the side and put out her right foot. 'Go on, then. If you add my name to the tweet, then I can retweet it for you.'

'Great!' Riley took out her phone and snapped at the woman's foot a few times. 'What's your name?'

'Marsha.' She looked slightly embarrassed as she tucked her long blonde hair behind her ears. 'My Twitter name is RizzlesticksM'

Riley smiled.

'I know, I know. I thought it would be funny at the time, but now I kinda like it.'

Riley stuck out her hand. 'Well, thank you so much. Lovely to meet you, RizzlesticksM. That's a great tote too, if I might say so.'

'Thanks very much! My friend designed it for me.'

'Did she?'

'*He* did.' Marsha took the bag off her shoulder and held it up so that Riley could see it better. The image was of a young woman standing in front of an easel as she put colour to her own painting. The attention to detail was incredible. 'We're both studying fashion and design at Hedworth FE College,' Marsha added. 'Frank's always designing new ones. I have several of them.'

A thought popped into Riley's mind. 'Do you think he would be interested in selling them at our shop? We could perhaps showcase them in the window.'

'Really?'

'Yes, do you have his contact details? An email, maybe?'

Marsha nodded. 'I do, as a matter of fact . . .'

CHAPTER NINE

Ash flopped down next to Riley on the settee. Riley's head was down as she wrote frantically in a notepad.

'What are you doing?'

Riley looked up momentarily. 'You know our shoes aren't fashionable enough,' she said, 'and Suzanne thinks we can sell anything, but we can't? I might have come up with an idea.'

Riley told Ash about stopping Marsha, taking a photo of her shoe and being shown the tote bag. She had emailed Frank and he was coming into the shop the following day.

'Wouldn't it be great if a fashion and design student put a display of their bags in the window?' Riley said, excitement clear in her voice. 'Especially if that person has a local connection, and then went on to make it big later on?'

'I think it would be a great idea, full stop,' Ash agreed. 'I'm sick of getting moaned at because people have to pay five pence for a carrier bag. Totes are going to be all the rage, you mark my word. All it needs is someone to come along with something snappy that everyone wants and we'll all be buying them. I just wish I could design one!'

'I was thinking he could work on a sale or return basis. If I made it sound irresistible, the chance to showcase the bags in our shop, he and Marsha might invite all their friends to Chandler's. I don't know – I'm just thinking aloud. We could do a display, in the shop and in the window.'

'And you could take a small cut if you sold any?'

'Yes. Do you think it would bring people into the shop?'

Ash sat forward. 'It's a great idea.'

'I have been known to have them.' Riley brushed her hair away from her face in dramatic style.

'But won't all that take time to set up?' said Ash. 'I don't want to put a downer on things, but you don't have long to run this stupid competition.'

'You're right.' Riley sighed again. 'What we need is something as well as the bags. A gimmick that will bring people into the shop.' She sat forward again to speak but changed her mind.

'What?' said Ash.

'What about sharing photos of shoes on Twitter? I could take a photo each day. Maybe I could do a roving reporter type thing, and everyone who gets a photo taken of their shoes goes into a prize draw. They could have a bag designed!'

'I doubt you'd get any money from Suzanne towards a competition.'

'There's a couple of ways round that. Either we could have a fee to enter, say a pound a photo – which goes to a local charity. That might shame her into giving something to us. Or me, Sadie and Dan could chip in. If we split a prize three ways, it won't be too much then. Do you think one hundred pounds will be enough?'

Ash nodded. 'And it's something that you could do really easily, too. But if you want to go the whole hog and create a media campaign, why don't you do something like a video and upload it to YouTube? Or a flash mob?'

'A flash mob?' Riley frowned. 'You mean like a group of dancers coming out of the crowd?'

'Yes. You could do it one Saturday afternoon when the High Street is busy. You remember Serena, who used to work with me in Jazz? She owns her own dance studio now. She might be willing to help you.'

Riley's mind went into overdrive as Ash continued.

'At the end of the dance, you could give out leaflets about the competition. Anyone who tweets a photo of their favourite shoes to Chandler's Twitter feed—'

'Including a hashtag,' Riley broke in.

Ash nodded. 'They can all be entered into a draw for a hundred pounds' worth of vouchers to spend in the shop, or to go towards designing your own bag.'

Riley's eyes widened. 'Brilliant. Everyone loves showing off their shoes!' Then she came back to reality. 'But how do we get a flash mob going?'

'Serena could help you with a dance. And' – Ash was getting excited now – 'if you were in it too, that would mean even more publicity.'

Riley drew her head back in surprise. 'I can't dance to save my life! It would take me years to learn a routine.' She grinned at the thought. 'But I do have some great moves.'

Ash laughed. 'Imagine if you had a few thousand hits, Riles? How much publicity it would bring to the shop. Especially if you run it with a competition. We could all tweet the video too, get more interest for your Twitter account.'

'Any interest on social media would be good.' Riley had checked the Chandler's accounts earlier on. 'Since I created the account, we've had twenty-seven new followers on Twitter – and some of those look dodgy – and only a handful of retweets.'

'What about Facebook?'

'Not much better. I wish I had something to advertise on there, though. So, this way, we could use a certain hashtag. How about 'put your #bestshoeforward, RT and follow?' That kind of thing might increase our followers quickly. Plus, if people share it, they will see a shoe and snap in an instant to join in!'

'People love doing selfies – we can invent the shoe-ies,' said Ash.

Riley laughed. 'I like that, although I'm still not sure about being involved in a flash mob. Knowing me, I'd fall flat on my face!'

'That would look good, too,' Ash laughed, reaching for her phone. 'Let me send a message to Serena. I bet she'll be able to persuade some of the kids to join in. If we can get a group to do it *for* you, you could walk on at the last minute and hand out the leaflets. It's perfect.'

Riley pondered. It did seem mad, even if they could get a dance group to join in at such short notice. But she had to admit, it might be fun.

'Imagine doing something in the High Street, stopping everyone in their tracks on a Saturday afternoon, having them all snapping photos to join in the competition,' Ash added. 'Maybe Ethan could help out with the filming?'

At the mention of his name, Riley's stomach flipped again. But although the thought of Ethan was a happy one, she didn't have time to think about anything other than the shop. She looked up to see Ash staring at her expectantly.

'It will take a lot of sorting out,' she said.

'You're the queen of organisation!' Ash grabbed Riley's notepad and held it in the air. 'It's perfect, and it will be so much fun! I might join in too. They always look so brilliant when you watch them back.'

'It couldn't cost us much, though.' As ever, Riley was the practical one. 'Wouldn't the dancers need to be paid?'

'I doubt it. Serena could use a well-rehearsed routine. Do you think Sadie and Dan would join in too?'

'Yes, I reckon they might.' It really was a mad idea, and it could easily backfire, especially if Suzanne got to hear about it before it happened. But if there was a chance – even the slightest chance – that it might work, they had to give it a go. She nodded at Ash.

'Okay, let's look into it.'

'Great! Now can we talk about Ethan? I'm dying to know how you're getting on.'

'I don't think so,' Riley pouted. 'You haven't even told me wonder boy's name. I'm beginning to suspect that you've made him up.'

'I haven't!' Ash shook her head. 'It's just early days yet. His name is Warwick.'

'Warwick? That sounds . . . young.'

Ash threw a cushion at her and stood up. She walked across the room on her tiptoes, hips swaying, bottom sticking out, shoulders held high. She swivelled as a model would do and walked the few paces back to Riley, her right hand sticking up.

'This is what you need to be concentrating on,' she said, keeping her face straight until they both burst into laughter.

Sadie stretched out her arms and yawned. She lifted her head up off the pillow. The room was fairly light as she glanced at the clock beside her. With a groan, she sat up quickly. She flicked the switch on and off but there was no power. Unexpected tears dropped down her face. This was all she needed after another night tossing and turning.

She checked her watch and shot out of bed.

'Damn,' she cursed. It was 8:30 a.m., the alarm hadn't gone off and for some reason Esther had slept through, too. Most mornings Sadie would find her awake in her room, reading a book or playing on her tablet. Christine and Paul had treated her to one for Christmas. Esther loved taking photos and putting them into folders. She was getting quite good at it – although, when Esther wasn't looking, Sadie had removed a few dodgy ones of herself that her daughter had taken.

'Esther.' She went into her room quickly. 'Come on, poppet. The alarm didn't go off and we're late.'

Esther's eyes opened. Just like her mum, she stretched her arms above her head and then sat up. 'Is it a school day, Mummy?' she asked.

'Yes, it is.' Sadie raced across to the wardrobe and took out a clean school uniform, laying it on the bottom of her bed. 'Get dressed quickly.'

'Why isn't the electric on?' Esther wanted to know.

'I don't know,' Sadie replied patiently. 'I'll have to ring Cooper to see if he can sort it out for us.'

'Yippee! Can Cooper take me to school?'

'No, poppet. He has to go to work.'

'But he is his own boss. That's what he tells you, doesn't he, Mummy?'

Sadie raised her eyes to the ceiling. It was exactly what Cooper kept telling her. When she worried that she was taking up too much of his time whenever she asked him to do anything for her, he would say he could work as he chose. She didn't want to rely on him too much but this was one of those occasions when she had to ask for help. She missed her dad as much as Ross when there was something she couldn't sort out for herself. And she certainly couldn't afford to get an electrician out. There would be an astronomical emergency call-out charge, and what if it was something as simple as a blown fuse, that she could fix herself if she knew how? Cooper would show her what to do if the problem was easy to solve, in case it happened again.

Tears pricked her eyes – would she always feel this helpless?

By the time Cooper's van pulled up outside the house, Sadie had managed to get in touch with Riley and explain that she would be late, praying that Suzanne wouldn't choose this morning to do a spot check, as she often did. It seemed that the electric had been off for a few hours. If Cooper could get it back on soon, everything in the freezer might possibly be safe.

Esther was sitting at the kitchen table, eating a bowl of cereal. Sadie was putting together a sandwich for her lunch box as Cooper knocked on the back door and came in.

'You rang, madam?' he spoke with a cheerful tone. Too cheerfully, for Sadie. Honestly, wasn't the man ever miserable? Pushing her self-pity to one side, she greeted him with a smile.

'Cooper!' shouted Esther as she spotted him, getting down from the table and running at his legs. She hugged his waist as best she could before running back to the table to finish her breakfast. 'We're very late!' she shouted.

Sadie rolled her eyes. 'If I needed kiddie power to run the house, I would be quids in,' she exclaimed.

'I'll just go and check the fuse box, see if anything has tripped.' Cooper jerked a thumb over his shoulder. 'It's outside on the wall, isn't it?'

Sadie nodded, following him. 'I need to know what to do if it's just as simple as a blown fuse,' she told him. 'I don't want to trouble you all the time.'

'It's no trouble,' Cooper gave a sigh.

'Oh, I didn't mean anything by it. I just have to be prepared to do things on my own. So it's useful to learn.'

'I don't mind helping you out.' He grinned. 'They don't call me Super Cooper for nothing.'

'They don't call you Super Cooper at all,' Sadie couldn't help but smirk.

A few minutes later, Cooper had indeed located a blown fuse. The circuit had tripped, and once he'd flicked it back on again they went around the kitchen testing appliances. When Sadie flicked on the kettle, the electricity went off again. She picked it up to discover water around its base.

'The kettle's leaking,' she explained.

'I always said you make a dodgy cuppa,' Cooper joked. 'I can get you a new one this afternoon and drop it off later, if you like?'

'I can get one from town,' said Sadie, not wanting to put him to any more trouble than necessary. 'A bloody kettle.' She shook her head. 'Thanks, Cooper.'

'That's what friends are for,' Cooper grinned. 'Now, as I can't have a cuppa, can I scrounge a piece of toast? And then I can give you a lift and drop Esther off at school on the way. Deal?'

'You'll make someone a fantastic husband,' she smiled, giving his arm a squeeze. 'And, as you know, I can make a mean Sunday roast but other than that I'm hopeless at cooking. So, would you like your toast half burnt or burnt completely?'

'Wow, I can hardly resist either, but half burnt sounds good.' He pulled out a chair and sat down at the table with Esther. 'What are you doing at school today, do you know?'

As she turned away at the intimacy of the scene, Sadie held in tears. Ross used to sit and talk to Esther for hours.

'Mummy, can Cooper come for tea tonight?'

Sadie swivelled round to face them. 'Of course he can.'

'I'm actually busy, sorry,' Cooper replied. 'Maybe tomorrow?'

Sadie nodded. Although she was secretly disappointed in not having any adult company, she didn't want Esther latching onto him any more than she already had. Cooper would eventually find a woman he loved and have a family of his own. She didn't want Esther getting too attached, mistaking his friendship for a father's affection.

She never wanted Cooper to feel obliged to come round all the time either. She had to learn to stand on her own two feet, no matter how hard that turned out to be.

CHAPTER TEN

At ten o'clock, Riley took an unofficial break, hoping that Suzanne, the praying mantis, wouldn't come by for a spot check and find her missing. If she did, Sadie and Dan had been told to say that she'd had to rush to the doctor's.

It had been a month since their competition had started and yet things were still slow. She took a bus out of the town centre and, only fifteen minutes later, was crossing the road towards Petrani's Insurance Brokers, as Ash had instructed her. Above the brokers' office, she could see large letters on skew-whiff coloured posters spelling out the name Streetwise. Serena's dance studio was on the first floor.

She pushed on a door and went into a small reception area with a row of chairs to one side and a desk against the far wall. Sat behind it was a thin young woman who didn't look old enough to have a job, her thick dark hair hiding most of her pretty face until she looked up. Her name badge said Rhianna.

'Hi, I'm looking for Serena,' said Riley.

'Hi, yes, she's expecting you.' Rhianna glanced at her watch. 'Her class is due to finish in a few minutes. Do you want to go up?' She pointed towards a staircase.

As she went upstairs Riley heard faint music, and imagined herself flying around the room like Jennifer Beals in *Flashdance*. Laughing to herself at the ridiculous image, she heard a thud, thud, the beat getting louder as she levelled with the first floor. She could hear a woman shouting 'Five, six, seven, eight. Good work, Jessica! And again. Two, three, four, and change!'

There was a narrow corridor ahead. On the left side, along its length, was a window at waist height, and she stood for a moment, entranced by what she saw. A group of children, she reckoned no more than six years old, were running around the room dressed as elephants. It was the cutest thing she had seen in ages and it brought a lump to her throat. One young boy, seemingly unfazed by the fact that he was in the minority, was racing round the room chasing the girls with his arm made out to be a trunk. Riley smiled when she saw him being chastised by the tutor.

'Now, now, Freddy,' the woman shouted. 'Let's not get carried away.'

Riley thought his name fitted him perfectly but wouldn't like to put a bet on which Fred he was most like – Krueger or Flintstone.

The woman clapped. 'Right, you lot of ugly mugs, back to mums and dads and I will see you next week. And remember,' she said, holding her arm out like an elephant's trunk, 'keep practising being an elephant!'

As the room exploded with the sounds of screeching and footsteps thundering across the floor, the woman turned to Riley.

'Peace at last,' she sighed. 'I do love that class but they try my patience, little imps.' She held out a hand. 'I'm Serena. You must be Riley.'

Serena reminded Riley of a young Gwyneth Paltrow. Her blonde hair was tied back in a ponytail, showing off her fresh complexion. She wore leggings under a loose, oversized T-shirt that slipped off one shoulder to reveal a flash of a shocking-pink bra strap.

Riley shook her hand. 'I'm the one with two left feet and a mission impossible, should you choose to accept it.'

'Oh, I will definitely choose to accept it.' Serena pointed to a room off the main hall. 'Let's grab a drink.'

Once Riley had gone over her ideas, she tried to apologise for coming up with such a ridiculous notion.

'It's a mad idea, isn't it?' she cringed.

'Let me be the judge of that,' replied Serena. 'A flash mob sounds exciting. Do you have a song in mind?'

'Yes,' Riley smiled in embarrassment. 'This is going to sound ridiculous, but whenever Pharrell Williams' "Happy" comes on in the shop, which isn't that often thankfully, we all stand in a line and do a dance.'

'A dance?' Serena's eyebrows went up questioningly.

'Yes.' She clapped her hands in the air and then down at her side. 'I know it's really silly, but we have the customers in stitches, most of the time – ourselves too.'

Serena paused momentarily. 'Can I have a think about what song might work with one of the routines they already know? That way there won't be too much preparation on my side, apart from drilling you and your staff into shape. I'm sure I can sort you out with something easy to do that will look spectacular.'

Riley beamed. 'Be my guest. I'm really happy that you agreed to see me, let alone want to do this.'

Serena handed her a mug of coffee. 'Are you kidding? I mentioned a flash mob to the group and I couldn't hear myself telling them the rest of the details as they were screaming so loud. They were so excited. I'm not sure how many of them will be able to keep it to themselves, though. But I suppose any publicity is better than doing this kind of thing and no one stopping to look at you.'

Riley agreed, though even just the thought of it scared her. 'So the dancers – what are they like?'

'They're aged between fifteen and twenty-one. We have fifteen girls and three boys. So with you three, plus me, and Ash mentioned that she'd like to be involved too, that's twenty-three people. I reckon we can put on a good enough show with that number of dancers. What do you think?'

Riley was still dubious. 'How long will it take us to work on our routines?'

'You'll only have a basic routine. I reckon you'll master it within an hour. For me, it's a matter of working out who appears when, and where from – perhaps a few shop doorways on the High Street. I suppose we'll need to do a couple of practice sessions here at the studio with all the dancers. Then you can practise whenever you get the chance. It'll be thirty seconds at the most.'

'And you're sure you don't want any payment?' Riley gnawed at her bottom lip. 'I don't mean to sound ungrateful, it's a lot of work for you.'

'I like a challenge.' Serena waved her comment away. 'Besides, I'll get some press coverage for my business. And as long as you stay on your feet during your performance, and don't go arse over tit, then it will be good fun for you too.'

Riley laughed. 'Thank you so much. I know a lot of people wouldn't have given up their time for something like this.'

'You're right. But if I can help someone who is willing to help me, then I'm all for it. I love two-way promotion. Plus the dance group need to be motivated every now and then and this is just the thing.'

Riley grinned. 'So, when can we start?'

'I have an hour free on Friday, around seven – does that sound doable?'

Riley nodded. 'I'm sure it can be sorted. We have a six-year-old girl that would have to tag along. Is that okay?'

'Do you think she will join in?' Serena pondered. 'The cute factor will be incredible if she did.'

'Yes, I expect so!' said Riley, knowing that Esther would love to be involved. 'I'll have a word with Sadie – that's her mum – and see what she says.'

'Perfect. I'll see you here on Friday. Dress comfortably, but bring heels that you will be wearing on the day.'

'Will do!' Riley headed for the door.

'You're gonna love this. If it gets seen, we'll all be laughing.'

'As long as it's no one laughing *at* us!'

Serena sniggered. 'I can't promise that. And it will depend on my song choice, which I will let you know on Friday. When do you want this to happen by?'

'The following weekend. Do you think that's possible?'

'I'll let you know on Friday when I've seen exactly how you dance.'

'I imagine we'll be really bad,' Riley admitted.

'I'll sort you out. We'll get the guys wanting more.'

'That sounds like the wrong kind of dance to me.'

Serena laughed. 'There are no poles to wrap yourself around in here.'

As Riley left the building, her steps were a little lighter. How kind of Serena not to want any payment. It had been one of her biggest worries. Riley loved someone who had an entrepreneurial streak in them.

She couldn't wait to get back to the shop. Now all she had to do was persuade Dan and Sadie to put in the time for a week, and then they could strut their stuff for the good folk of Hedworth. And on Friday, they would learn their fate, determined by Serena's choice of song.

The High Street would never look the same again after this.

'So what do you think?' Riley looked at Ethan with the wonder of a child, hoping that he didn't think she'd gone mad. After all, he hadn't known her long. This could put their fledgling relationship into serious jeopardy.

She'd called him once she had seen Serena, to see if he was available for a quick coffee.

He stared at her straight-faced for a moment, and then laughed.

Riley felt unsure whether to smile or frown.

'I think it's a brilliant idea!' he said. 'But why do you need to promote the shop that much? Didn't you say it was doing well?'

'I might have exaggerated a little.' Riley looked sheepish. 'I thought maybe the paper wouldn't want another feature on a shop that was being threatened with closure.'

'You might close?' Ethan reached across the table for her hand. 'I had no idea things were that bad for you.'

'For all of us. It's our livelihood.'

'It's not all about the money for you, though, is it?'

Riley shook her head. 'Nor for the other staff, if I'm honest. I've seen people on the news where factories have closed and I've always thought, oh, that's a shame, and I hope there are other jobs out there for most of the people. What I hadn't thought about, until now, was the effect it would have on our lives away from work. It pays the bills but we're a team too, Ethan – we work so well together, but we're also really close outside of office hours. You mentioned office politics – we don't have that for a reason. We're like an extended family and I— I don't want to lose that.' Tears welled in her eyes and she looked away quickly. 'Sorry.'

'Hey.' He paused until she looked at him. 'I think the passion that you have is amazing. If I can help in any way, I will.'

A tear escaped and slid down her cheek. He wiped it away, still staring at her.

'I can set up the filming, that isn't a problem. I can also get Kim involved – she is brilliant with PR. If it's something we can spring on people, even better. I'll check with my boss and let you know.'

'You can do all that?' Riley hadn't thought further than the flash mob.

Ethan nodded. 'How long will it be before you're ready to do it?'

'We've agreed on next Saturday at two o'clock. There should be a fair number of people around at that time. I can set everything up by then but I doubt we'll be ready.'

'From what you're telling me, you have a twenty-second slot at the end, and then you're handing out leaflets.'

'Yes, but—'

'Parkinson's Law,' said Ethan. 'Whatever time you have in which to do something, it will be done in that time. So if you set a date, you'll hit the deadline.'

'I wish I had your faith.'

'You don't need faith, Riley. You have courage and desire.' He gazed at her. 'So, now that you have a date for the flash mob, do we have another date too?' He leaned forward and planted a kiss on her lips. 'I need my Ethan time too.'

She nodded again, this time smiling. Ethan time – she liked that. Then she began to panic.

'It won't go viral, will it?' she asked. 'I'd hate for people to see me make a fool of myself.'

'If you can sit in a shop window looking like Cinderella, I think you can do this. You're made of strong stuff.'

Riley really did hope so. Because if it went wrong, not only would she bring unwanted attention to Chandler's, she would also be the laughing stock of Hedworth.

CHAPTER ELEVEN

'How did you get on?' Dan was the first to ask Riley when she got back to work later that morning.

'Really great.' Riley shrugged off her jacket and went behind the till. 'Are you both free on Friday evening?' she asked.

'I can be,' said Dan. 'I doubt I'll have any exciting dates to go on at this rate.'

'I can be, if I can get Christine to keep Esther with her for a while longer,' Sadie said, joining them once she'd finished serving a customer.

'No need. Serena says she can come with you, if you like.' She threw Sadie a grin. 'Serena is happy for Esther to join in with the dance, if that's okay with you?'

'Really?' Sadie frowned. 'Do you think she'll cope with a dance routine?'

'She'll be more than capable,' sniggered Dan. 'It'll be us that will take some teaching.'

'Serena suggested that she came on at the end to do one simple move,' said Riley.

'Maybe she could carry a sign with the Twitter hashtag on it?' Sadie suggested.

'That would be great! I'll make a list of what we need and what we have to do before next Saturday. I did tell you we're doing the flash mob a week on Saturday?'

'What?' Sadie and Dan spoke in unison.

'But we won't be anywhere near ready by next Saturday!' Dan complained.

'Coffee anyone?' Riley grabbed their mugs as the other two threw excuses at her. But just as she was about to disappear downstairs, she spotted Marsha coming along the High Street. She went to greet her, and the two people she was with, at the door.

'Marsha,' said Riley. 'It's so lovely to see you again.'

'These are my friends.' Marsha pointed to a girl dressed almost identically to her, with long blonde hair and pale features. The only colour on her face was a dash of deep purple lipstick. 'This is Ruby and,' she pointed again, 'this is Frank.'

A young man who seemed as if he would be more comfortable on a beach in Newquay grinned at Riley. He looked like a fresh-faced surfer boy without the tan, his dark hair in messy dreadlocks, a tattoo of a bird on his neck and a ring through his bottom lip. His eyes were welcoming, putting Riley at ease. She couldn't help but glance at his clothes, instantly loving the sense that his baggy trousers, Converse trainers and slash-necked jumper with thick-ribbed cuffs had all been thrown together to create the perfect look.

'I've been looking forward to meeting you,' said Riley, pointing to the seating area. 'Have you brought any bags with you?'

'Yeah, I've got a few.'

Marsha held up another tote bag, decorated with picture postcard motifs. 'A bag full of bags.' She laughed as she handed them to Frank. 'We'll be back in about twenty minutes.'

'Thanks,' said Riley. She pointed to the back of the room.

While Dan and Sadie took it in turns to look after the shop, Frank showed Riley several bags. They chatted amicably about how he came up with particular designs, why he used certain colours, how he drew some pictures and used motifs for others.

By the time he had shown her the fourth bag, Riley was sold. These were just what she needed to attract people's eye to the shop window.

'Are you able to work on a sale or return basis?' she asked next. 'I can't pay upfront at first but if you have some to display, and they sell well, we could always order some in then.'

'Yes, I'm up for that.'

Riley watched Frank's dreadlocks bounce around as he talked animatedly. Up close he was really attractive and she wondered how he would look without all the hair. She could imagine him in a sharp suit but, equally, knew that he would look drab in it compared to the way he looked now.

'How does forty per cent sound?' asked Frank.

'And you say they will retail at fifteen pounds?'

'For starters, yes. Once I get more well-known, the price will go up. "Designed by Frank" is going to be the bag to be seen with. I have other plans too, and—'

Riley signalled for him to stop. 'Twenty per cent and you have a deal.'

'I was after at least thirty.'

'If it was exclusive, I might run to twenty-five . . .'

'Exclusive for how long?'

'Shall we try three months?' Riley knew that the shop might not be open that long but she wasn't going to tell him that.

Frank paused for a moment before nodding his head. 'Twenty-five per cent it is, then. Three months exclusive to you. Do you have a website?'

'Not yet, but I'm working on it. We also have plans to promote the shop over the next few weeks, so I'm sure you'll get some coverage.'

Frank held out his hand. 'Great, we have a deal.'

Riley shook his hand and stood up. 'Are you leaving these with me or do you want to display them yourself?'

'I'd like to display them, but I'll need to think about how, now that I've seen your window. Can I come back tomorrow?'

'Yes.' Riley beckoned Marsha and Ruby over as they came back into the shop. 'Ladies, can you give me some advice on these sandals I'm thinking of stocking?'

Riley showed the two girls the sandals, her smile widening as she saw their excited faces.

'Ooh, they are cool. How much are they?'

'Twenty pounds.'

'Twenty pounds! That's a bargain,' said Marsha. 'I love the blue ones.'

'They are my favourites, too.' Sadie came over to join them after the last prospective customer had come and gone, empty-handed.

'Are you going to buy some in?' Marsha wanted to know.

Everyone looked at Riley. She would be going against Suzanne if she did stock them. But with Frank's tote bags on display, and the bright colours of the sandals, Marsha's age group could be a target market for Chandler's to concentrate on. It could bring in some much needed trade. She nodded vehemently.

'Yes, I think I am.'

'Great, would you save me a pair in size six, please? I definitely want those blue ones.'

Riley jotted down the details.

'Me, too. I'm a size five, please,' said Ruby, smiling shyly. 'I reckon half the girls on the campus would like them, too.'

Riley grinned as they left the shop. Half the girls on the campus sounded great to her. And along with Designed by Frank tote bags, their window was going to look very inviting.

She just hoped Suzanne wouldn't be too annoyed with her for taking control.

Frank had been gone no more than twenty minutes when Suzanne came into the shop. Riley was showing Sadie some of the designers she was following on Twitter, pointing out some of the crazy shoe designs. Dan was serving a man who needed a pair of shoes to go with the suit he'd just purchased. He was going to his father's funeral. Dan had been giving him extra time as he chatted.

Riley sighed, putting down the cup of coffee that Sadie had just made for her. Typical, they would be caught on a break.

Suzanne walked past, leaving behind the smell of something sweet and sickly.

'Riley, come with me,' she beckoned, curling her index finger. 'Chop-chop.'

'Chop-chop?' Sadie mumbled. 'Who the hell does she think she is?'

Riley rolled her eyes and picked up her drink again. She wasn't missing a cup of coffee for anything. 'Into battle I go,' she said quietly before following behind Suzanne.

Suzanne twirled around in a flash when Riley joined her in the staffroom. She pointed to the competition chart, on the wall to her right.

'There don't seem to be many sales added to this, I see.'

'It's the beginning of the week,' Riley explained. 'We make most of our sales at the weekend, sometimes Thursdays as it's late-night shopping in the shopping centre.'

'That's something we need to look at,' Suzanne nodded, still staring at the chart. 'If we do keep the shop open, despite the abysmal sales you've racked up between you, then we'll need to think of staying open longer during the week as well as starting to open on Sundays. Until seven each weekday evening, at least.'

Riley didn't feel like protesting. She wondered what Suzanne meant by "we" – it definitely wouldn't include doing extra hours herself. And Riley was willing to bet that the pay would remain the same either way. Really, was there any point? It was worse than being at school.

'Have you thought of any more ideas for how to increase sales?' Suzanne looked at her now. 'It's been three weeks and, even with the article in the local news, nothing has impressed me so far. I think you need to motivate the staff more, or make them work harder. It's your responsibility. I need to see you pulling your weight.'

'I *am* pulling my weight. I want Chandler's to stay open, and I want it to do well, but I don't think threats will help.'

'Threats?' Suzanne looked insulted. 'I'm not threatening you.'

Riley said nothing, deciding instead to take a sip of coffee.

Suzanne folded her arms. 'I'm trying to save your skin, so I expect you to be a little more grateful.'

Riley clenched her teeth to stop herself spitting out anything about the flash mob. 'I just don't know what else we can do to drum up more trade,' she said, finally.

'I'm sure you'll think of something.' Suzanne glanced at her watch. 'I have an appointment for a manicure in ten minutes. I might call in later to see you, or it may be tomorrow.' She tapped a finger twice on the chart. 'This needs to improve, and quickly, or I might just tell Max to go ahead with his plans when I next speak to him on the phone. He wants to close before the three months are up. That's not what you want, is it?'

'Do you know what, Suzanne?' Riley put her coffee mug down with a bang on the table. 'I just might tell Sadie and Dan that Max came round quite a few times on his own last year. I know he was taking money from the till because I saw him.'

Suzanne paled.

'He told me to mind my own business and I didn't even ask what he needed the money for. Maybe that's the reason things aren't as good as they seem. If he paid back what he took, then—'

Suzanne held up her hand. 'Whatever money went out of the till would have been taken because Max needed something for the business.'

'Great, then if you can just drop off the receipts, I can enter them into the accounts.'

'This has nothing to do with you.' Suzanne narrowed her eyes, her nostrils flaring. 'And it had better go no further, do you hear?'

Riley said nothing. It was clear something was going on between the two of them, something that Suzanne didn't want anyone to know about. She wondered if it had anything to do with Max not being around. It wasn't unusual for him to go overseas, but it was strange he hadn't been seen since last year. And Suzanne didn't bring his name up in conversation as much as she used to.

Suzanne glared at her once more before flouncing out of the room as quickly as she had arrived. Once the door closed behind her, Riley's shoulders drooped. At least the flash mob was still under wraps. If word of that got out, Suzanne would try and stop it. And they were too close for that now.

Friday night came around quickly. Riley was filled with a mixture of fear and giddy excitement as they made their way to Streetwise Dance Studios. A different girl was on the reception desk and pointed them upstairs.

'Hi, guys, come on in!' Serena opened the door and held out her arm. 'Welcome to the room of pain.'

'Sounds a bit *Fifty Shades of Grey* to me,' Dan quipped.

'Believe me, you will be in pain by the time I've knocked you into shape.' Serena pulled him inside the studio. 'Hey, Ash.' She gave her friend a hug.

'This is Dan and Sadie.' Riley pointed to them both in turn. Serena smiled, then stooped level with Esther. 'And who might you be, miss?' she asked.

'My name is Esther,' she said. 'I'm my mum's lucky mascot. I was the apple of my daddy's eye, but he died.'

'I— oh,' Serena looked perplexed.

'Come on, poppet.' Sadie flashed Serena an apologetic look. 'Maybe we can show Serena how well you can dance. What do you say?'

'I want to go on *The X Factor*, Mummy, not *Strictly Come Dancing*.' Esther trotted forward, loving the sound of her feet clicking on the floor. She watched herself in the mirrored wall at the back of the room.

'Tell everyone my dirty secrets, why don't you?' Sadie smiled. 'I am a reality TV show fanatic, guilty as charged.'

'There's nothing wrong with a bit of Simon Cowell within reason,' said Riley. She walked to the side of the studio, putting her bag on the floor and slipping off her coat. 'Come on, Serena, put us out of our misery, and tell us what song you've chosen for us.'

Serena had been teasing Riley since her first visit. Each day, she had sent her a text message with a different song choice, threatening to use each one if they didn't get everything sorted well in time. One of them had been Abba, 'Dancing Queen' – a complete and utter no. The next one had been Queen, 'I Want to Break Free' – another no. When she had suggested the Spice Girls, 'Wannabe', Riley had called to give Serena a categorical no. As Serena cackled down the line, Riley had realised that she'd been winding her up. So she was excited, yet apprehensive, to hear the final choice.

'Wait and see.' Serena pointed to the middle of the floor. 'I want you all in a line here.'

Riley, Dan, Ash and Sadie obliged. Esther held on to Sadie's hand.

'Are you ready?' Serena asked.

'Come on,' cried Riley 'We're dying to find out.'

'Okay, here we go.' Serena pressed a button on a remote control and raced to the door. 'I won't be a minute,' she cried, before disappearing through it.

'What's going on?' said Sadie.

Before anyone could reply, the music started. Riley grinned as she looked at Dan.

'It's Pharrell Williams.' He clapped his hands in delight. '"Happy".'

The door opened and in walked three girls. Dan's mouth dropped open as, dressed in the highest of heels and the tightest of mini-skirts, they strutted across the floor and began to dance in front of them. Esther clapped her hands too, jumping up and down next to Sadie.

Another two lines of the song went by before the door opened again. Three more girls appeared, this time in leggings, hoodies and trainers. They did their own style of dance before moving to join the others and all six did the same routine. Over the next two minutes, every few seconds, two or three more dancers came into the room and joined in.

Riley looked first at Sadie, and then at Dan, and then beamed. 'This is great!' she cried as the door opened again and three more girls came in, this time wearing rave gear.

As the chorus started up, the dancers moved around the room using every inch of the floor. Riley and Ash began to clap. Sadie held out Esther's hands and she clapped too.

Finally, the door opened for one last time and Serena was led in by a male dancer. He was slightly older than the rest of the group, dark-skinned with tight brown curls. He wore a tuxedo and held on to Serena's hand as she sashayed across the room in the highest of heels.

As the record came to an end, the couple came up close to Riley, Dan, Sadie and Esther. Serena twirled like a ballerina and then came to a stop in the male dancer's arms. She arched backwards and threw out her arm. In her hand there was a card. She thrust it at them.

It said '#BestShoeForward'.

The music stopped and the dancers caught their breath. There was a moment of stunned silence before they all started clapping.

'That was fantastic!' said Riley, clapping too. 'It was – beyond words.'

'Yes, wow!' agreed Dan. 'I'm not often speechless but that was *amazing*!' He frowned then. 'Which part do we have to do?'

'Just the bit at the end that I did with Anthony,' Serena replied. 'You'll all be partnered up with an experienced dancer.'

'Once we've finished, we could hand out flyers about the competition,' suggested Ash.

'Yes,' agreed Dan. 'We could even have a separate word on each card. I do like Best Shoe Forward, though.'

'I can't believe you wound me up about all those songs!' Riley narrowed her eyes at Serena. 'You knew all the time that you would use "Happy", didn't you?'

'Yes, sorry.' Serena nodded. 'I couldn't help but tease you.'

Riley smiled. 'This is going to be amazing!'

'Good, I'm glad you like it.' Serena clicked her fingers. 'Because this is where the hard work begins.'

'Isn't that a line from *Fame*?' Dan whispered to Riley, who hushed him with a mock-glare.

'We'll never learn that in a week,' said Sadie.

'Of course you will,' Serena encouraged. 'You're going to learn it now and then it's practice, practice, practice!'

'Are you sure?' said Riley.

'I'm absolutely certain.' Serena waved over three boys and a girl. 'These are your partners. So, in the words of the late David Bowie – bless him – let's dance!'

CHAPTER TWELVE

After the rehearsal, Cooper had picked them up and they all went back to Sadie's house. It was 7:30 p.m. As they had gone straight from the shop to the dance studio, there had been no time to eat, so Cooper and Ash had now gone to collect a takeaway.

Riley was getting anxious now. At everyone's insistence, Ethan had been invited along too. Although he'd briefly met Sadie and Dan, Riley had been pleased when Ash had wanted to meet him too. Yet, when Sadie invited him to her house, Riley knew the pressure it would put on him – and on them. He would be under scrutiny, even if only in a playful way. She prayed her friends wouldn't grill him too much.

Although Riley had known Ethan for less than a month, everything had seemed to slot into place for the two of them. It felt like she'd known him forever, yet at the same time as if they had only just met. The familiar stomach flip caused by excitement and apprehension took Riley by surprise whenever she thought about the next time she would see him. And when she got home, she sat wanting to remember every minute of each date, like she'd done many times as a teenager.

Although it was making her nervous, shouldn't she take a chance? She thought back to when she had met Nicholas. It was hard to get that kind of feeling when meeting someone no more than two nights a week. The relationship and the butterflies didn't tend to build up as quickly.

And, if it weren't for Ethan, there probably wouldn't be a flash mob. If he hadn't offered to film it for them, Riley would most likely have given up. He'd even got the backing of the newspaper now. Kim was going to go big around the secrecy of it all, dropping hints on the paper's Twitter feed on Saturday. *Hedworth News*'s Twitter feed had over 20,000 followers! Riley had thrown her arms around Ethan's neck when he'd told her, so grateful for his support. He could have thought it was a mad idea and therefore not want to join in. But he hadn't – only time would tell if he'd made the right decision or not.

Riley checked her watch and saw that he'd be arriving in less than ten minutes, so she grabbed her bag and dashed upstairs. Sadie had said she could take a shower. She'd have to be quick, and just freshen up her make-up, but at least she could wash away the sweat she could feel on her skin and change her clothes.

'I can't believe how much I'm aching,' said Dan when she rejoined him in the kitchen. He was sitting at the table, rubbing the bottom of his back. 'I'm going to be good for nothing in the morning.'

'You're aching?' Riley prodded him in the shoulder as she walked past him towards Sadie. 'You didn't have to do as much as us girls. And you certainly weren't flung like a whipping top across the floor. I swear I haven't stopped spinning yet. So I think you can count yourself lucky.'

'*And* you get double practice time as there are two of us in the shop,' Sadie joined in as she took plates out from the cupboard. 'You should have the routine nailed in no time, while we,' she pointed at Riley, 'have no chance.'

'We'll get there,' said Riley. 'Even if we have to practise night and day. I'm determined to stay on my feet and not make a fool of myself.'

'I got a special part, didn't I, Mummy?' said Esther, reaching her arms up to Sadie.

'You certainly did, madam.' Sadie picked her up and began to waltz around the kitchen with her.

Esther burst into fits of giggles as the doorbell rang. She shimmied down Sadie's legs, shrieking, 'I'll go!'

But Sadie pulled her back. 'Let Riley go,' she said.

'I want to see Cooper!' Esther protested, trying to wriggle from her grip.

'It might not be Cooper, and you're in your jim-jams.'

'I'll go,' said Dan. 'Save you blushing when I bring Ethan in.'

Riley grinned, already feeling her skin hotting up. Ash and Cooper had texted to say they were minutes away, and she suddenly felt nervous about introducing Ethan. After being unable to share Nicholas with them, the last time they had met one of her dates had been when she'd first introduced them to Tom. When they had split up, the dynamics of the group had changed a little, as Ross and Tom had got on really well. The same had happened when Sarah and Dan had gone their separate ways. But no one had thought for a minute, back then, that Ross wouldn't be around now.

Dan brought Ethan into the kitchen. 'Here she is, all fresh and lovely. Whereas I stink like a kipper after all that hard work.'

Riley walked over and greeted Ethan with a kiss.

'Don't take any notice,' she told him, holding onto his hand. 'He hasn't stopped moaning since we finished.'

'Thank goodness the flash mob is next weekend, then,' Ethan sympathised, grinning.

'Are you talking about the big dance-off?' said Cooper, appearing in the doorway, Ash behind him.

Esther ran into his arms. 'Cooper!' she cried. 'Do you have any chips?'

'I do.' He picked her up. 'You can have . . . five.'

'Five? I want more than that,' she giggled.

'You're not having many,' said Sadie, taking her from Cooper. 'And then it's off to bed for you. It's way too late for you to be up.'

Stomach awash with nerves again, Riley introduced Ethan to Cooper and Ash. She needn't have worried. They did indeed welcome him into their fold as she had hoped.

'Ash has been telling me all about the dance,' said Cooper. 'I think they should show us, don't you?' He looked at Ethan, who nodded.

'You must be joking,' Riley cried.

'I'm up for it.'

Dan pulled her into his arms and they began to dance around the kitchen. Three seconds in, they were all feet and laughing at Ethan's expression.

'Is that it?' he asked, incredulously.

'We're not showing anyone all of it until the day,' said Riley.

'Is it worth watching?' Cooper looked as doubtful as Ethan.

'You'll just have to come and watch us.' Ash prodded him hard in his arm.

'Oh, I wouldn't miss that for the world,' Cooper said, as he held up the greasy brown paper bag he was carrying. 'I don't suppose any of you want this, now that your bodies are your temples?'

Everyone decided to leave quite quickly after the food had been eaten. It was plain to see that Riley and Ethan wanted to spend time alone, so Cooper offered to give Ash a lift home and then come back. Sadie wasn't quite sure why, but she was glad of it.

By 9:00 p.m., the dishes had been done and the house was her own again except for Cooper, who was making a coffee before he left.

Sadie went through to the hall. Even though Esther had been put to bed over an hour ago, she could still hear her in her room. She beckoned Cooper to the bottom of the stairs.

'Listen,' she whispered, grabbing his arm.

Esther was singing 'Happy', clapping her hands. She had some of the words and some of the tune but not exactly in the right order.

They tried not to laugh in case she heard them.

'She's so cute,' whispered Cooper.

'She won't be when I can't get her up in the morning,' Sadie whispered back. 'Esther?' she shouted up the stairs. 'Bed, young lady.'

They heard her run across the room in a fit of giggles.

Sadie smiled at Cooper. Without warning, she felt tears well in her eyes, and found she couldn't do anything to stop them falling.

'Hey.' Cooper drew her into his embrace.

'I miss sharing things like this with Ross,' she sobbed. 'He would have found that so funny.'

'He would have tried to dance with her, too,' Cooper soothed, rubbing her back. 'I can't do that. I definitely have two left feet.'

'I miss him so much, but sometimes I can't even remember the sound of his voice. I can't remember his laugh. I go to sleep and ache for him to be by my side in my bed. I get up thinking of him, I go to bed thinking of him. He's been gone ten months now. I wish I didn't feel so lonely. '

'Grief is a thing you get over in your own time. There are no rules to say how long it takes. You'll go through different stages before you accept it.'

'Is that why I still feel guilty?' She pulled away from him.

'What do you mean?'

They moved back to sit in the living room. Sadie wondered whether to tell him to leave. She couldn't burden him with her feelings. But she couldn't stop the words from tumbling out.

'I was terrible to him before he died,' she admitted. 'All I did was shout and get angry all the time. Why did I want to inflict such pain on him? He was the one who was suffering. Okay, I was suffering too, but I had no right to take it out on him. He couldn't do anything. He was lying there, just waiting to die.' She looked up through more tears. 'And now I'm left with this pain. I have to hide my grief from Esther, and I have to hide my feelings when I'm at work. I try to hold it all in but sometimes I can't. Everywhere I go, I see happy couples. I see people in love. It's so unfair. Sometimes I want to run out onto the High Street and scream at everyone.'

'It's a natural reaction,' said Cooper softly. He reached for her hand but she pulled it away.

'Why can't I get over losing him? I *have* to get over that before I can move on with my life. And now that the shop might close, what am I going to do without Riley and Dan, to get me through the days? I— I can't do this on my own.'

'You don't have to,' said Cooper. 'You have us to help you.'

'It's not enough.'

A silence fell upon the room. Sadie hoped she hadn't offended him with her outburst.

'Ross wanted me to live my life without him,' she tried again to explain. 'He wanted me to go on and do everything we'd done before, but with someone else. He wanted me to be loved again.' She looked at Cooper. 'I told him I didn't think I could do that, and he got angry with me for a while, and then he calmed down.'

'He loved you so much,' said Cooper.

Sadie nodded. 'I feel desperately lonely without him, yet I also feel that I'm being selfish if I show that. I have Esther to think about. I shouldn't be feeling sorry for myself. But I— I can't do this without him.'

Again, Cooper drew her into his arms and let her cry until her tears had dried up. It was so good to have his arms around her. She felt a physical jolt as she realised it was what she missed: being loved by someone, held by someone, belonging to someone. She missed being part of a couple.

Afterwards, she pulled away slightly, embarrassed by her outburst.

'Sorry about that.' Sadie reached for a tissue. 'Sometimes I just can't keep it all in.'

'I've told you, anytime.' Cooper stared at her. 'Don't forget that. I do worry about you.'

A thought struck her, causing her to gasp. 'You don't think you're a substitute for Ross, do you?'

'Of course not.' Cooper shook his head. 'I really wish I could fall in love with you and marry you and make you and Esther happy, but I can't do that. It would be like sleeping with my sister.'

'Eww.' Sadie wrinkled her nose. 'That's gross.'

'I can still make you smile.' Cooper kissed her gently on the forehead. 'And I can look after you just the same.'

'Mummy, are you all right?' Esther's head popped round the door frame.

'Sure I am.' Sadie wiped at her eyes, as she beckoned her over. She pulled her daughter onto her lap and held her close. 'I thought you were asleep.'

'I'm too excited.'

'But everyone knows a good dancer needs her beauty sleep,' Cooper told her. After a moment, he took Esther's hand. 'Come on, I'll tuck you in.'

As they left the room, Sadie held back tears once more. Thank goodness she had supportive friends around her. She really was lucky.

Once Cooper had gone, she would write in her journal, then maybe log on to Grieve Together. If Tanya was around she might be able to have a quick chat. Tanya would understand.

And then she might be able to get a grip, even if just for Esther's sake.

CHAPTER THIRTEEN

Jimmy was sitting in the armchair in the window when Riley and Ethan arrived at his house. Before they'd got through the door, he had leapt from the chair and rushed to them. His barking was insane as he dived around their feet, following them into the living room, jumping on every seat before sliding along the laminate flooring.

'Jimmy, me lad,' Ethan cried, trying to stop him jumping up at Riley. 'Calm down, will you? You'll do yourself an injury.'

'He's fine.' Riley sat down quickly. 'At least he's welcoming. Hey, boy,' she smiled as Jimmy placed his chin on her knee, and she stroked his head. 'He must really miss you when you're working.'

'My next-door neighbour has a key and checks on him during the day. I don't know what I'd do without her, given the often irregular hours of my job. I know most of the time it's daytime hours, and if I get called out it's likely to be during the night, but she lost her dog last year and Jimmy seems to have filled the hole Ralph left behind. She often takes him round to her house for a few hours, especially in summer when it's hot indoors.'

'Lucky fella.' Riley continued to stroke Jimmy's head.

'So, this dance?' Ethan looked at her pointedly. 'Will you be practising in your bedroom, watching yourself in your wardrobe mirror?'

'No!' Riley blushed. Serena had told her to visualise herself doing the dance in her mind. Sadly, every time she did, she saw herself falling over at the last minute, like Bridget Jones when she came down the fireman's pole showing off her knickers.

'Although I do hasten to add that maybe if I did something stupid, it might work out in my favour – people would share the video more then!'

'You'll be fine,' said Ethan.

'Or maybe everyone will be too busy cooing over Esther looking so cute next to all the grown-ups.'

'I still want to see some of your moves.' Ethan's voice turned husky. 'I can't wait to see what you can do.'

Riley felt a shiver pass through her as he reached for her hand. They hadn't slept together yet, but they were both keen to. Their kisses had turned more passionate with every date. She was surprised she had held out this long, really. She was the one holding back, so hurt by Nicholas's betrayal. She couldn't take that out on Ethan forever, though. It wasn't fair to him, and it would feel as if she didn't trust him.

It wasn't fair to herself, either.

More to the point, she *did* want to move things along, and she was looking forward to getting closer to him, even if she was a little nervous. Surely that was par for the course? She wasn't the type of person who would rip her clothes off as soon as she met someone. She wanted to know that it was right before giving herself to anyone, even at the age of thirty-two. Especially after the Nicholas debacle. She'd told Ethan she had some demons, and he'd said he understood.

But yes, she was ready now.

'No time like the present.' Her voice was soft. 'I'm not doing the dance, though. That is strictly for a one-off performance.'

'A one-off performance is definitely something I am *not* interested in. But . . .' Ethan pulled her to her feet and into his arms. 'Back to the dance – it isn't anything like *Dirty Dancing*, is it? Because I could definitely carry a watermelon.'

Riley laughed as they waltzed around the room.

'Ow!' she cried as he stamped on her toes one too many times. 'You're worse than I am.'

'Well, they do say practice makes perfect.'

Ethan twirled her one more time and then wrapped his arms around her as she faced him.

Riley looked up, noticing his dilated pupils, the curve of his lips and the gap between them. She glanced at his eyes, then his mouth, then back to his eyes.

Time seemed to stand still as he dipped his head towards hers. Their mouths pressed together as if it was the first time. She wrapped her arms around his neck, running one hand through his hair, feeling his body responding as a groan escaped his mouth. His lips began to travel to her neck, his hand to her breast. She pulled at his shirt, wanting to feel his skin. He groaned again, and pushed her down onto the settee.

Dropping on top of her gently, he went to kiss her.

'Aren't you forgetting something?' Riley asked.

'What?'

Riley nodded her head in the dog's direction.

Ethan grinned. 'Oh. You don't want an audience?' He scooped Jimmy up and carried him out of the room. Seconds later, he was back in the same position he'd left. His look was intense as she gazed back at him.

'Where was I?' he said, before dipping his mouth to find hers.

Over the next few days, every spare minute at work or at home was spent practising the dance. At home, Riley waltzed around her living room to the song as she streamed it on YouTube. At work, she and Sadie took it in turns to practise with Dan whenever the shop was customer-free.

By the time Wednesday evening rolled around, they were as ready as they would ever be. They were all at the dance studio, taking a breather after rehearsing for over an hour.

'Let's go again from the top!' Serena cried for the umpteenth time as she clapped her hands at the group.

As the dancers trooped back out into the corridor, all excited and pumped up with adrenaline, Riley stood at the front of the room, bent over, hands on knees, trying to catch her breath.

'Honestly, I don't think I've ever worked so hard in my life,' she exclaimed through ragged breaths. She held up a hand. 'I'm going to be super-fit after this.'

Sadie leaned on her shoulder. 'Me, too. I'm glad Esther is having a sleepover at Christine and Paul's tonight. I'll be fit for nothing but the sofa as soon as I get in. But only after a long hot bath to ease the aches I know I'm going to have in the morning.'

'What time is Cooper picking us up?' asked Ash, leaning on Dan's shoulder, her face covered in red blotches and glistening with sweat.

Sadie checked her watch. 'Another half an hour yet! That's about ten more rehearsals.'

'We can do it,' said Dan, taking her and Sadie by the hand. 'Come on, Riley.'

Riley followed behind them, flashing a smile in Serena's direction before heading out of the door. As soon as they were in the corridor, the music started again and two dancers went through the door.

Although Riley was tired, and thinking that she would never get the dance moves perfected in time, she couldn't help feeling proud of what they had set up and what they had achieved in such a short space of time. Setting the date had made them focus rather than dilly-dally around, thinking they had lots of time to spare. It had been a perfect deadline. They were lucky to have Serena and Ethan helping them.

Ethan.

Her mind flicked back to the night before, when they had finally got down to getting to know each other. The sex had been good, a little nerve-racking at first, but the second time had been much better. Riley had felt herself relaxing, thinking of him only, and enjoying the moment, putting that slimeball Nicholas out of her mind completely.

She pressed a finger to her chin, feeling the slight stubble rash Ethan had created. He was picking her up after the dance session, and they were going back to his house again. Tonight would be the first time she had stayed overnight with him.

'You'll miss your place if you're not careful!' Dan clicked his fingers in front of her face.

For a moment, Riley tuned Ethan out of her thoughts as she heard the beats where she, Dan, Ash and Sadie were supposed to enter the room. Ryan, her dance partner, reached for her hand again. He was just how you'd expect a young dancer to be: tall, lean, tidy hair and an angelic face. His hands and feet were always poised in the right position, and he had the patience of a saint, bringing Riley back whenever she went wrong, almost leading her through the dance. He'd told her he'd have his own dance studio by the time he was twenty, and she didn't doubt him for a moment. Riley already knew he had a special knack for teaching. She was certain that she could nail it on the day, with him by her side.

Sadie's dance partner, Will, pushed the door open for the final time and they followed after him. Dan and Ash, with their dance partners, came in behind. This time the dance routine was flawless, none of them faltering, none of them messing up their steps.

'Nice work!' Serena clapped. 'At last! The moves weren't all perfect, but they were in the right order.' She reached for the remote control for the music deck. 'Again, from the top. Just to check that wasn't a fluke.'

Riley groaned. It was bound to have been a fluke. Knowing Serena, she would make them do it again and again and again. She'd be pirouetting in her sleep at this rate.

Serena turned back sharply. 'Did I hear someone complaining?'

'Me?' Riley looked all innocent. 'Not at all. I meant to do a little . . . "yay!", but it came out wrong.'

Serena grinned. 'You're doing fine,' she told her. 'You just need a little more practice. Shoo.'

'Ha ha, nice one,' said Dan.

Serena looked puzzled.

'Shoe?'

'Talking of which,' Serena pointed to their feet. Sadie and Riley had been told to wear trainers until they were accustomed to the moves. 'Pop on the heels you'll be dancing in. It's time to add the glamour.'

'Are you sure we're ready for that?' Ash questioned. 'I've only just learned to stay on my feet. Adding heels to the equation may definitely result in me tripping over my toes.'

'Better to do it now than on Saturday,' said Serena.

'You have a point.' Ash joined Sadie and Riley and changed into her heels.

'Time to make a fool of myself,' Riley muttered as they lined up in the corridor once more. 'If I stay up on my feet, I'll eat my hat.'

'If I stay up on my feet, I'll eat my shoes!' laughed Dan.

CHAPTER FOURTEEN

'Well, I'm not sure if that was fun or medieval torture,' said Dan, after they'd finished for the night and said their goodbyes to Serena and the dancers.

'It's all for a good cause,' said Sadie, trotting down the stairs behind him.

'Yes, I'm bound to lose a little bit of weight too!' Dan shouted. 'That can't be bad.'

'Depends how many takeaways you eat afterwards,' added Riley.

'Damn, I was just going to ask Cooper to go home via the chippy,' Dan remarked.

'I'll ask him instead,' said Ash. 'I'm starving after all that exercise.'

'You're always starving,' pointed out Riley. 'Beats me where you put it all.'

'Here.' Ash grabbed her waist. She pinched the tiniest bit of flesh. 'That was the curry we had the other night.'

Cooper and Ethan were standing chatting as everyone went out into the car park. Over their own chatter, Riley could hear the two men laughing, and was pleased to see they seemed to be getting on really well. It was mid-April, Easter the weekend after next, and after the recent warm spell the blustery weather was back again. Riley pulled her coat around her before she took off.

'What are you two laughing at?' Ash asked as they reached the waiting men.

'You beat me to it,' said Riley, grinning wildly at Ethan. 'Hi.'

'Hi, you.' He pulled her into his arms to shouts of 'Get a room!' from Dan.

'We were just taking bets on which one of you would fall over first,' said Cooper.

'And who did you say?' Ash replied.

Cooper pointed at her, trying to keep his face from breaking out into a smile.

'O ye of little faith!' Ash cried. 'I'll have you know, I've just stayed on my heels three times.'

'She fell off them at least fifteen times before that,' whispered Dan loudly.

Ash pushed him. 'Do you want to walk home?' she asked him.

'It's not your car,' retorted Cooper.

Apart from Riley, Cooper was giving them all a lift.

Ash grinned. 'I know, but I'm your co-pilot.' She turned to Riley and raised her eyebrows. 'I suppose you're going to the love shack?'

Riley blushed again. 'You're only jealous,' was the only thing she could think of to say.

Ash gave her a hug. 'You're so easy to wind up,' she whispered.

After saying their goodbyes, Ethan and Riley headed out of the car park amidst shouts of 'Be good' and 'Don't do anything I wouldn't'. It was all so childish but ridiculously funny.

Yet as soon as Riley got to Ethan's house, she suddenly felt nervous again. Luckily, Jimmy made a fuss of her, so she could dip her face towards him and hide her burning cheeks.

'I have pizza or cheese on toast,' Ethan shouted through from the kitchen.

'Pizza, please,' Riley shouted back. 'Although I really need to start eating normal food again. I've never eaten so much fast food in such a short space of time.'

With the pizza in the oven, Ethan walked towards her, removing his jumper before his lips found hers.

'The food is on low,' he whispered.

'I need a shower,' she whispered back.

'We'll take one together.' He took hold of her hand and led her out of the room.

An hour later, they were curled up on the sofa. The pizza had been eaten. Riley's hair was wet and she was wearing Ethan's dressing gown.

'So, are you ready to share your past with me yet?' Ethan asked.

Riley frowned at him.

'I just wondered what your story is, who hurt you recently? I can tell it took a while for you to trust me enough to . . .' He raised his eyebrows up and down.

Riley clammed up. 'I don't want to talk about it just yet,' she said. 'It will spoil a good evening.'

'So shall I tell you all about my sordid past instead?'

Riley's mouth dropped open.

Ethan laughed. 'I have a few scars too. I escaped a toxic relationship just over a year ago now. The woman I was seeing, Clarissa, I was with her for nearly two years. She'd always been the jealous type, but during the second year she became *extremely* jealous, of everything.' Ethan's smile faded. 'You know my job. I photograph people, I have to banter with them. But I'm a one-woman man. I could never cheat on anyone. Clarissa is a model. She was always being photographed, so she said she knew what went on.'

'That seems a bit unfair,' said Riley.

Ethan nodded. 'I take photographs for the local news: she modelled lingerie and swimsuits. There's a huge difference.'

'I bet she was beautiful.' All of a sudden, Riley felt inadequate.

'Beauty's only skin deep. It doesn't matter how good-looking someone is if the relationship is going nowhere because of it. She was really vain, constantly comparing herself to other women. Always accusing me of eyeing them up too – which I never did.' Ethan looked away for a moment, as if he couldn't bear to recall the memories.

'She began to follow me around,' he continued. 'Accused me of having an affair every time she saw me with a woman. In the end, her possessiveness got too much to handle. Even when I finished things, she made my life hell. She just wouldn't accept it was over.'

'That sounds awful,' said Riley. 'I don't think I could cope with anything that intense.'

'She was always calling me,' he said. 'She'd send me emails, texts and messages on social media. She damaged my car, kept ringing me at work after I changed my mobile number. The receptionist was going mad.

'She started leaving me written messages then. Everywhere I went they would appear, slipped under the windscreen wipers of my car. I had to have it out with her in the end, and then I stopped all contact. I haven't seen her for a few months now.'

'Ouch.' Riley reached for his hand when she saw how upset he was. 'That must have been terrible to go through.'

He nodded. 'But now I have you to think about instead. I like that – how about you?'

Even though Riley didn't want to tell him about Nicholas yet, it did seem tame in comparison to what he'd gone through. 'I think my story can wait for another night.' She leaned over, pulled him towards her and kissed him lightly on his lips.

Although it was a small town, there were lots of places to eat in Hedworth. Dan had seen the inside of most of them during the past couple of months. Date after date, meal after meal, he'd eaten and drank whilst each time trying to watch his weight. He could never resist a sticky toffee pudding, though, try as he might.

He sat in a booth at the Red Lion pub, nursing a glass of orange juice. Tonight he was meeting Ronnie – short for Veronica, so her profile said – thirty-one years old, divorced, no children, thank goodness (her words, not his), and looking for a man with a good sense of humour who liked going on walks, eating out and having fun. Well, he supposed if you counted all the times he covered the shop floor each day, that must surely be equivalent to a walk.

Ronnie was already ten minutes late and he wondered if she was going to show up at all. *Please let her arrive soon*, he thought, not wanting to be stood up.

Although, to be fair, she might already be here and watching him, and he might not recognise her, if his last two dates were anything to go by. Lorraine, especially, hadn't looked anything like her profile picture, so much so that he was actually thinking of complaining to the dating site for false advertising. At his reckoning seventy per cent of the profile pictures were probably a few years out of date.

His mind flipped back to the night before, when he had been chatting to a woman named Anna. He hadn't mentioned anything to Riley or Sadie, but he'd been talking to her on the website for a few nights now. Last night, they'd sent some private messages – nothing corny, just getting to know each other. She seemed a laugh, although he was disappointed that he couldn't see her face as she hadn't added a photo to her message.

Dan had decided to be honest and had taken a selfie to upload. He couldn't see the point in meeting with someone if you weren't being your true self. It just made the night uncomfortable and a waste of time and effort. Before the Lorraine fiasco, there had been Alice the month before. She had moaned from the minute she opened her mouth – about her life, her job, her family, her car, her flat, her pet rabbits. Dan had nearly lost the will to live when she began to go into great detail about how long it took her to clean out Jekyll and Hyde's cage every day. Why have pets if you didn't want to look after them? And didn't she realise how lucky she was to have her own place?

'Dan?'

He looked up to see a woman standing in front of him. Ronnie wasn't much like her profile photo either, he sighed inwardly. Dressed all in black, with hair the same colour and a pierced lip that he couldn't recall seeing in her photo, she reminded him of someone from *The Walking Dead*. Pale skin and dark make-up finished the look.

He took a deep breath and smiled.

'Yes.' He stood up and held out his hand, long ago giving up the notion that a peck on the cheek was more welcoming. 'Hi, Ronnie.'

Ronnie shook his hand, shirked off her coat and sat down with a thump. 'That's enough of the introductions. What shall we eat? I'm starving.'

Put off a little by her abrupt manner, Dan smiled nonetheless as Ronnie studied the menu. She seemed to light up as she ran her finger over the choices.

'Ooh, they do so much here, don't they?' She looked up, eyes wide with exhilaration.

Dan wondered if there was human blood on the menu. He snorted, then changed it into a cough as she stared at him. 'They do,' he said, after clearing his throat.

Ronnie's head went down again, a finger lovingly stroking down the list of main courses. 'What are you having?' she asked as she snapped it shut a few seconds later, making him visibly jump.

'I think I'll go for chicken and pasta,' he said. 'You?'

'It has to be steak for me, with all the trimmings. Don't skimp on anything, especially onion rings. I'll have an extra portion of those.'

Dan gasped. This dating lark was becoming very expensive. Even though he would never let her, he was annoyed that she hadn't even offered to contribute.

The waiter came across and took their order. 'Could I add an extra portion of chips to it?' Ronnie asked just as he was about to walk away. 'And heavy on the mayo, too. Ta.'

'Have you been here before?' Dan asked when they were alone again, for want of something to say.

'Yes, lots of times,' Ronnie nodded. 'I prefer mid-week, don't you? More choice on the menu and cheaper, too. We can have two for a tenner. Actually, I usually have two for myself for a tenner.' She laughed loudly at her own joke. 'I do love a bargain when I'm eating. You should have ordered some chips with your chicken and pasta.'

'Oh, I couldn't manage both.' Dan tried to keep his annoyance at bay, outraged by the fact that she thought he could eat all of that.

'No, for me.' She laughed again.

They had to wait an excruciating thirty minutes, making small talk, before the food arrived. Dan tried not to scowl as he realised he was going to have to watch her eat all of it, too. By the way she was eyeing the plate on the next table, practically drooling as she watched a woman spooning food into her mouth, he knew she'd be a messy eater.

As soon as the plate was put down in front of her, Ronnie began to devour the food, sawing into her steak and shovelling it in as if she hadn't eaten in months. She chewed the meat like a cow chewing grass, speaking between mouthfuls and washing it all down with lager.

When she saw he wasn't eating, Ronnie stared at Dan's food longingly.

'Don't you want that?' she asked.

'I'm not very hungry.' Dan put down his fork.

Without being asked, Ronnie leaned over, grabbed the dish and tipped the remainder of his meal onto her plate. 'Waste not, want not,' she grinned, before popping some of it into her mouth. 'Have you decided what you're having for pudding?'

Just the thought was enough to make Dan want to throw up on the spot. Again, he found himself glancing at his watch, figuring out how long he'd have to stay before it was acceptable to make a move. It was too early to leave politely. This called for emergency measures.

He put his hand out, purposely clipping his pint glass. It flipped over, the liquid dropped over Ronnie's meal.

She pushed back her chair, her face a mask of horror as she surveyed the ruined food.

'Look what you did!'

Dan felt like a young Macaulay Culkin in *Home Alone*, when he tipped coke all over the pizza. He wouldn't have been surprised if she'd called him a little jerk.

Everyone in the restaurant turned to look his way. Mortified, he stood up quickly. 'Let me grab a cloth.'

He rushed across to the bar and asked for something to wipe down the table. While he waited, he saw a couple come in. They were laughing as they chatted, hands reaching out to find each other's as they waited to be shown to a table. He sighed: that's how a date should be.

Suddenly, he made a dash for the door. Stuff it, he wasn't waiting around to be insulted. Ronnie could pay for her own food, too. The greedy cow.

Out in the fresh air, he felt elated as he giggled at his courage in walking away. Another dating disaster. Another woman to cross off his list, but at least it hadn't cost him a penny.

CHAPTER FIFTEEN

On Friday evening, Sadie had invited everyone over to her house for a final rehearsal of the dance routine. Until now, Riley had felt confident that they might just be able to do it, but doubt was beginning to creep in and they couldn't seem to get anything right.

'Be careful!' she cried as she practised with Dan, who was flinging her around a little too energetically. 'I want to stay in my heels tomorrow.'

'Sorry,' he replied, 'but I want to make sure it's perfect. I don't want to let Chloe down. She's such a good dancing partner and I'm such a bad one. I'm expecting someone from the crowd – if there is a crowd – to hold up a score card and it definitely won't be a se–ven!'

'I'm not sure I can even wear my heels tomorrow.' Ash bent down and slipped her shoes off. 'My feet are red raw from all the dancing this week. Whatever gave me the impression it would be good to join in with you lot?'

'We'll all be sensational,' Dan retorted, ever the optimist. 'It will be a huge success and everyone will join in with the competition and save our skins.'

'If only it were that easy,' said Riley, flopping onto the settee. 'I feel like Baby in *Dirty Dancing*. I don't know the lifts, we haven't rehearsed the pliés. I would rather someone put me in a corner!'

'At least you don't have to lift me up above your head,' Sadie laughed. 'I don't think anyone would be capable of that.'

'Seriously, Riles,' said Ash. 'It'll be fine. And if it isn't, then let's hope no one makes too much fuss about it. We don't have to promote it on social media if it goes wrong. Ethan said he needed time to make the video look good afterwards, so as long as no one uploads anything from their own phones, we'll be laughing.'

'We'll be laughed *at*, more like,' muttered Riley. 'If something does go wrong, you can guarantee that lots of people will be filming us and uploading it and then that will go viral.'

'You sound more pessimistic than me.' Ash got to her feet again and held out a hand to Dan. 'Come on, let me practise with you.'

Dan pressed play on his iPad, whizzing the song forward to the place they needed to begin. 'Right, here we go again.'

Riley glided around with him afterwards too, as best she could in the space they had. After three attempts, they succeeded in doing it faultlessly. Twice more they repeated it and by the end she felt a little more confident.

Yet when she got home to her flat that evening, the nerves were back. She was praying that Suzanne wouldn't show up unannounced. Although it was unlikely, knowing their luck she would turn up just as they were about to join in the dance – at the exact moment they were shutting the shop for ten minutes to do the flash mob.

It seemed strange to come home to her flat after staying with Ethan for a couple of nights. He'd dropped her back at home each morning and she had gone to work with Ash as usual, but just being part of a couple again had felt good. Ethan had told her he was an exceptional cook, and when they had more time, after the flash mob, he was going to cook her a meal. He'd said she would be dessert – now *that*, she couldn't wait for.

Now that she was home, all she wanted to do was share the day's events with him in person, rather than chat to him over the phone. Not that he would be remotely interested in an order of sandals, but she couldn't contain her excitement.

It had been touch and go, but her order had finally arrived that afternoon and they had spent time displaying them in between serving existing customers and drumming up followers online. Riley had moved everything around several times before she had been satisfied.

The sandals were sure to be a winner – she'd even put pairs aside for herself and Ash. They had a thick-ribbed sole and one large strip of leather to push feet into, which enabled the toes to peep out. A delicate thin strap held the shoe in place around the ankle but it was the marbled heel that made them stand out. She'd ordered them in three colours so far: white, orange and the blue that Marsha and Ruby had favoured. She couldn't wait to see what people thought of them.

Frank's bags were looking sensational, too. He'd even designed one with a pair of black heels and the hashtag, which was perfect for their competition. Remembering how great the chair in the window had looked in the photo that had appeared in the *Hedworth News*, when she had sat in it, Riley had popped the chair back on display and draped the bags over the arms, with the sandals on the seat and underneath, both in and out of their boxes. Sadie had suggested putting a pair of sandals into a bag, too. It had the added effect of creating the colour, and the element of fun, that she had imagined. She hoped Frank would be pleased when he saw them.

Riley sank down on the settee with a glass of wine and a huge grin, tired but elated. Her sense of adventure over the past couple of weeks had completely surprised her, taking on a life of its own. She was about to do something crazy, something that could potentially be amazing. Something that might save her job, perhaps even the shop, if they got a big enough crowd on the High Street. It could keep her friends together and the business she loved open.

And the competition seemed like it could be a lot of fun, too. Deciding not to ask Suzanne, they'd each put £50 into the fund. The prize money stood at £100, and the leaflets they'd had printed to promote the competition had cost another £50. The winner would also have a bag exclusively designed for them. What could be more personal than that?

She took a sip of wine and relaxed her neck, letting her head sink back into the cushions. It seemed things were starting to look up, at last. Organising the flash mob had filled her with new confidence. It had given her the get-up-and-go that she had been missing for a while. This campaign, and the flash mob, had given her the opportunity to make a name for herself. She was thinking less and less about Nicholas and more about Ethan. She was moving on, and she liked it. Who knows what other opportunities would come from all this? She couldn't wait to find out.

Riley felt apprehensive as she caught the bus to work the next morning. It was *the* morning. Although not too warm, the sun shone brightly in an only partially cloudy sky. She'd checked the forecast earlier and seen that there was a dry afternoon on the horizon, with no rain anticipated, and hoped that it would be right. If it rained, everyone would probably disappear into the shopping centre and they'd either have to postpone the flash mob or perform for a few daredevils who didn't mind getting wet. And that wouldn't look good on a video, if no one was watching the dancing.

'Are you nervous?' asked Ash, sitting beside her. For once, she didn't have her earphones in. 'I'm more excited, really. It's going to be so much fun.'

'I hope so,' Riley replied. 'I really am scared of falling over in front of people we know, never mind the people we don't!'

Over the past week, they'd each been dropping hints about the flash mob all over town. When she had called in at the chemist's, and some of the other smaller shops on the High Street, Sadie had mentioned that something exciting might be happening on Saturday. Riley had confided in Ray, as she needed a place for the dancers to meet up beforehand. Ray's Café was on high alert, and they were also going to be responsible for playing the music out into the street. Dan had gone further into Hedworth, to the barber's in the town square, to Blundred's Bakery, and to some of the shops in the shopping centre.

Riley had been to the indoor market to visit the girls on the fruit stall. As well as Nicci, there was her sister, Louise, and Sam, the owner. Riley had gone to school with Louise and Sam, so knew them well. She'd dropped into conversation that something would be happening on Saturday afternoon, and asked them to spread the word to build up a buzz. Sure enough, it had worked a treat and several people had come into Chandler's to ask them what was going on.

'Do you have any big followers on your Twitter feed who would retweet and maybe get some interest?' said Ash, as the bus pulled into the station. 'Any names from Hedworth?'

'Yes, I made a list. Of local people too. I'll have another scan through when I get to work.'

They split up at the top of the steps on the High Street. It was strange to see it deserted as Riley walked along, and to think that by that afternoon they might hopefully have brought a little fun to the place.

'How are you feeling?' Sadie asked when she arrived at the shop.

'I feel like I'm going to throw up,' Riley admitted. 'I'm excited, but scared too. You?'

Sadie held out a shaky hand. 'Nervous,' she admitted. 'Christine is bringing Esther here half an hour before, so that she can't spill the beans. She's so excited.'

'What happens if there aren't enough people around? We have a four-minute window. If people hear about it after the dance has started they won't get to us before it's finished.'

'There will be.' Sadie gasped. 'My stomach has just lurched again. This will either be great fun or a total disaster.'

'I can't wait to see which one.' Riley smiled as a text message arrived from Ethan. How are you feeling about your big dance debut?

Terrified, if you must know. Do you have a minute to talk?

'I'm just going to speak to Ethan.' As her phone rang, Riley went outside for a moment. Maybe Ethan had some ideas for how to get the word out about the flash mob without mentioning what exactly was going on.

'Well, there's Danny Warrington, the football player. And what about Urban Angels . . . surely they'd be interested in shoes?'

'They won't bother with the likes of a small shop, surely?' Riley wasn't convinced.

'They might. I'll see if I can get them tweeting for you. One of the journalists is sure to know them. Maybe Kim. Don't say anything for now, though. I'll do my best.'

'Okay, thanks. What time will you be here?'

'Missing me already?'

Riley pictured him smiling at the other end of the line.

'No,' she fibbed. 'I meant what time will you be here for the flash mob?'

'I'll be there about one. That should give me time to set everything up by two.'

'Thanks for doing this on your day off.'

'You can pay me in kind, later.'

Riley sniggered before saying goodbye. When she went back indoors, Dan was flicking through his iPad. He caught her eye.

'I think we should go all-out this morning and let people know there's something happening later,' he said. 'That way we can create a buzz about it all day. What do you think?'

'That's what Ethan has just said,' Riley replied. 'He says we've put too much effort into it for it not to get seen. Plus we want people on the High Street to start taking photos of their shoes and putting them on Twitter to enter the competition.'

Dan gave her arm a squeeze. 'We're going to have a blast.'

'I do hope so,' said Riley. 'Do you fancy a quick rehearsal before we open up?'

Dan took off his jacket. 'Sure, we can do that. Just let me get changed into my gear. If you're going to tweet from Chandler's account, and I'm dressed differently, people might keep a look out.'

Sadie nodded. 'Great idea. Do you think we should all do that, Riley? Maybe close the shop for half an hour here and there? I'm sure it can't do any harm. Although I doubt I'll be able to walk in my heels all day, and then dance too.'

Riley shook her head. 'Let Dan do it for now, in case Suzanne decides to pop in. That way, we can say he's dressed to give out leaflets in the street.'

'Hey, that's a great idea anyway,' Dan nodded. 'I could do that as you are tweeting.'

Riley agreed. 'As long as we don't need you inside. Ethan is ringing the local radio station and letting them in on it, and Kim knows already.'

'I'm surprised it hasn't leaked by now,' said Sadie.

'It isn't a top secret military operation,' laughed Riley. 'It's just a dance.'

'But there *is* a lot depending on it,' Sadie said. 'We need to keep our jobs, to ensure that the shop stays open. I don't want to go anywhere.'

'I don't want to go anywhere that you two won't be, either.' Dan stood between them and draped an arm around each of their shoulders. 'All for one and one for all, remember?'

'Yes, d'Artagnan,' laughed Riley.

CHAPTER SIXTEEN

Serena arrived at 1:30 p.m. She looked superb in her outfit of black skinny jeans, ripped at both knees, a bright yellow T-shirt, fake-fur multicoloured gilet, and red heels swung over her shoulder as she came through the door.

'That High Street looks very busy.' She narrowed her eyes. 'Have you been giving hints of what's to come?'

Riley nodded. 'We don't want to dance without an audience. Although I'm not sure I want to dance to *any* audience at the moment. My nerves are getting the better of me.'

'You'll be fine,' Serena soothed. 'It'll be all over in a flash . . . mob!'

'All my leaflets have gone!' Dan came rushing in, empty hands raised in the air. 'There's a definite sense that something is going on,' he added. 'I've had lots of girlies asking me about the competition. Have you checked the Twitter account, Riles? They've been tweeting photos to Chandler's.'

Riley took out her phone and was astounded at how many notifications there were. She opened the Twitter app and flicked through them. Shoe after shoe appeared.

'Wow, it's working already!' She beckoned them over. 'Look at all these.'

Ethan arrived while they were still scrolling through the tweets. 'I'm all set up outside. Are you ready for the big moment?'

Riley turned round and beamed. She beckoned him over.

'Look at all these photos.' She thrust her phone in his face. 'We've got over fifty already, thanks to Dan.'

Dan polished his fingernails on his chest. 'It didn't take much to persuade them to join in,' he said. 'Seriously, you women and your shoes.'

'Says the man who wears a different pair of boots every day!' exclaimed Sadie.

'You should take a photo of your own shoes,' suggested Ethan. 'All of them in a circle. Tweet it right before the flash mob.'

'That's a great idea! Come on, everyone, best shoes forward!'

'Here, let me take some too.' Ethan got out his camera. 'Souvenirs of a time before the flash mob.'

'You mean you want something to remember us by before we run off screaming in embarrassment, never to be seen again,' laughed Riley.

'I've just had word from Ray at the café that all the dancers are there, ready and waiting,' said Serena. 'Shall we take our positions?'

Riley's stomach flipped over at the thought of what they were about to do. She tried not to think about making a fool of herself, as they locked the shop up and took their positions. They'd decided to stand on the pavement and that the dancers would come and get them when it was their cue. That way, they would be amongst the shoppers, and hopefully surprise some of them when they were whisked away to join in.

'Break a leg,' Serena said, before giving Riley a quick hug. 'And remember to smile, look as if you are enjoying yourself. It's going to be *fun!*'

With that, she was gone.

'Good luck,' said Ethan, giving Riley's hand a quick squeeze. 'Although I'm sure you won't need it.'

'Oh, I think we will, said Riley, her heart racing.

'I think I'm going to faint,' said Dan, standing beside her.

Ash nudged him, putting a finger to her lips as someone turned to look his way.

Riley's dance partner, Ryan, walked up to Riley. 'Excited?'

'Nervous,' she whispered. He too gave her hand a squeeze as he held on to it.

The first notes of the song made Riley's stomach lurch. She grinned excitedly at Ash. She glanced down the High Street, looking for signs of the first three dancers. They were pretending to window-shop at the chemist's. Then they began to dance, running out into the middle of the pedestrianised area of the street.

Three more dancers on the other side of the road ran to join them. People on the street began to stop what they were doing.

When three more female dancers joined in, Riley spotted phones being taken out of bags, as shoppers began to take notice. A group of girls squealed and started to join in, clapping their hands. 'It's a flash mob! I've only ever seen them on YouTube,' said one.

'Quick, get your phone out!' said another.

'Are you sure Esther will be okay with you?' said Sadie, holding on to her daughter's hand for dear life.

'She'll be fine,' said Serena, smiling down. 'Won't you, missy?'

Esther nodded. 'I can see Nanny over there too.' She pointed to where Christine was pretending to look in the window of the butcher's.

'This is brilliant!' A young woman turned to Riley with a huge grin. She began to dance, clapping her hands to the beat.

Riley laughed inwardly: she had no idea that they were about to join in. She looked through the crowd and spotted Cooper, who gave her the thumbs up.

As the tune rolled towards their cue, the crowd swelled. More people joined in, dancing and clapping. Some were singing too.

It was such an infectious song. Staff and shoppers came out of shops and stood in doorways, some joining in with the clapping.

Ryan turned to Riley. 'Ready?' he asked.

She gulped and nodded. He led her by the hand out onto the pavement, the others following behind.

Riley took a deep breath and, with head held high, sashayed across the High Street to the astonishment of the people who knew her. People began to point and whistle when they recognised the staff from Chandler's dancing past.

Without a moment to think, she performed her part perfectly, pirouetting to stand in a line with the others, her face breaking out in a huge grin as she achieved what she'd set out to do.

With one last move, the four of them arched their backs, dropped down in a line and held out their cards. They'd changed their minds at the last minute about the hashtag.

#ShoeLove

Esther danced onto the street, finishing with a twirl in front of Sadie, holding a sign with the hashtag written on it.

#ShoeLove

Ethan gave a thumbs up as the music stopped, and the dancers caught their breath.

And then the applause started.

'We did it!' Riley laughed as she was pulled into Ash's arms. Next came Dan and Sadie and Esther.

'We deserve a group hug. That was amazing!' cried Dan.

People around him urged them all to take a bow with the dancers.

Riley searched out Serena and gave her a hug. 'I can't thank you enough,' she said, as the dancers began to hand out leaflets to the crowd. 'That was incredible, and it *was* so much fun.'

'That's what it will be remembered for,' said Serena. 'You'll have everyone on Twitter adding their shoes to the feed now – absolutely perfect PR.'

'We couldn't have done it without you.' Riley hugged her fiercely. 'Thank you so much for your time and expertise.'

'You were great!' Cooper enthused as he joined them all. 'I wasn't sure you'd pull it off, but I have some great bits on video.'

'You were indeed,' echoed Christine. 'It looked so much fun.'

'Can I get some photos of you all together before you leave?' said Ethan, coming up behind them. 'The five of you at the front and the dancers in the background. Good job, everyone, by the way. This will go down a storm.'

As everyone talked around her, Riley eyed Ethan. His natural knack for making everyone feel at ease was taking over. Before long, he had them all saying stupid words to make them smile for the photo.

The crowd showed no signs of thinning, and Riley could see people checking their phones, taking photos of their shoes. Serena was right. It was a PR dream come true. She hoped the video would look okay when Ethan had finished with it.

Finally, she had time to catch up with him.

'You were amazing,' he said. 'I don't think I'll need to edit this much. I'll have it done by the time you finish work. Shall I bring it into the shop to show you all?'

'No— Yes! No!' Riley laughed. 'I mean, I want to see it but I don't want to see it. What if it's so embarrassing that we can never show our faces in the town again?'

'Then you'll have to practise more and go on *Britain's Got Talent*. If it doesn't turn out right that time, Simon Cowell and six million viewers will tell you.'

Riley wanted to throw her arms around his neck and kiss him with a passion, but she knew that would create a different kind of scene. She couldn't wait to get him alone again tonight.

Instead, she got out her phone. 'I have over two hundred notifications on Twitter!' she said. 'I wonder how many you need to start trending?'

'What does trending mean?' asked Sadie.

'It means lots of people are tweeting about it at the same time.'

'Did you add your own photograph?' asked Ethan.

Riley gasped. 'I forgot! I'll add it now, as a kind of competition reminder, and then pin it to the top of the feed. And I'll add the hashtag as a reminder too. If they don't use that, I'll never keep up with everyone.'

Sadie had reopened the shop and taken Esther out of the crowd with Christine. From where Riley was standing, Chandler's seemed to be pretty full, even though she knew most people would be joining in with the competition rather than buying anything. But it was a start. And a great moment to show off the Designed by Frank bags.

'Great job, Riley Flynn,' she said to herself, tapping a finger to send her tweet:

@RileyFlynn Tweet us a photo of your favourite shoes to be entered into the £100 prize draw. Don't forget to use the hashtag! #ShoeLove

Riley stayed outside with Ethan for as long as she could. She couldn't believe there was still a small crowd some half an hour after the flash mob had ended. Dan had gone back inside, but she'd had to stay outside as news of the competition got out and everyone wanted details.

People had been coming up to her, taking photos of her shoes to tweet, taking selfies with her and also taking photos of their own shoes. Riley was encouraging them to share the photos on social media. Everyone thought it had been a great idea. Now she hoped it would create some interest around the shop.

'I hope this continues for long enough to gather some momentum, rather than be just a PR stunt that everyone has forgotten about come Monday morning.'

'Stop worrying.' Ethan planted a sneaky kiss on the end of her nose. 'I'm surprised you stayed on your feet, though. I thought you might fall over on purpose, for viral appeal.'

Riley pouted. 'I wasn't going to pull a stunt like that just to get attention.'

'Shame,' he whispered, moving closer so only she could hear what he had to say next. 'I wouldn't have minded a flash of your knickers.'

She smiled at him, then sighed when she looked back across the High Street. She could see people still milling about outside the door. 'I'd better get back to the shop.'

'Yes, no rest for the wicked,' said Ethan. 'Time to meet your public.'

'If they would all buy something, that would be good!'

Riley went back inside the shop, pleased at having to squeeze past a few people gathered in the doorway.

'At last! Here's Riley,' announced a harassed-looking Dan as she joined him behind the till. 'It's been manic.'

'I take it you mean competition entries rather than shoe sales,' she grinned.

'Well, your sandals are going down a storm and people are loving Frank's bags, but not only that.' Dan reached for his iPad from underneath the counter and showed her the Chandler's Twitter feed. 'That's what I mean. It's gone crazy!'

Riley gasped as she scrolled through mention after mention on their Twitter feed. There were lots of photos of them dancing, even a few small grainy videos that had been taken by onlookers. But more than that, there was photo after photo of shoes with the competition hashtag #ShoeLove. The campaign seemed to be working.

'This is amazing.' Riley reached down to take off her heels before doing a jig in her bare feet for a couple of seconds. 'If we don't get any sales from this, then we never will.'

'I hope Suzanne will be pleased,' said Sadie as she came across to them with a box containing a pair of white sandals. 'This is my third sale of these in the last half-hour, so something is working, for today at least.'

Riley gave Sadie's arm a squeeze before checking the time. 'Two hours until closing. We'd better get a move on. Or should I say, best shoe forward!'

By the end of the day they were all glad to see Riley flip the sign on the door from 'open' to 'closed'.

'What a day,' sighed Dan, as they congregated around the leather cubes. 'My feet are killing me!'

'You should try dancing in heels and then walking around in them afterwards,' said Riley.

'Your fingers will be aching after checking all those tweets for the competition. I can't wait to sit down and go through them. Are we each going to pick a favourite one and then narrow it down to one winner? You know, like they do on *The X Factor*?'

'It depends how many entries come in,' said Riley. 'It'll only perhaps keep going over the weekend. Once the video has been circulating for a while, it will be old news. We'll have to think of a way to keep the buzz going.'

'What are everyone's plans for this evening?' Dan asked. 'Anyone want to join me in a celebratory drink or two? All I need is a house to come to. I'll bring the supplies.'

'Not for me,' said Sadie. 'I just want to curl up on the settee and slob out with Esther.'

'Riley?' he looked expectantly.

'Sorry, I'm going to Ethan's. Maybe we could do a night in the week?'

Dan slapped his thighs before standing up. 'No worries. I'll go home all by myself and sit with my mum and dad. Oh, how I love the single life.'

'You could always go on the pull with the lads again,' grinned Riley.

'I would rather pull my own teeth out,' snorted Dan. 'Remember last weekend?'

Dan had a group of friends he'd known since school, who regularly did a pub crawl around Hedworth. All single men, they were looking for women, made no bones about it, and often left Dan with a severe case of embarrassmentitis as they tried to chat up woman after woman.

'One day soon, you will meet your Mrs Right.' Riley chucked him under the chin.

'After that last date with Ronnie, I'm thinking of cancelling my membership. Honestly, I doubt anyone normal joins a dating agency. It's just full of rejects and losers and no-hopers. I reckon I'm pretty much the only honest person on there.'

'Then maybe you should start fibbing, too. The sky would be your limit. Just think – you could say you were anyone! Who would you like to be?'

'I'm not sure. But I do know that I don't want to be me, if it means going on another ridiculous date like the last one.'

CHAPTER SEVENTEEN

After she had finally closed up the shop for the night, exhausted but elated, Riley went with Ethan back to his house. While Ethan took Jimmy out for a walk, she showered and changed. Then, while Ethan was sitting at the table with his laptop, editing the video, she made a quick meal of pasta and salad with some leftover cold roast chicken.

Riley loved the space in Ethan's house. An old two-bedroomed terraced house, it had lots of original features as well as modern quirks too. Ethan told her it originally had three bedrooms until he'd moved the bathroom upstairs. The old bathroom had been removed and the kitchen extended, allowing for a bigger dining area. New units had been added, and the handle-less, glossy, champagne-coloured cupboard doors created a sense of more space. A dash of blue made the whole look less clinical, and a warm wooden floor finished it all off. It was the kind of kitchen Riley would love to have. She liked to mingle the old with the new.

'Are you ready with it yet?' Riley asked. 'I'm dying to see it.'

'Just give me a couple more minutes.' Ethan's phone beeped. He picked it up, read the message with a frown and pocketed his phone again.

'Everything okay?' Riley asked, noticing his expression.

'Hmm?' He looked distracted for a moment, but then his face lit up with a smile. 'Yes, everything's fine.' He swivelled his laptop round to face her. 'Are you ready?'

'Hit it.'

Ethan pulled her onto his knee. Riley covered her eyes, leaving gaps between her fingers as he pressed play. The music filled the room and she watched the dancers, group by group, move into the middle of the High Street. She dropped her hands as she became enthralled.

'Ethan, it's incredible!' She hugged him as they continued to watch. 'You're so good at your job.'

'Wait until you see the stills I've taken from it,' he replied, a tinge of red appearing on his cheeks. 'You'll have some fantastic photos to share on social media to keep the competition going.'

'Brilliant!' Almost holding her breath, she waited to see herself on the screen. But as she caught the familiar beat, she looked away.

'I can't watch!' she said, laughing.

'You have to!'

Riley shrieked when she saw the four of them coming into shot with their partners. Jimmy, who had been around her feet ever since the food had been dished out, ran from the room before creeping slowly back in again.

'We look great!' She pointed to the screen as she waltzed around with Ryan.

'For ten seconds at least,' Ethan teased. He pressed a few keys on the laptop, bringing the image into focus a little more, and then nodded. 'That's better.'

The video continued. As all four of them arched over, one after the other, in a row in front of the camera, the words on the cards came into view.

'It looks like I can actually dance!' Riley said.

Finally, the pièce de résistance, Esther, pirouetted in front of all of them. Once she had finished, she held up her card with the competition hashtag on it.

The applause when the music finished was deafening. Riley clapped too – she couldn't help herself.

'It's really good,' she told him. 'I can't thank you enough.'

Ethan pressed a few more keys. 'If you're happy with it, I can send it to the paper. What do you think?'

'Do it!' Riley got out her phone and began to text Dan and Sadie. 'I'll have to send the link to Suzanne, too. She's probably going to go nuts.'

Ethan took the phone from her. 'Let's eat first, before I send the email and you get in touch with people. I'm starving.'

Riley grabbed the plates and took them over to the table. They chatted about the best bits over dinner. She knew everyone involved was going to be pleased, which meant they would all share it on social media. Since the competition had started, they'd gained a lot more followers on Twitter and Facebook, so perhaps they could even get it trending for a while. If it was picked up and retweeted, they might get a few more competition entries. And if it wasn't, she would share it more herself over the next few days. Despite the grilling she would likely get from Suzanne, Riley wanted everyone in Hedworth to be talking about Chandler's.

Sadie woke up with a start and sat up in bed, tears pouring down her cheeks. Some days she'd cry several times, the slightest thing setting her off. Others she didn't cry at all. She hoped this wasn't the start of a bad run.

She lay back down, glancing at the clock illuminating the time. It was five past three in the morning. She could almost guarantee that she wouldn't get back to sleep again now.

The dream she'd been having was so vivid that it made her even more upset to find that Ross wasn't lying beside her when she woke. She ran a hand over his side of the bed, pulling herself over to it and curling up in the space that used to belong to him.

This had all come about because she had enjoyed the flash mob. It reminded her just how much she had wanted to share it with Ross. He would have been so proud of her and Esther for strutting their stuff, learning the dance by heart and then being on a video that might be shared far more than any of them had anticipated. There were so many competition entries, and she had wanted to come home and show Ross, flick through some of the photos, show him her favourite so far.

Dreaming about Ross made it all real again. It was as if she was going to wake up to find him lying next to her. 'I'm right here,' he'd say and pull her into his arms, rocking her to sleep again.

In some ways, he *was* still here with her. She felt his presence throughout the house, and whenever Esther smiled. Every time she looked at things, he was there. She wanted to be reminded of him but also wanted to forget the pain. The loneliness. The guilt.

Ross had been in the hospital, and the hospice, for the last few weeks of his life. At times it had been so hard to come to terms with his pain, his deterioration, his end-of-life care. All the staff had been so good to them, yet she still felt guilty. She remembered all the times she had moaned when she'd got to his ward after being stuck in traffic, complaining about how long it had taken her to get there, how long it had taken her to park, only to moan more when it was time to go home because she couldn't bear to leave him there.

Every time she'd left, she'd convinced herself that it would be the last time she would ever see him. That she wouldn't be with him when he died, not able to say goodbye before he left them for good. She'd heard people say that they knew when someone was passing away, but surely that was because they could see the rapid deterioration over hours and days rather than weeks and months. Sadie had borne Ross's pain and her own. She'd had to deal with the idea of being left a widow at thirty-five, with a five-year-old daughter who wouldn't understand that Daddy would be leaving them soon and she would never see him again.

Sadie cried as she recalled the moment they had been told that the cancer was terminal, and that Ross had less than three months to live. He'd run from the consultant's room, unable to deal with the news. They'd eventually found him in the children's play area, sitting with his back against the wall, tears pouring down his face. She'd tried to put her arms around him but he had pushed her away. He said she needed to leave him there. The consultant had sat down too, and they had both spent twenty minutes talking to him, trying to reassure him that every day was worth fighting for.

He'd died exactly three months later. His body had deteriorated to such a point that there wasn't much left but skin and bone, but at least they had been given sufficient warning so Sadie and the rest of his family could be there when he died. Esther had sat on Sadie's knee as she'd held on to his hand, not wanting to let it go. Christine and Paul had been there too, sitting on the other side of the bed. Sadie had felt their loss, as their only child slipped away. No parent should see their child die. It just didn't seem right.

The days between then and the funeral were like being in limbo for her. She had wanted to scream at the injustice of someone so young being taken away; yet she also wanted to celebrate Ross's life and wear a brave face for Esther.

Once the first tears had dried, Sadie functioned as best she could. It was then that Esther developed a habit of talking to the urn, as if Ross was magically inside it and would one day come out like a genie from a lamp if she rubbed hard enough.

Grief. It affected everyone differently, and for different lengths of time. Sadie was dreading the first anniversary of Ross's death. It was seven weeks away now, and bearing down on her. No matter what, she had to stay focused on Esther. She needed to be a happy mummy, not a sad one.

She wiped the tears from her face and got up. Even though it was early she would face the day, when it came, with a smile. For Esther's sake, she would keep her grief hidden. The nights were for crying, remembering, hating, longing, raging.

Downstairs, Sadie made coffee and stared at a pile of ironing that she hadn't managed to get to during the week. Turning her back on it, she got out her journal. She wasn't supposed to be awake now so she would make this time her own. And it might do her good again to empty her mind of all the thoughts running around in it.

> I remember everything so plainly, Ross, even though it has been ten months, one week and two days since you left me. I can remember the pain and the suffering that you went through, so dignified, just to stay with me and Esther for as long as you could.
>
> I don't blame you for leaving us. I just regret that it was so soon. You were in so much pain, coughing up all that vile black stuff, losing weight, you were like a bag of bones at the end. Yet you always kept your sense of humour. I loved that about you, Ross. You were my rock, you always will be my rock, even though you are no longer around. I will never replace you, ever.

Sadie put down her pen as she struggled to see through her tears. She really didn't know what she would do without her writing. At first she had done it to keep a record for Esther when she was older, writing down memories that they both might look back on in later years. But then the journal had taken on a life of its own. Writing about Ross, what he meant to her, had given her great comfort. She'd been able to write out all the things she couldn't begin to tell people, personal thoughts and feelings. Maybe they'd be too raw to show Esther, even when she was grown up, but until Sadie decided otherwise the journal was staying. For now, it was her secret. It wasn't meant to do anything but be a place to let go of her emotions and enable her to pack them away until a time when she felt she could deal with them.

Even though it hurt now, she'd been blessed to have fifteen years with Ross before he died. Five of those had been shared with Esther. Four and a half of those years had been the best of her life.

At least she had that to be thankful for.

CHAPTER EIGHTEEN

The first hour until midday after Chandler's opened the following morning was spent dealing with a flurry of people coming into the shop to join in with the competition, and lots of photos being tweeted. Overnight, the campaign hadn't fizzled away as Riley had anticipated. The video had been viewed more than 8,000 times and she'd had to switch her phone to silent, as so many notifications were coming through that it had sounded like a heart monitor.

The experience had given her a great boost and a feeling of achievement. But she was also filled with trepidation wondering how Suzanne would react to the email she'd sent the night before.

'I can't believe it's gone so mad,' said Dan, as he walked back to the till after selling another pair of sandals to a student. The shop was finally empty, except for a woman and her son who'd just come in for a browse. 'Look at this photo for the competition!' Dan said, gaping at his phone. 'Neither of you would be able to walk in them. Do you think they are real?'

'Let me see,' said Riley.

Dan was looking at a pair of pillar-box red shoes shown in a photo on the Twitter feed for Chandler's Shoes. Their heels were metal and shaped like the barrel of a hand gun.

'I doubt they'll ever have been walked in,' said Riley. 'I bet they're car to pub shoes.'

'Car to pub shoes?'

'Gorgeous to look at and be seen in but excruciating to walk in, so they are only viable if you are going from the car to the pub with no long walk to a venue.'

Their smiles dropped when Suzanne came into the shop. She marched up to them, her mobile phone in her hand.

'My phone has been going mad since last night, everyone congratulating me on the YouTube video.'

'Oh, that's great news!' said Riley, without thinking.

'Is it?' Suzanne all but snorted. 'I had to pretend and go along with it all until you sent me the link. Why wasn't I informed before this happened?'

'I thought it wouldn't be a problem,' fibbed Riley. 'And, as you gave us free rein to get people into the shop for *our* competition, it also gave me the idea of running another one and getting the general public involved too.'

Suzanne glared at her. 'It was done on *my* time.'

'It was only a few minutes and we were working.'

'You shouldn't have uploaded it to YouTube without my permission.'

Riley dropped her eyes to the floor for a moment. The reason she hadn't asked for permission was because she knew she wouldn't like the answer.

'Have you any idea how much publicity the video has brought to the shop already?' interrupted Dan.

'Suzanne's right, Dan,' said Riley. 'I should have asked.'

Dan stared at Riley. 'Show her.'

'Show me what?' Suzanne folded her arms.

'How many hits the video has had.' Dan used his fingers to count. 'How many people are joining in with the competition on social media. How many people are talking about Chandler's Shoe Shop because of it. It was a genius idea.'

'It's had thousands of views,' Sadie joined in. 'You couldn't get more publicity than that. And the competition is really gathering momentum.'

'Thousands of people looking at it, you say?' Suzanne paused long enough for them all to think she was coming round. 'And how many sales have you had since? I wasn't exactly beating customers out of my way to get through the doors just now.'

'We've been really busy since we opened at eleven,' said Riley. 'It's only just gone quiet.'

'You should have seen it yesterday,' added Dan. 'We sold loads of stock.'

'Stock, as in those sandals I saw in the window?' She pointed at Riley. 'The ones I told you were too tacky for Chandler's?'

'I know you said not to order any in, but I thought I'd try a few pairs. The local students love them!' Riley defended her choice. 'I can't believe how many we've sold, actually.'

'And the bags,' added Sadie.

'It's all well and good having one busy day,' Suzanne huffed. 'I want the people in the shop all the time.'

'If we had a website, more people could have been looking at that, maybe buying something online,' said Riley.

Suzanne rolled her eyes. 'We do not have a website and we are not getting one. Websites are expensive, and I— I mean, Max and I don't want to spend another penny on the shop if it isn't making money.'

'But we are making money!'

'Riley.' Suzanne pinched the bridge of her nose. 'You've gone way above your station with this. I told you not to order those shoes. And those bags in the window? Remove them. This is a shoe shop, not a bag stall at a market.'

Suzanne flounced past them and down into the staffroom.

'Well, that went as anticipated,' Dan muttered.

But Riley hadn't finished yet. She went after her.

'Suzanne! Wait.'

Suzanne was at the bottom of the stairs by the time Riley caught up. She sighed loudly. 'What do you want now, Riley?'

'I'm sorry if you don't approve of what we did, but it was all well-intentioned,' Riley explained. 'We thought if we did something different, bought in some new stock, then we might get some attention. The competition has had over five hundred entries so far. Everyone is adding photos of shoes to Twitter, which means that everyone is talking about Chandler's.'

Suzanne stood quietly, so Riley continued.

'How many of them had heard of Chandler's last week? And how many people have heard of us now?'

'How many of them are actually shopping and making me money?' questioned Suzanne.

Riley said nothing. The flash mob would certainly be getting Chandler's name out there, and the summer sandals had helped with sales for now. But unless they could keep it that way, it would all be a waste of time.

But Riley wasn't done trying yet. 'I'm sure it will make a difference,' she reiterated.

Suzanne paused for a moment before nodding her agreement. 'But if anything goes wrong, it's on your head.'

Riley went home from work that afternoon with a huge grin on her face. Despite her run-in with Suzanne, they seemed to have pulled off the flash mob. As soon as she got back to her flat she checked Twitter to see what was going on and sat down with a bump. There were hundreds more tweets with the hashtag #ShoeLove. It seemed to be catching on.

Riley scrolled through some of the photos, stopping to like her favourite ones. There were some fabulous designs. There were some funny photos. There were messages from a few trolls who had joined in to spoil the fun, but she didn't take them to heart. She blocked a few of the more offensive ones. Honestly, why couldn't people get a life!

She sent text messages to Dan and Sadie before calling Ethan. She was meeting him later for something to eat. Sadie had gone to her in-laws, as they were looking after Esther.

'It's definitely working on Twitter,' she told Ethan, excitedly.

'I had no doubts it wouldn't. Did you?'

'Of course I did.'

'O ye of little faith. When I get to work in the morning, I'll check the stats on the paper's website again. The feature will be in tomorrow evening's print edition, too.'

'Brilliant. I can—' She heard traffic noise. 'Sorry, you're not driving, are you?'

'No, I'm out with Jimmy. I'm just heading back home now. I might have a surprise for you. Pick you up in an hour?'

By the time Ethan called for her, Riley was dying to know what he was up to. The tweets had started to die down, although she was still getting the occasional one, and she showed him a few before they headed off.

Ethan drove to a pub a few miles outside of Hedworth, down a winding, and very narrow, lane. The Moat and Salmon seemed dark and dingy from the outside but inside it was modern, with bright lights and tiled flooring.

'When did you find out this was here?' Riley asked as they were shown to a table that Ethan had booked.

'A couple of years ago. There was a fire and I was sent to cover the story. A lot of the old pub was damaged beyond repair but the landlord wanted as much as possible restored exactly as it had been before. Hence the dark and dingy exterior to a modern pub. The food is delicious.'

'Not smoked, I hope,' Riley teased. The waiter took their order and they sat back with a drink each.

'I thought you'd want to see what's happening shortly.' Ethan got out his phone. 'I just need to check my Twitter feed. I asked them not to tweet until I was here with you so I could see your reaction... Yes!' He gave the phone to her. 'I've just got you the biggest tweet yet.'

'Who?' Riley was intrigued. Her eyes widened in disbelief when she saw who it was. 'Roxy from Urban Angels!' A few heads turned her way. 'Sorry,' she grimaced as she glanced around. Then she turned back to Ethan with a smile. 'How the hell did you pull that off?'

'A mate of mine. I found out that his younger brother is dating Roxy. I've known him for years, so I got in touch with him last night. They're all going to tweet photos of their favourite shoes this evening, too. Roxy has even retweeted the video link.'

Riley didn't know how to contain herself. She wanted to scream out loud. 'Do you know how many followers she has?'

'Over a million. Do you think they are all real, though? It's easy to buy fake followers.'

'It is, but you don't believe they'd do that?'

Ethan shook his head. 'They're huge in the UK, and from what I heard they're heading for America next.'

'I don't suppose they'd need to,' Riley agreed. 'It was good of them to join in.'

'And there are four of them, all with over a million followers each.'

'*And* you managed to get them to join in with the competition. Well, the hashtag. I guess they won't be interested in a measly one hundred pounds for shoes. I bet they pay a fortune for theirs! Oh, that must be the life. I'd love to sell more fashionable shoes in Chandler's.'

Riley quickly rummaged in her bag for her own phone.

'I have over five hundred notifications! Ethan, this is fantastic,' she said. 'I can't keep up with them!'

She leaned across the table and gave him a kiss. 'Has anyone ever told you you're a genius?'

'Several times, but you can tell me again.'

'Wait until Dan and Sadie hear about this!' she laughed.

CHAPTER NINETEEN

Dan wiped his hands on the sides of his jeans as his palms began to sweat. He was sitting waiting in the restaurant for Anna to appear. Since sharing a few more messages with her online, he couldn't wait to see if they gelled as much in real life. This was going to be a blind date, however, as Anna still hadn't added a photo to her profile. Dan had wondered whether it would even be worth meeting her, especially after his dates with Lorraine and Ronnie had been disasters, but over the past couple of weeks he felt he'd gotten to know Anna a little bit. And even if he didn't know what she looked like, her personality had shone through in those messages. She seemed witty, liked a few of the same things he did, and was the same age – which he hoped she wasn't fibbing about as Lorraine had.

When she'd asked to meet, Dan had initially decided against it but then changed his mind. How would he feel if Anna had been the one and he'd turned down his soulmate? So, at the last minute, he'd said yes. They'd arranged a date for this evening and now here he was.

Dan hid a smirk as he looked at the menu. He was setting himself, and the date, up for failure before he had even seen Anna. He perused the menu. Carlo's restaurant was one of his favourites in the town. The Italian eatery had a good reputation and it was often hard to get a table, but because it was situated just off the High Street Dan often saw the owner out and about and knew him well. He always gave Dan a discount too, and a free dessert. So, even if the date went wrong, he knew he was guaranteed to have a good meal out of it.

Almost every table was full. Chatter could be heard over the music playing low in the background. The smell of garlic set Dan's taste buds tingling. By his side, a table of four were all laughing, and a table of eight were celebrating a fiftieth birthday, balloons bobbing in the middle of the table. To his left, several tables were occupied by couples. He hoped Anna wouldn't be too long.

He chanced a look at his watch, hoping not to seem too desperate. And then he froze. Standing waiting to be shown to a table was his ex-girlfriend, Sarah. He hadn't seen her in a good while, almost making her as distant as she was familiar. Her brown hair had been cut a little shorter, and highlights added to it, making it shine. The bright red blouse she wore suited her olive complexion, and it stung to think that he hadn't seen the blouse before.

He glanced around the room: who was she meeting? He wouldn't be able to stay here if it was another man. It would be too awkward. Maybe Anna wouldn't mind going somewhere else. He'd be honest with her and tell her why he wanted to leave. After all, they had met on a dating website. Everyone on there had baggage, surely?

He bobbed his head down quickly. Maybe her table was booked for a later time. He prayed it would be at the other side of the room. Either way, he didn't want her to see him.

He peeped over the top of the menu. The waiter was walking straight towards him, with Sarah following behind. He ducked his head again, leaning to his side as if he had dropped his napkin. When he'd given them enough time to pass, he sat up straight again.

They had stopped in front of his table.

'Your guest, sir.' The waiter spoke to Dan as he pulled out a chair for Sarah. She sat down and he handed a menu to her and left.

Sarah's smile was nervous as she waited for Dan to speak.

'You have got to be kidding.' His voice came out as a high-pitched squeak, and he cleared his throat quickly. 'You posed as someone else?'

Dan felt his whole body going rigid and he clammed up. How could she have tricked him into saying all those things online?

'Did you know it was me?' he asked, holding his breath.

'Yes. After the video of the flash mob went online, my friend Felicity said that she thought she'd seen you on Dates Online. She showed me your profile, so I joined too. I suppose it's a bit of a shock to you. I've been wanting to contact you for a while now, so I thought it was fate. There are a lot of dorks and weirdos on that site, aren't there?'

Dan felt a flicker of a smile. 'There are a few, I fear. But why pose as Anna?'

'I wasn't giving away my details until I was sure what the site was all about. Besides, I only wanted to chat to you.'

'I half-wish I had done that too,' said Dan, missing her point completely. 'Honesty isn't always the best policy.'

'I wasn't sure if you'd want to see me again,' Sarah pressed her point. 'Talking to you online was fun. I felt that old spark, and I thought maybe it was worth trying to meet with you.'

'If you'd been less selfish, we might still be together.' Dan wouldn't let her walk all over him.

'Ooh, I love it when you talk tough.' She smiled shyly.

'Stop taking the piss.'

'I'm sorry. I'm really nervous and my mouth is running away with me as usual.'

Dan was quiet for a moment. He couldn't help thinking that he had walked into a time warp. Or maybe someone was going to jump out with a hidden camera and say this was all a joke.

Had he really been chatting to his ex online and not known it? Sure, dating hadn't been much fun, but did he want to revisit the past with Sarah? She seemed so sure of herself, so much fun to be with.

Had they just lost sight of what they'd had together?

He was quiet for a moment longer while he decided what to do.

'You really want to pick up where we left off?' he asked eventually.

'We could try.' Sarah reached across the table and put her hand over his. 'Seeing as we are here.'

Dan hesitated again. He should really shout her down in the middle of the restaurant for tricking him into this date. But part of him had to admire her guts. Much to Sarah's surprise, he nodded.

'We can at least be civil this evening,' he told her.

It had been over a week since the video went online and Riley was shocked to see how many competition entries were still coming in. Over 500 people had joined in so far. It was incredible – and really hard to keep track of. Luckily, just searching the hashtag #ShoeLove brought up shoe after shoe. That made life a lot easier.

Since Urban Angels had joined in the Twitter conversation, things had become even more hectic. Riley had been asked to write a few articles for blogs and online magazines. She'd been invited to speak on local radio. She'd even been tweeting with Roxy and the other three band members quite often. They had tweeted photos of lots of their shoes. There was talk of them visiting the shop the next time they came home to Hedworth. Now, that would be a scoop. She would have to get Ethan to take lots of photos if it happened. She loved their music, despite the fact that the girls' average age was just twenty.

The shop's own sales competition was looking good, too. Sales had improved, so Suzanne didn't have reason to complain. In another few weeks the shop would be doing better, which meant none of them should lose their jobs.

As she served a lady at the till, Riley noticed another woman looking at her. She was tall and her long blonde hair was as thick as her make-up. She wore a knee-length black coat and nude-coloured high heels that she tottered around in.

Riley noticed her again a few minutes later, once her customer had gone, studying the last pair of the new sandals. After helping Dan to locate a pair of missing shoes in size five, she caught the woman looking over again. Riley frowned, but by the time she had reached the woman it had morphed into her regular customer service smile. Up close the woman was a little older than Riley had first thought. She reckoned she might be in her early thirties.

'They're great, aren't they?' Riley said. 'If you're looking for them in your size, I'm sorry, that's the last pair.'

'I'm just browsing.' The woman glared at her. 'I doubt you'd have anything to suit my requirements in here.' She held the strap of the shoe between her finger and thumb as if it was covered in cat poo, before placing it down again.

'Well, if you need any help, just give one of us a shout.' Riley forced a smile before turning back to the till.

'Yes, you're great at helping, aren't you?' the woman spat.

Riley turned to her with another frown.

The woman pointed a manicured nail at her. 'You don't mind helping yourself to anything.'

'I'm not sure what you mean,' said Riley.

'I've seen you and your social media campaign. I saw the stunt you pulled at the weekend.'

'It wasn't a stunt. It was a—'

'You were kissing *my* boyfriend!'

People in the shop, including Dan and Sadie, had turned to stare. A silence fell as they watched the scene unfold. Riley's shoulders drooped as everyone continued to stare at her.

'Ethan is . . .' She paused. 'You're Clarissa?'

'Yes, and I happen to still be going out with him.'

'No. He told me your relationship was over.'

'It isn't. He's still seeing me.' Clarissa looked Riley up and down snidely. 'I thought he was only seeing me, but now I know that you're around too I'd call him a two-timing bastard.'

'I'm not sure what's been going on, but Ethan said that he has nothing to do with you any more.'

'Is that so?' Clarissa opened her coat.

Everyone in the shop shared a gasp. Riley thought the woman must be at least seven months pregnant.

'He doesn't want to see me any more,' Clarissa went on, 'because he doesn't want to acknowledge that this is his baby.'

'He didn't tell me that . . .' Riley's hand flew to cover her mouth.

'Of course he wouldn't say,' Clarissa almost screeched. 'He accused me of harassing him, can you believe that? He's been ignoring all my calls and my emails. But all I wanted was to tell him my news. When I did finally see him, he said the baby wasn't his. He's wrong. I know he's the father.'

'But I thought your relationship ended well over a year ago,' Riley finally managed to say.

'It did. We bump into each other occasionally, and we always end up in bed together.' Now she had an audience, Clarissa was becoming far more theatrical. She pressed a hand to her stomach. 'This was one of those times.'

'I— I—' Riley stuttered.

'You don't believe me?' Clarissa pointed her finger in Riley's face. 'Ask him about the time when we met up at Rembrandt's and he took me home afterwards.'

Riley frowned. Ethan had told her he didn't like Rembrandt's, so she wasn't sure he would meet anyone there, let alone Clarissa.

'Ask him!' Clarissa folded her arms and rested them on her bump. 'You'll see he's lying then. He's nothing but a two-tim-ing—'

Riley didn't want to listen any more, especially when every-one in the shop was listening too.

'Dan,' she said, beckoning him over. 'Would you escort this lady out of the shop if she doesn't want to buy anything, please, while I—'

'That's it, run away.' Clarissa waved her off. 'But you can't hide from the facts. Ethan should have told you that he's going to be a father soon. It's a good job you did this flash mob thing. If it wasn't for that video, I wouldn't have been able to warn you off him.'

Riley was halfway down the stairs, yet she could still hear Clarissa shouting after her. She hoped Dan would be able to remove her from the shop without causing a scene. Wow. Ethan had warned her about Clarissa's jealousy, but she had never thought she would go to such lengths to get him back. She got out her phone.

Yet, as she waited for him to pick up, the image of Clarissa's pregnant stomach kept flashing before her eyes. It couldn't be true. Ethan would have told her.

Maybe Clarissa was trying to get her to argue with Ethan and then finish things with him so that Clarissa could get him back.

She needed to speak to him, to put her mind at rest. But his phone went unanswered, switching to voicemail.

'Ethan, it's Riley. Could you call me when you have a mo-ment, please?'

CHAPTER TWENTY

Riley sat in the staffroom while she wondered what to do. Ethan had told her how jealous Clarissa was, and she was inclined to believe him over his ex. He was a nice guy, not like Nicholas. Nicholas had made a fool of Riley, and she shouldn't take that out on Ethan.

Yet, she wondered whether she should be so quick to believe him. She hadn't known him long, and Clarissa was definitely pregnant. It might not be his baby, but Riley needed to know for sure. She was still hoping this was all a mistake.

Ethan hadn't called back and she would be needed out on the shop floor soon. But she couldn't face anyone yet. Her hands shook as she made a cup of sweet tea.

A few minutes later, she was just about to go back upstairs when her phone rang. It was Ethan.

'Hey, what's up?' he asked. 'How's the competition going?'

'Good,' she replied. 'But it brought the wrong kind of publicity today. I've just had a most bizarre exchange with someone named Clarissa.'

She heard him groan. 'She came into the shop?'

'Yes, she's accused you of seeing both of us, and says that the baby she's carrying is yours. She's just shouted me down in front of a shop full of people. Why didn't you tell me she was pregnant?'

'Ah.'

Ah?

'The baby isn't mine. She's been saying it is, but it can't be.'

'But why didn't you tell me? I made a total fool of myself when I saw her.'

'We split up over a year ago.'

'Yes, but . . .' Riley paused. She was about to accuse him of something he may not have done.

'Did she tell you we've been having casual sex since we split?' Ethan asked.

'Yes.'

'It isn't true. I would have told you if it was. She's been harassing me since the weekend.'

'But I thought you'd blocked her?'

'I have. She's opened another Twitter account. I blocked that one, too. She keeps setting up new ones. I can't keep up with blocking them all.'

'But why has it got so bad all of a sudden?'

'She must have seen you in the video. For some reason, she wants to mess with me.'

'So the baby isn't yours?'

'No. Ask Jimmy if you don't believe me.'

Riley felt herself relax at his attempt at a joke.

'Though I do feel sorry for the man who *is* the father – I doubt she'll ever tell me his name.'

Dan came into the staffroom. 'Riley, I think you need to see this.' He held up his iPad. 'Your Twitter feed has gone wild again – but not in a good way.'

'I'll ring you back, Ethan,' she told him. 'Something's happening on Twitter.'

She disconnected the call before he could speak again. Her heart sank as she looked at the tweets displayed on Dan's iPad.

@RileyFlynn You slimeball, Can't believe you'd sleep with another woman's man. #Howcouldyou? @RileyFlynn

@RileyFlynn All this competition stuff was to cover up what you're really doing. #Slut

'Why are they saying that?' Riley looked up at Dan with a frown.

Dan scrolled up the screen and showed her the tweet they were all referring to. It was from someone with the Twitter handle @Clarissapops. Riley looked at the avatar on the account and saw a photo of Clarissa.

@RileyFlynn stole my man for publicity campaign. Don't buy your shoes from Chandler's Shoe Shop!

'How the hell can everyone talk like that without knowing the facts?' Riley questioned.

'That's social media for you,' said Dan. 'Happy or sad news, if they see it, every loony in the world can comment on it.'

'But why would Clarissa try to sabotage the campaign?'

'I don't think she's doing that deliberately.' Dan continued to scroll through more tweets. 'She seems as if she wants to get back at Ethan, through you. I hope Suzanne doesn't see this, though. Clarissa's bringing ill repute on the shop as well as you.'

'Do you think it will blow over soon?' Riley glanced at the Twitter feed again. 'Things on social media don't last long. Do they?'

'Depends who it's aimed at,' Dan shrugged. 'Loonies love to join in if someone else is being slagged off.'

Riley gave him back his iPad. 'We need to get retweeting and sharing some competition entries, take the attention off Clarissa's tweet. Show some shoes – stay positive. Come on.'

'Are you okay, Riley?' asked Sadie as Riley came back onto the shop floor. 'What was that woman talking about? It isn't Ethan's baby, is it?'

'No. That was Ethan's ex-girlfriend, though.'

Sadie's hand shot to her mouth. 'Oh Riley, what a cow!'

'I'm inclined to believe him over her,' Riley sighed loudly. 'Whatever's happening, it will all blow over soon.'

Sadie touched Riley's forearm. 'Keep your chin up. I think you may have found a good one in Ethan.'

'I hope so.' Despite the circumstances, Riley broke into a smile. 'Because I really like him.'

They shared a hug. Behind them, two young women walked in.

'Can we enter the competition?' said one of them, walking over to the till with a leaflet in her hand.

'Of course you can,' said Riley.

'Are those the bags in the window?' the other said. 'They are well cool. I'm definitely buying one if I don't win.'

Riley suddenly found her faith again. This was the goodness in social media, right here. No matter what the likes of Clarissa did, there were a lot more good people.

It had taken Suzanne an hour to hear about the trouble on Twitter and to come into the shop. Riley took her downstairs to the staffroom.

'Just what the hell is going on?' Suzanne barked. 'It's one thing for you to say this social media lark is good for publicity, but quite another thing when it starts bringing bad press to the shop. Who is' – she peered at her phone – '"Clarissapops"? And why is she hell-bent on causing you misery?'

'She's my boyfriend's ex.' Riley cringed as she explained. It felt weird to call Ethan her boyfriend, and a little immature, but she couldn't call him her partner yet. They hadn't been together long enough for that.

'And what has she got to do with Chandler's?' asked Suzanne.

'Nothing at all. She used to go out with Ethan and has been harassing him over the past few months since they split up.'

'From what I can see, it doesn't look like they have split up at all. The woman is having a baby!'

'It's not his,' said Riley. 'She's just being vindictive and trying to get him back. I'm ignoring all her comments, and concentrating on the positive things being shared. The favourite shoe competition is really working.'

'And are sales improving?'

'Yes, we've had more footfall since the video went live.'

'That's not what I asked.'

Riley knew exactly what she meant. 'I don't think we can judge these things on a daily basis. Things will look better week by week, month by month if we have more time.'

Suzanne shook her head.

'What does Max think about all this?' Riley decided to bring his name into the conversation. Max was beginning to feel like the elephant in the room, with Suzanne hardly mentioning him at all.

Suzanne's shoulders rose. 'Max agrees with me, of course,' she snapped.

'When is he due home?'

'He's in Italy, on a six-week residential course. It hardly seemed worth him coming home at the weekend to go back on Sunday evenings, so he's staying there until he's finished.'

'Which is . . . ?'

'None of your business. Why are you asking?'

'No reason in particular,' Riley shrugged.

'It was a last-minute opportunity.' Suzanne glanced at her watch. 'I must dash.' She stared at Riley for a moment. 'I trust I can leave you to sort out the mess with this Clarissapops?'

Riley nodded, stifling a giggle at the face Suzanne pulled at Clarissa's Twitter handle.

'Good. I don't wish to see Chandler's' name bandied about on social media, or anywhere else for that matter – not in a bad way. Any more nonsense like that and I will close the Twitter account.'

'You can't! What about the competition? We've worked so hard at it.'

'You'll just have to make sure the ex-girlfriend keeps her comments to herself then,' Suzanne told her sharply. 'You know I had my doubts about social media in the first place. I thought that you might have proved me wrong. But as far as I'm concerned, it seems to bring nothing but trouble.'

Riley couldn't agree more. 'Before you leave, am I okay ordering in some more of those sandals? They've gone down a storm with the local students, and schoolgirls have been coming in with their mums too.'

Suzanne paused. 'I suppose so, if they're selling.'

'And the tote bags? Frank can't make them quick enough. I know they don't bring in much profit, but it's about what else customers buy on top, isn't it? We've actually got a waiting list and I can—'

'Like I said, I'm putting the onus on you if anything goes wrong,' Suzanne interrupted. 'If this social media thing gets out of hand, I'll be forced to close the shop before the three months are up.'

When Ethan rang that afternoon asking if she wanted a lift home, Riley declined his offer. Throughout the day, the trolling had gathered momentum and she had been called every horrible name she knew, as well as some that she hadn't come across before.

How could everyone side with Clarissa? Was it because she was pregnant and all they saw was a helpless woman? Because, to Riley, Clarissa seemed far from helpless. She was very much in control.

Ash drew Riley into her arms for a hug when they met at the bus station.

'I'm sorry,' Ash told her. 'I had no idea she was such a psycho. Did you?'

Riley shook her head. 'Ethan says she's been unstable for some time now, at least two years.'

Ash paused for a moment. 'Do you believe he would lie to you?'

'Of course I don't.'

'Then stop this right now – go online and dampen the fire. If you don't respond to the accusations, you'll look guilty. You don't need to get involved with all the tittle-tattle, just say your piece and leave it at that.'

'Won't it make things worse?' Riley asked.

Ash shrugged. 'It's possible, but you still need to be seen to be trying to limit the damage. A baseball bat around the head might suffice.'

Ash was trying to make her laugh, but Riley wasn't in the mood. She sat on the bus, head hung low, desperate to see Ethan but not wanting to incite the trolls again. The internet made everyone a target. Everywhere you went people could film you or photograph you and it could be online within seconds, around the world in the same. Riley had marvelled at the speed with which the competition had grown legs, but now she could see the darker side of things too. And the story Clarissa was spreading wasn't even true.

How was Riley going to quell the rumours?

CHAPTER TWENTY-ONE

Sadie put down her wine glass and wiped the tears falling from her eyes, but it was no use. For some reason, she couldn't stop thinking about the night she and Ross met. She had been eighteen and carefree, out with her work colleague in the local nightclub. It had been called Tiffany's and was in the building that Rembrandt's now occupied. It was before she had started work at Chandler's, long before she knew Riley and Dan. She and Lucy had been on the dance floor, energetically flinging their arms around, and had accidentally bumped into a group of men standing at the side. One of them had been Ross.

Sadie had paired up with him for a good kissing session, they'd fixed a date for the next evening, and their life as a couple began. Lucy had eventually married a man from Liverpool and had moved away. She and Sadie kept in touch with the odd text every now and then. Sadie and Ross were married three years after they met, just after her twenty-first birthday. They'd spent fifteen fabulous years together before the illness had taken him away.

She logged on to Grieve Together to see if Tanya was around. There was a message waiting for her.

Tanya: *I'm so glad I'm online. You sound so upset. I wish I could give you a hug. I'm here if you want to rant.*

Clara: *At least I have poppet to help me through it all. Although even that is bittersweet as we had been trying for another baby for a while.*

Sadie paused. She hadn't told anyone that before. She and Ross had been keen to have another child, but now she was glad that they hadn't. It was one thing to have one child, an independent six-year-old who looked after herself more and more each day, but to throw a baby into the mix as well would have made things more than twice as hard. Of course, Christine didn't mind looking after Esther, as she could have the day to herself while she was at school, but a baby would have been another matter. Maybe then Sadie would have had to give up her job completely and be a stay-at-home mum until they were both at school.

Tanya: *Oh, no! That's so sad to hear.*

Clara: *Yes, when they found out that he had cancer, everything stopped. It sounds selfish but I'm glad now that we didn't have another baby. I don't know how I would have coped with two children to look after.*

Tanya: *Do you have family to help with poppet? It must be hard to do it all by yourself.*

Clara: *Yes, Ross's parents are great. I'm very lucky, really, as my own parents live out of the area.*

Tanya: *It's good to hear that you have people to confide in. Although I find it's better to chat to people who don't know you, sometimes. Look at how we've bonded.*

Clara: *You're right. I can't confide in either of them. My mother-in-law often gets upset when we talk about him. Besides, there's too much personal stuff. And imagine if they thought I wasn't getting over his death and that I am taking advantage of them!*

Tanya: *I'm sure they wouldn't think that. I expect they just want to help as much as they can. And being around poppet might help them both, too. Until you're ready to be with anyone else, welcome their help!*

Clara: *I don't want to find anyone else.*

Tanya: *Of course you do! You're too young to stay on your own for long.*

Clara: *I'm hardly marriage material: a single parent with a six-year-old. And no one can take the place of poppet's daddy, can they?*

Tanya: *Of course not. I wasn't suggesting that.*

Clara: *And would I even want that? Ross told me to find someone else to love.*

Sadie recalled what Ross had said to her on the morning before he'd died. 'Find yourself someone else, another top man.' He'd tried to laugh at his own attempt at a joke. 'Don't be on your own, and don't feel guilty – someone else needs to love you as much as I do.'

Clara: *I can't do that yet.*

Tanya: *I understand. It's hard to think of the future when it's all so raw, but you will get there one day.*

Sadie closed the laptop. She knew in time that she would have to try – to give Esther a good upbringing as part of a family. Maybe she might meet someone else who had children?

Would she cope with stepchildren? She couldn't see why not. She would have liked more children, but she wanted them to be hers and Ross's.

More tears fell. Her mind was so mixed up. How would she get past the anniversary of his death? The first year without him. She still hadn't decided what to do to mark the day. She could either go somewhere with Esther on their own, or involve everyone else.

Was it something she had to do solely with their daughter, or did she need to include family and friends? After all, they'd known him just as well, and they would be grieving too. She wasn't the only one who had loved Ross and been left with a huge hole in her life. She could tell that Cooper was feeling it – coming round here, thinking he had to look after her because he had promised Ross that he would.

That was another thing she felt guilty about, especially after her outburst before the flash mob. One day, Cooper would have a family of his own, rather than trying to look out for her and Esther. She had been lucky that he was unattached. No girlfriend would let him spend all the time with her that he did at the moment without being jealous. She wouldn't understand why they had such a close bond.

Sadie reached for her wine again. Talking to Tanya had made her feel a little better about the tears she had shed.

She tried to settle down and watch the television. Maybe catching up on *Coronation Street* would make her forget her own worries for a while, if she concentrated on someone else's.

She scoffed. If only it were that simple.

Dan had hardly been able to contain himself at work that day. Despite his misgivings about Sarah, he had decided to meet her again. And now that the initial shock had worn off, he found himself looking forward to seeing her that evening.

It had been like seeing a ghost when she had walked into the restaurant, and there was no denying that his heart had pounded when she smiled at him, sitting so close. She had kissed him at the end of the evening, before giving him a lift home. It had been a nervous kiss at first, tentative, daring even. Then they'd both relaxed into it, and it seemed as if they had never been apart. They'd pressed their bodies together, as good a fit as before. Breathless, they'd then pulled apart and gone their separate ways.

Yet, for some reason, he hadn't been able to share his happiness with Riley and Sadie. Dan supposed it was a case of 'once bitten, twice shy'. Getting back together with her would make him look like a fool. He didn't want to chance it yet. He'd tell them when he was more comfortable with it himself.

He was a few minutes late when he pushed open the door to the busy bar and, glancing around quickly, was glad to see that Sarah was already there. She waved as he made his way over to her. There were two drinks already on the table.

'How are you?' He leaned over to kiss her, the familiar scent of her cloaking him.

'I'm good, thanks.' She smiled, taking his hand in hers. 'How's your day been?'

'Hectic!' Dan grinned. 'I'm not getting trolled as the fat dancer, though, thank goodness. It's Riley I'm worried about. She's still getting the odd nasty comment, but we're trying to keep everything positive by tweeting about the competition. There are some great photos of shoes coming through. Here, let me show you some.'

Dan got out his phone and scrolled through some of the competition entries, showing Sarah a few local celebrities who had joined in with the hashtag.

'It all went a bit wild after Urban Angels joined in,' Dan explained. 'It's been really busy in the shop, but it's been great fun too. Everywhere I go, people start singing "Happy". I get stopped in the High Street all the time.'

'You're a celebrity!' Sarah's laugh was friendly. 'I can't believe you, of all people, did that dance.'

'Why ever not?'

'You never wanted to dance whenever we went anywhere.'

'That's because I didn't realise I *could* dance.' He took a sip of his drink. 'I've been thinking about taking classes. Serena, the dance instructor from the flash mob, has mentioned that I could join one of her regular groups. I thought it might help me to shift this too.' He prodded his protruding stomach. 'It's a great way of keeping fit.'

'Nonsense.' Sarah put a hand on his chest. 'I, for one, like you just the way you are.'

An hour later, they were still chatting but the mood had changed. There was a feeling of anticipation, a sense of urgency and the desire to be alone. Dan was the first to bring it up.

'It's busy in here, isn't it?' he said, glancing around the room. There were a few groups of people milling about the bar and most tables were full, but it wasn't uncomfortable.

'We could always have a coffee back at the flat?' Sarah suggested.

'I thought you'd never ask.' Dan knocked back the last of his drink and stood up.

As Sarah parked her car outside his old home, a feeling of déjà vu washed over him. The last time he'd been to their old flat was to collect the rest of his belongings after he'd moved in with his parents, after Sarah had confessed to cheating. Pushing those thoughts to the back of his mind, he got out of the car. Now wasn't the time to think about the past. He didn't want anything to spoil the evening.

He held open the communal front door for Sarah to walk through first. Walking behind her up the two flights of stairs, he began to get excited. But stepping into the flat was a little weird, almost like being a stranger in his own home yet feeling as if he'd never been away.

The flat was exactly as he had left it. Nothing had moved. He sat down on the large leather corner settee they'd bought to create more space in the living room, glancing around at the wallpaper and paintings they'd hung together. There was even a photo of the two of them, taken in London last year, on the side unit.

'So, do you want me to come dancing with you?' Sarah shouted through from the kitchen, while she waited for the kettle to boil.

The question took him by surprise and he went in to her. 'Well, yes, I suppose.'

'You suppose?' Sarah looked mock-insulted. She took one of his hands and put it around her waist. The other she clasped in the air. 'I can do a mean tango,' she said, proceeding to lead him across the tiny kitchen floor.

'You don't do it like that.' Dan pulled her nearer and rested his cheek on hers. Then he strode across the room with her, humming a tune as he did so.

Sarah laughed as he turned. She followed his lead and they did it again. After a minute, laughing as they tangoed and then waltzed around the kitchen, they stopped, staring at each other while they caught their breath. The air was full of anticipation.

Sarah leaned forward and kissed him. It felt so good that for a moment he forgot to kiss her back. Within seconds, she reached for his jumper and pulled it over his head. He gasped as she touched the bare skin on his back. It was as if he'd been woken from a very long sleep. Sarah took his hand and led him through to the bedroom. As they removed each other's clothes, Dan felt the passion building. They began to caress each other, knowing exactly how to give each other maximum pleasure. It felt so good to be together once more.

Afterwards, for a moment it was awkward again, until Sarah spoke.

'That felt . . . strange,' she admitted. 'Kind of familiar but new at the same time.'

Dan nodded. 'I was thinking the same thing.'

Sarah sat up. 'Perhaps we should stay in bed and then do it again in a little while – you know, just so that it seems more natural. What do you think?'

Dan grinned. Oh, he was all for that.

'I can't see any harm in it,' he said, as he pulled her into his arms again. How he'd missed doing that, holding her, making love to her.

And the next time, he was going to take the lead.

CHAPTER TWENTY-TWO

'How are you feeling this morning?' Dan asked Riley when they got into work. 'I was checking Twitter last night. It seemed to be dying down a little.'

'I'm okay,' said Riley. 'At least I'm today's chip paper, so to speak. Someone else will take a battering online today, no doubt. How about you?'

Dan beamed.

'Don't tell me you've had a date that's gone well!'

Then he blushed.

'Oh!' Riley gasped. 'You've had a second date, haven't you?'

Dan checked to see that Sadie wasn't in hearing distance before looking back at Riley. 'I have, and I haven't.'

'That sounds ominous.' She beckoned him over to the till. Sadie was busy trying to persuade a three-year-old girl to take red pumps when she really wanted blue. There were only red ones left in her size and Sadie was trying to persuade her that red was a special colour.

Seeing Dan gnawing on his bottom lip, Riley knew that he wanted to speak but was unsure of the reply he'd get.

'Come on, spill,' she encouraged. 'If she wasn't the Bride of Godzilla, then what was she like?'

'My blind date last week . . .' Dan paused for a moment. 'Turned out to be Sarah.'

Riley frowned before her eyes widened in disbelief. 'As in, *your* Sarah?'

Dan nodded and quickly told her what had happened.

'So why the long face?'

'Because I wasn't sure how you'd react.'

Riley snorted. 'Like I'm the one to give out relationship advice.'

'But you and Sadie were so pleased when I finished things with her.'

'That was because we knew how hurt you were and we took your side. If you feel that you can make a go of things again, it doesn't matter what anyone else thinks.'

'Sure it does! You are my friends. I value your opinions.'

'You don't need our approval! And we'll always be here for you.'

'I know, but I was hoping that you would swear and slag her off and tell me not to go there again so that I would stop seeing her and—'

'What are you so scared of?' Riley wasn't one for mincing her words. She put her hand on his arm. 'Getting intimate again?'

Dan's face reddened in a second.

'Oh,' Riley grinned. 'That *was* the second date. How do you feel about that?'

Dan smiled. 'It was okay, actually. But . . . I don't know. It was right. So familiar. But at the same time it felt so wrong. It was as if I was going backwards rather than moving forwards.'

'Maybe it will take a little time to adjust.' Riley patted him on the arm. 'For things to slip back into place.'

'What if it doesn't work out, Riles?'

'But, what if it *does*? Sarah knows she hurt you so much before. She won't do it again, surely?'

Dan shrugged.

'Anyone can make a mistake. It takes a lot of guts to say you're sorry and to ask for forgiveness.'

'I guess.' Dan sighed.

An elderly gentleman in a dapper suit came into the shop and approached them.

'If you feel you want to try again with Sarah, then do it,' Riley said to him quickly. 'Life's too short, Dan. And, if it doesn't work out, we'll be here for hugs and pizza and cake— Hi there, can I help you?'

Riley had only been back from her lunch break for twenty minutes when a woman came in, walked straight up to her as she was checking through a list of invoices, and prodded her on the shoulder.

'Do you enjoy going after other women's men?' she hissed.

Riley was taken aback by the woman's tone. She didn't recognise her at all. Late thirties at a guess, with blonde hair cut in a layered bob and red glasses that suited her face. Her clothes were smart and she was well turned out.

'Hey, what do you think you're doing?' Dan was over to them in a flash.

The woman ignored him and continued to speak to Riley. 'You were the one sleeping with my husband.'

'I— I beg your pardon,' Riley stuttered. Then she paled. Oh no, please, no. She couldn't be talking about Nicholas. And if she was, how the hell had she found out? Ash was the only person she had told about what had happened. This was all she needed, with the farce that Clarissa had started still continuing online.

'I saw your video,' the woman continued, pointing a finger at her. 'At first, I thought it was an excellent idea. I was even going to come down here myself and support you! But then I looked a little closer at you and I knew I recognised you from somewhere else.' She pulled her mobile phone from her bag. 'It was only last night that it came to me. It took me a while to check on his phone but, yes, there you were. Here, take a closer look. That's you and him, isn't it?'

Riley looked at the screen. It was a selfie of her and Nicholas. The woman must have copied it to from his phone to hers. It had been taken at Riley's flat. She could remember the evening. She'd been happy then, not knowing any of his sordid secrets.

The stupid idiot – why the hell did he still have it?

The shop went silent as everyone waited for her to speak. What could she say but the truth? Which she had a feeling the woman wouldn't want to hear.

'It's Liz, isn't it?' Riley said, quietly.

'Yes.' The woman nodded curtly.

'He didn't tell me he was married.'

'And you expect me to believe that?' The woman folded her arms.

'But it's not how it looks in—' Riley began.

'If what you're suggesting is that Riley had an affair with your husband,' said Dan, coming to her defence, 'I suggest you get your facts straight first. She wouldn't do that.'

'I agree.' Sadie stepped forward. 'Riley isn't that type of person.'

'Thanks, Sadie.' Riley tried to keep the shake from her voice. It had been bad enough when Clarissa had come into the shop and blasted her down in front of everyone. She wasn't going to take it a second time.

'I didn't do anything wrong. Nicholas lied to us both.'

She saw Dan and Sadie share a look. Her shoulders drooped a little as she realised she had a lot of explaining to do once Liz had gone.

'Do you want to come through to the staffroom and we can chat in private?' she asked Liz, knowing that it was the lesser of two evils. She didn't want her to cause more of a fuss in the shop, nor for it to spread out onto the High Street. It would be better if she could explain in private what had happened.

Liz stood still for a moment before nodding.

Feeling her skin flush as all eyes were on her, Riley led Liz through to the back, down the stairs and into the staffroom. She pointed to the small table crammed into the corner. 'Please, sit down. I could do with a coffee. Would you like one?'

Liz shook her head. 'I just want to know what's going on.'

'*Nothing* is going on. I haven't seen Nicholas since last year.'

Liz frowned. 'But I thought . . .'

The silence that fell became claustrophobic.

'How long have you known?' Riley asked eventually.

'Since New Year. I found a present – I assume it was for you. It was shoved in the bottom of the wardrobe.' Liz laughed snidely. 'The idiot hadn't even got the brains to hide it somewhere I wouldn't find it, or even throw it away. It was wrapped in Christmas paper and had a tag with your name on it.'

Riley cringed inwardly. The stupid idiot, indeed.

'When I confronted him, he said that it was for a woman at work. He said the gift was to thank her for helping him out with a business deal that had brought in a lot of money. It was a token gesture.'

'And you didn't believe him?'

Liz shook her head. 'He's cheated twice before. Both times I took him back because I don't have the financial means to cope on my own. With two children under five, I know the law is on my side, but where would I go? I can't throw him out of the house.'

Riley kept her expression neutral, fuming inwardly. He'd done it before? But of course. It was obvious.

'So you checked his phone and found the photo of me?' she asked.

Liz nodded. 'How long did the affair go on?'

'Four months. I only saw him a couple of times a week.'

'Let me guess. Tuesdays and Thursdays?'

'Yes, and the odd Friday.'

'When he told me he was playing squash.'

Riley grimaced. 'He told me he worked away, so couldn't see me any more regularly. It was when it came to Christmas that it fell apart. I wanted to share Christmas Day with him.'

'I don't understand.' Liz looked up with tears in her eyes. 'How could he have left us at Christmas? How could he do that to his children?'

'He couldn't.'

'Sorry?'

'If you want to make your marriage work,' said Riley, 'that's what you need to focus on. He couldn't leave you for me.'

'That doesn't excuse what he did to us both!'

'Maybe not. But when it came down to it, he didn't want to leave you and the children.'

'He didn't want to rock the boat, you mean,' Liz scoffed, folding her arms. 'It was easier for him to walk away from you than it was to walk away from two children and a marriage. Don't take this the wrong way, but he'll probably have moved on to some other woman now. He can't keep his dick in his trousers. He's always been selfish, always wanted the best of both worlds.'

Riley looked away, tears welling in her eyes as the emotions came flooding back. She could spare Liz her tears at least.

'Does he know that you know?' she asked instead.

Liz shook her head. 'Not yet. But his balls will be black by the time I've finished squeezing them.'

'I am sorry,' said Riley, sinking down into a chair opposite Liz. 'Despite what you may have read about me lately, I would never have started an affair with a married man. He was deceitful to us both, but he was disloyal to you.'

'Much more than you'll ever know.'

'I suppose you need to ask yourself how much you love him. Or how much you love what he can give you. If that's enough, then great. But I suspect it isn't.'

Liz shook her head. 'He doesn't think I'll ever leave him. He thinks I'll play along with it.' She sat up tall. 'He's right about one thing, though. I *won't* leave. I've put my heart and soul into our house, and looking after the children is my job. *He* can find somewhere else to live.'

Riley couldn't help but smile. 'Good for you,' she said. 'It won't be easy, but it's a start.' Her smile slipped then. 'I really am sorry.'

Liz nodded. 'I should have got my facts right before I walked in here. But I was so angry when I saw you on YouTube.'

'It's forgotten.' Riley waved the comment away, wishing everything else could be forgotten as easily.

They sat in quiet for a moment while Liz regained her composure. She stood up.

'I'd better go. Leave you to your work while I sort out my own mess.' She laughed awkwardly. 'Maybe I should dump him by social media. It would serve him right.'

Riley balked. 'Please don't share that photo. I've had enough bad press with someone else blaming me for—'

'I wouldn't do that.'

'Thanks.' Riley's shoulders dropped. 'You should definitely dump him, though,' she agreed.

Once Liz had gone, panic overtook Riley. Although she knew it was unlikely that Clarissa would find out about Liz and Nicholas, she hoped that none of what had happened today would leak out onto social media. Because if it did, it would just add more controversy.

And Suzanne didn't need any more ammunition to call off the competition.

CHAPTER TWENTY-THREE

'What the hell am I going to do about everything, Ash?' said Riley as they got on the bus that night after work. 'If anyone else comes into the shop and says I've run off with their man, I'm going to run off myself!'

'Oh, Riley,' Ash soothed as she shuffled along the seat.

Riley sat down next to her. 'Thousands of people on social media think I'm a home-wrecker. I hate that word. And I'm not one, full stop.'

'It will all die down.'

'Not for a while. Clarissa is trying to keep it going as long as she can. I know it's getting better, and thankfully she won't hear about today's fiasco, but all the same. I'm going to get myself a reputation and I haven't even done anything.' Riley shrugged. 'Anyway, let's change the subject. How are you and wonder boy getting on?'

'Oh, we're doing okay,' Ash grinned.

'Ready to introduce him to us yet?'

'No, I bloody am not! I need at least another year before that.'

'It's only fair. You've all met Ethan now. I can't see what the big secret is.'

'I want to be certain of things before I unleash my friends on him. I'm going to get enough stick about being a cradle-snatcher as it is.'

'He's not a teenager!'

'But there is an eleven-year age gap. If I do stay with him, things will get complicated.'

'Not necessarily,' Riley snorted. 'If I've learnt one thing over the past few weeks, it's to live your life and don't let anyone else stop you. I doubt you'll get as much fuss as I'm getting.'

Ash sighed. 'I can't believe Nicholas's wife came in to see you. I bet you wanted the floor to open up and swallow you whole.'

Riley nodded. 'If it wasn't for the flash mob, I could have easily gone on living my life as it was. Now, everyone knows me. I can't hide anywhere.'

'You shouldn't have to hide,' said Ash. 'You've done nothing wrong. If anyone is to blame, it's Nicholas for being such a selfish bastard, and Ethan for being a pushover. And now you're getting the blame for both their messes.'

Riley smiled. It was just like Ash to stick up for her, and try to make her smile too.

'So, where are you off to this evening?' she wanted to know.

'Out for a drink, I expect.'

'I'm surprised I haven't bumped into Warwick visiting you. I might have to pop upstairs for a cup of sugar.'

'Ha ha. Well, if you do pop round this evening, Cooper will be here. I've got a problem with my electric fan in the bathroom and he's coming over to look at it on his way home before I go out. Are you seeing Ethan later?'

Riley nodded. 'Yes, I think so.'

'Staying in or going out?'

'Staying in! I want a bit of peace and quiet.'

'Oh, is that what they call it nowadays,' Ash teased.

Riley smirked. She was so lucky to have Ash. After Liz had left, Sadie and Dan had been trying to console her, but she couldn't tell them what had happened with Nicholas. It was good of them to leave it alone, as she knew they would both be dying to know what had happened. She'd tell them soon. There was nothing to be gained by keeping it to herself now. And at least her friends wouldn't think she was a fool.

Despite everything that had been going on online, Riley spent a pleasant evening with Ethan. They'd chatted about Clarissa and put the world to rights. On the surface everything was good again; but underneath, there was an uneasiness between them. Riley wasn't too sure that she should tell him about Liz and the events of the day, so she kept it to herself.

The shop was fairly quiet the next morning, but at least another batch of the sandals had arrived. Sadie was wiping down a shelving unit before putting them out on display. Dan was supposed to be helping her but he was busy looking at his phone.

'Anything nasty yet?' asked Riley. She hadn't checked her phone in a good while, for fear of the trolls' comments getting her down.

'There are still lots of competition entries coming in.' Dan glanced her way before his head went down again. 'Lots of not-so-nice tweets about you, too.'

Riley sighed as she got out her phone. She was just about to go on Twitter and block a few people when a text message arrived. Covering her mouth, she held in a gasp. It was from Nicholas.

I'm outside. If you don't come and speak to me, I'm coming in.

Riley looked up to see him loitering on the pavement on the other side of the street. What the hell did he think he was doing, turning up unannounced at her place of work?

'I'm just nipping outside for a few minutes,' she said, quickly grabbing her purse from the drawer beneath the till. 'Either of you want anything from the newsagent's?'

'A Crunchie, please,' said Dan. 'And a bag of cheese and onion . . . no, just a Crunchie, thanks.'

'Sadie?'

Sadie shook her head. 'I'm okay, thanks.'

When Riley got out onto the pavement, Nicholas jogged across the road towards her. Surprised to feel her heart skip a beat, she tried not to look at him, but her eyes were drawn to his face. His wife was right. He would no doubt have moved on to some other gullible woman by now. He was so good-looking that he could take his pick, and conceited enough to know it and to try his luck. She remembered kissing those full lips, having those blue eyes stare into hers with such adoration that they brought tears to her own, running her hands through his thick hair...

But she hated what he had done to her. He'd turned her into someone who couldn't trust another man for fear of being hurt again.

Quickening her step, she continued on towards the newsagent's.

'Riley, I only want to talk,' she heard him say.

She turned her head slightly as he drew level with her, moving away as he tried to touch her arm. 'You have a nerve coming to see me,' she snapped.

'You wouldn't have let me if I'd asked.' Nicholas marched to keep up with her.

'Too right, I wouldn't. I had enough to deal with when your wife turned up yesterday.' She manoeuvred round a woman with a pushchair, almost colliding with Nicholas and then moving away as if burnt. 'Why the hell didn't you delete your photographs?'

'I didn't want to. They were happy memories.'

'And how many other happy memories have you got on your phone?'

'Liz was lying.' He looked shamefaced. 'There hasn't been anyone else.'

'You expect me to believe you?' Riley smiled at Ray as he came out of his café onto the pavement as they passed. 'Morning, Ray.'

'Morning, Riley. Looks like being a grand day.'

Nicholas scuttled along after her. 'I loved only you,' he insisted.

'No!' She stopped suddenly and prodded him in the chest, just as Liz had done to her the day before. '*You* were in love with the idea of having a bit on the side and I was in love with a lying, cheating bastard. Why didn't you throw away the gift?'

'Because I thought one day I'd be able to give it to you in person.'

She walked off again.

'Riley! I'm—'

'She came into the shop,' she turned to him again, 'shouting at me, telling me it was my fault! Can you imagine how I felt?' She pressed her index finger and thumb together. 'This small.'

They had reached the newsagent's now. Riley pushed the door open and marched inside, leaving it to close on Nicholas. But he followed her in. Ignoring him, she grabbed chocolate bars for herself and Dan then went to the till.

'Hi, Riley, diet over then?'

'Never even started, Stefan,' she laughed, as she searched in her purse for the correct change for him.

Nicholas was still behind her. 'I'm sorry,' he whispered. 'But it's over between me and Liz now. My marriage has been stale for a while and . . . I was thinking, maybe you and . . .'

A look from Riley silenced him.

Riley heard Stefan snigger under his breath. She paid for the chocolate and turned to leave. 'You've been thrown out, haven't you?' she asked Nicholas, not bothering who was listening.

'No, it was my choice to leave. Things hadn't been working for a while.'

Riley rolled her eyes, although glad that Liz had managed to go through with her resolve to give him his marching orders.

'And now you have the audacity to think that you can come back to me, four months later, and move in because you have nowhere else to go. You piece of lowlife!'

'But we were so good together! You can't deny that.'

Riley couldn't. Their fling had been short but very intense. She pushed past Nicholas again and was back out on the pavement in a matter of seconds. She'd almost reached Chandler's when he grabbed her arm and twirled her round to face him again. She landed against his chest with a thump.

The familiar closeness made her gasp and she stopped in her tracks, breathing in the familiar scent of him. It would be so easy to let him back into her life, feel his arms around her and his mouth on her lips.

Coming to her senses, she shook her head. This man had hurt her. She wasn't going to turn down the chance of happiness. And even though she and Ethan were on rocky ground because of Clarissa, she wouldn't give up on him yet.

She pushed Nicholas away, but he kept hold of her arm. Pulling her close again, he pressed his lips to hers. Her eyes widening, she pushed him away and slapped him hard across the face.

'Get away from me,' she said, almost snarling at him. 'You don't own me. And you certainly don't have the right to do *that*, ever again.'

'Riley, I'm sorry,' Nicholas cried after her as she raced away down the street to the safety of Chandler's.

Turning at the door, she saw that he had followed her, but at walking pace, giving her a bit of distance.

'Keep away from me,' she told him, before disappearing into the shop, back to her colleagues. She almost threw the chocolate at Dan as she ran past him. Dan twirled round but she had already disappeared down the stairs.

In the staffroom, Riley began to cry, as it all became too much. Nausea rushed over her and she sat down before her knees gave way. This week was going from bad to worse. How had everything become mixed up so quickly? How had it all spiraled out of control?

There was so much running through her mind that she didn't know how to process it all. She needed to talk to someone, but she didn't know who. Dan and Sadie didn't know the full story about Nicholas. In fact, until today, they hadn't even known what he looked like. Ash was at work and it was past lunchtime so she couldn't treat her to a bite while she offloaded. There was no one else except Ethan – and she certainly wasn't going to share this with him.

But then she began to calm down and think rationally. Things had just got out of hand, that was all. Just a lot of misunderstandings because of other people's interference.

She sent a message to Ethan. Had a great night last night. Can't wait to see you again. Rx

She saw there were numerous notifications for her again on Twitter. She wondered if someone had added a photo of a crazy shoe. There had been some really great ones that had been shared simply because they were so unique.

But it wasn't a photo of a shoe that met her gaze as she scrolled down her Twitter feed. Her shoulders drooped and her blood ran cold. It was a photo of her with Nicholas earlier.

She peered more closely at it. It hadn't been taken when she was pushing Nicholas away, nor when she'd slapped him. It had been taken when Nicholas had been kissing her.

Someone had taken it deliberately to stir up trouble.

That someone was Clarissa. And she had tagged Ethan, too.

#LiarRiley @RileyFlynn @HedworthEthan

Riley put her head in her hands and sobbed.

CHAPTER TWENTY-FOUR

Riley sat in Sadie's living room, a glass of wine in hand, trying to keep back the tears that were threatening to fall. After seeing Nicholas earlier, Dan and Sadie had been really worried about her and Sadie had insisted she phone Ethan and tell him she was coming home with her that night for dinner. Riley couldn't deal with a confrontation with him once he saw Clarissa's tweets, so she'd messaged him again, saying that she wasn't feeling too good. After that she'd switched off her phone. She knew she'd have to address the situation with him, but she couldn't cope with it just yet.

Sadie was putting Esther to bed. She could hear them upstairs, Sadie trying to cajole Esther into brushing her teeth. Riley twirled the stem of the glass, trying to concentrate on the television, but it was no use. She couldn't focus on anything.

It had been a while since she had felt this low. Everything had been so good last week and now, only a few days later, everything that could go wrong had done so.

How on earth could things change so quickly? She'd been thrilled with the flash mob, as well as the marketing campaign that would possibly save Chandler's and their jobs. The competition had been getting some decent coverage. What's more, lots of people now knew of Chandler's, especially since Urban Angels kept tweeting photos of their shoes every day, so the hashtag #ShoeLove was still active.

Now, the flash mob felt like the worst thing that could have happened. In the space of two days, Riley had been accosted by Nicholas *and* his wife. She wondered what lies he'd told Liz when she'd confronted him. Riley wondered if Liz believed her when she had said she didn't know Nicholas was married. She was the right age to be a mistress. Mistress, she scoffed. Even the word sounded horrid.

Before that had come the showdown with Clarissa, and the online smear campaign that she had started. And again, this afternoon, with the photo of Riley with Nicholas. What did she gain by being so nasty? Riley was certain she wouldn't get Ethan back that way.

She sighed. All the hard work everyone had put into Chandler's marketing campaign had been tainted when people had started to tweet nasty things about her.

Why did some people prefer to be negative rather than spread good news? She would never understand people who fed off other people's misfortunes. They were like vultures, ready to pounce and make a banquet out of bad news. Parasites, that was a good word for them too.

None of this was her fault. It had all started with exes. And Nicholas was the lowest of them all. Imagine him thinking she would go back to him after all that had happened.

Riley flicked away a tear as Sadie came back into the room and dropped onto the settee beside her. 'You need to talk and I'm all ears,' she told her.

Riley shook her head, but her tears defied her and fell in streams. Sadie listened while she let it all out.

'It's all gone wrong,' she said in between sobs. 'I don't know what to do.'

'What really happened with Nicholas?' asked Sadie, once Riley's sobs had slowed. 'You seemed so happy before Christmas. None of us could believe it when you said you'd ended it. We hadn't even met him.' She frowned. 'Did you know he was married?'

'I had my suspicions that something wasn't right. I suppose that's why I never introduced him to anyone. Not that he would have been willing, anyway.'

'Gut feeling?'

Riley nodded. 'I thought it was because I didn't want to tie myself down, being on the rebound from Tom. You know how much he hurt me. So seeing Nicholas a couple of nights a week was perfect at first. He told me he lived in Newcastle, that he only came to work here during the week. But the nearer it got to Christmas, the more I wanted to see him, and that's when I realised I was falling for him.'

'You mean the L-word?'

Riley nodded.

'Did you know how Nicholas felt about you?'

'He said he loved me, but that he had to keep the relationship long-distance because of his job.'

'Which is?'

'A sales rep.' Riley almost snorted. 'Or so I thought.' She suddenly realised how stupid she had been, how gullible for believing him.

'So he never asked you to go to his place at the weekend?'

'No. I asked him lots of times. Now I know why I couldn't go. In the end I thought he saw me as just a casual thing, for fun whenever he wanted it when he was down in Hedworth on business. I was right about that – but I hadn't thought it was because the bastard was married.'

'You had no idea?'

Riley shook her head. 'I did think about it at first, but then I thought he was just scared to commit. He told me he'd recently had a divorce and was still reeling from that. He said he needed time to get over her, the usual rubbish. I think I believed him at first because I wasn't ready to commit to him. I wanted a bit of fun, I suppose, with no ties. But that never works for me in the long term, so when I did eventually want more, he wasn't happy. That was when I tried to finish it.'

'You did?' Sadie sat wide-eyed.

'Yes. Early December, I told him I couldn't look forward to the New Year while not knowing whether he wanted to be with me or not. I said that Christmas was a time to be with a loved one, and if he didn't want to share Christmas Day with me, then the relationship should end now. He told me there was nothing he wanted more than to spend Christmas together, so we started to plan.'

'Oh, Riley,' Sadie said quietly. 'He didn't turn up, did he?'

Riley shook her head, tears falling again. 'We planned everything. Christmas Day was just going to be the two of us. We would cook dinner together, open presents together, get drunk together, and – well, you know. I thought he was fine with it.

'At six thirty on Christmas Eve, when I had done all the preparation I could, and he was due to arrive at half seven, he rang me to say he wasn't coming. And not only did he tell me that, he also told me the reason why. That he was spending the day with his wife and two children.'

'Small children?'

'Yes, although he'd lied about that too. He said they were grown up.'

'He told you that on Christmas Eve?' Sadie raged. 'The bastard!'

'I think he panicked. He couldn't get away with saying he was working over Christmas so he came up with lie after lie to tell his wife. And then he backed himself into a corner. He didn't want to disappoint me, but knew he couldn't stay with me.'

'He humiliated you!'

'It wasn't nice what he did. I didn't want to be anyone's bit on the side. I couldn't stop thinking of his wife and children for ages after I had found out.' Riley shrugged again. 'I don't think he had any intention of hurting me. He wanted to please too many people because he'd only thought of himself up until that point. When it all came tumbling down, I was the collateral.'

'What a snake.'

'No, being a snake was when he then wanted to resume the relationship in the New Year, just see me once or twice a week, whenever he wanted. That's when I found out he didn't live in Newcastle at all, but had been living in Hedworth all the time. That's when my world shattered. It took me a long time to get myself back together.'

'Why didn't you tell me?' Sadie asked.

'I didn't tell anyone but Ash. You had your own problems, with Ross dying. I couldn't burden you with any more pain.'

'But you were there for me when that happened!' Sadie sounded hurt. 'I would have been there for you, too.'

'I'm sorry.' Riley gave a faint smile. 'It was just . . . I still miss Ross too. Maybe it was because I'd lost him, after losing Tom, that I clung on to Nicholas?'

'It's possible. Ross meant so much to all of us.'

Riley reached for Sadie's hand and squeezed it. 'It was like losing a brother for me. I don't know how you cope.'

'Oh, I do okay.' Sadie's smile was faint too. 'I have to, for Esther's sake. I'm sure if I didn't have her, I wouldn't be so calm, though.'

Once Riley had left, Sadie sat down with her laptop and logged on to Grieve Together. What a day. She still couldn't believe what had happened with Riley, and how the public had reacted. When Dan had shown her what some people had been saying online, it had shocked her. She couldn't believe how vindictive trolls could be. He'd had to stop her from replying, telling her that it would make things much worse. His advice was to let it die down, ignore it and not fuel the fire.

Instead, they'd all been using their personal Twitter accounts to share photos for the competition. It had worked to a certain extent, but they had all had to block several people who had tried to keep Clarissa's tweet going. Why did a few people want to spoil things for the majority? It was a sad world they lived in.

She checked her private messages, wondering if Tanya had been online. Yes, there was a message. She clicked on it to open it.

Tanya: *How are you? You had a better day today? I've been having a rough one. I can't stop thinking about James. It's been nearly two years and I still cry when I think of certain things that he did. I hope you've had a good day, though. I hope everything is going okay at work. I know how well you've been getting back on your feet since Ross died.*

Clara: *Hey, I'm good, thanks. Just another busy day! The good thing about being busy is that my mind is occupied. We've been rushed off our feet since the competition started, but it's good fun. And I've just polished off a pile of ironing, so it's feet up for me now. I hope you're feeling better now.*

Sadie put down her laptop and picked up her pen and journal. If she didn't write her feelings down, she would carry them round in her head for the rest of the evening and that was never a good thing to do. But a message popped up from Tanya.

Tanya: *Have you been writing out your thoughts? I know you've found it useful so far.*

Clara: *I was just about to. Spooky! Yes, although I do worry about ever showing my journal to poppet. Wouldn't it be morbid?*

Tanya: *I don't think so. I think she will love the connection between her parents, how you felt about Ross. Lots of children don't have that when they are young. My mum and dad were always arguing. At least poppet has lots of happy memories, and she can be reminded of them by you writing them down.*

Clara: *But at what age do I show the journal to her? Ten, fifteen, twenty? When would a child ever want to know about her dead father?*

Tanya: *I think you'll know the right time. And I suppose he is very much alive in her memory still at the moment.*

Clara: *You're right. I'm scared that poppet will forget him if I don't do this.*

Tanya: *She won't. You won't let her. And you'll be glad you wrote it all down when you do get around to showing her. Although, maybe you should make sure that she doesn't find your journal when she's older, before you do tell her!*

Clara: *She won't find it. It's underneath a plastic box I use to store cleaning products under the sink. Once I fill one notepad, I'll hide it away in the loft or something. I'll get a box, I think, maybe put some of his things in it for her.*

Tanya: *That sounds a great idea! Something positive to think about, too.*

Clara: *Sometimes I hate myself for being so weak, though. But now, I realise that I must have been quite strong to cope with him dying, and getting on with everything to make life as normal as possible for poppet. She was a gem through it all, a very good girl, and I feel so lucky to have her now. I honestly don't know what I would do without her.*
I guess that's why I can't figure out what to do on the anniversary of his death. I want to do something for me and poppet, and I want to do something with Ross's family too. And then there are my friends.

Tanya: *I think you should make it special for his family as well as your friends. As long as you can deal with the day, do whatever it takes.*

Clara: *Yes, it's going to be painful, but I can get through it. If I can get through Ross dying, I can get through anything life throws at me.*

Sadie logged off Grieve Together and closed down her laptop. Just lately, she'd wondered if being a member of the site was helping her to move on and deal with her grief, or if it was keeping it alive far more than she needed. It was great to have Tanya to talk to, but maybe this was prolonging her struggle to face life without Ross. The first anniversary of his death was playing on her mind. Once she got past that, she would decide whether to stop using Grieve Together or not. She'd probably stay friends with Tanya online, maybe via emails instead, though.

She really hoped she was doing the right thing by writing her journal. She wasn't able to keep Ross's memory alive any other way, so this seemed the right thing for her to do.

Because now all she had were those memories.

CHAPTER TWENTY-FIVE

Riley walked home from Sadie's house. It was a good thirty minutes, but her head didn't feel any clearer when she got back to her flat.

She walked across the car park, heard a car door slam and looked up. Her heart faltered. Ethan was coming towards her. His face was like thunder. She wasn't in the mood for this now.

'What's going on, Riley?' said Ethan, flashing his phone at her. 'Who the hell is this?'

'It's not how it looks,' she told him. 'This is your ex's attempt to sabotage everything for me, again.'

'She says you're a liar. What does she mean by that?'

'I don't have a clue. I didn't even know her three days ago, so I'm not sure how much she knows about me.'

'But these tweets.' Ethan held up his phone again. 'They're saying you were seeing a married man. Is that the man you were so hurt over?'

'If I was, it was before I met you.'

'That's supposed to make it okay?' He shook his head in dismay.

'Look, can we go inside?' Riley pointed to the entrance. 'Despite being splashed across social media, I don't want everyone to know my business.'

Going indoors gave Riley a little time to compose herself before speaking to him again. From the tone of his voice, Ethan was angry enough to believe that everything was true.

'I didn't have an affair,' she started, after she had made them coffee. She sat down and told him what had happened with Nicholas, and what had happened over the past two days.

'When Clarissa took the photo, Nicholas was trying to kiss me,' she said. 'What it doesn't show you is that two seconds later I pushed him away and slapped his face. No one takes advantage of me like that.'

Ethan had the decency to look shamefaced. 'I just thought—'

'You just jumped to the same conclusions everyone else did!' Riley's tone was sharp. 'Thanks a million. And aren't you going to question why it was your ex who took the photo? I had no idea that Nicholas was going to turn up at the shop today. I haven't seen him since last year. Don't you find it strange that Clarissa just happened to be around to take a photo of us together? She must have been spying on me.'

'She might not have taken it. She might have had it sent to her.'

'Which makes it even more devious that she should put it on social media! She's clearly not going to leave us alone. What will she do next? Take photos of us leaving the flat? Or *in* the flat? I wouldn't put anything past her.' She pointed to the window. 'She could be watching us right now.'

'She won't be.'

'But even more so, I can't handle the fact that you were angry with me over something that was out of my control.'

'I'm sorry. Now that you've explained everything, I realise how wrong I was.'

'You didn't believe me.'

'You can hardly blame me. I saw that photo and thought you were kissing him!'

'You're a photographer! You of all people should realise things can be misrepresented and then blown out of proportion.'

'A bit like you're doing now?'

Riley turned to him sharply. 'What do you mean by that?'

'You're blaming me for what Clarissa has done.'

'You accused me of seeing someone else.'

'I didn't know who he was!'

'You should have asked me first!' She looked at him. 'I think you should leave.'

'Riley.' He reached for her hand but she moved away.

'I'll be fine. I just want to be by myself right now. I'll call you tomorrow.'

Once she was alone, Riley fell back onto the settee. What a day. Surely things couldn't get any worse? She hated falling out with Ethan but he shouldn't have accused her of seeing someone else. He should have tackled Clarissa first, or, if not, asked her who was in the photo rather than jumping to conclusions.

But she couldn't put all the blame on Ethan. They both should have been grown up enough to work things out for themselves. Perhaps if they had been seeing each other longer, this might not have happened. But their relationship was new. They hadn't even passed the lust stage yet. There hadn't even been a mention of the L-word.

Riley went over to the window and looked down on the car park. Was Clarissa hiding behind one of the cars? She squinted, trying to see out into the dark. Then she cursed, and drew the curtains shut on the night.

Although none of this would look okay in the morning, all she wanted to do right now was go to bed and forget about everything.

As she suspected, nothing looked any better the next morning. Riley had hardly had any sleep, getting up twice in the night to make a drink and sitting on the settee for a while before taking herself back to bed.

When she got to work everything seemed calm, but she knew it wouldn't last long. Once Suzanne got wind of the last bit of scandal, Riley would be in for it. She kept looking at the door, waiting for her to burst through it in dramatic fashion.

Her mind not on her job, Riley stared out onto the High Street and wondered how many of the people were happy. The man with the briefcase, rushing past, not seeing anyone. The woman who had gone into the newsagent's, who owned a stall in the market. The women who owned the sandwich shop over by the shopping centre.

Was anyone truly content, or did they all trundle through life thinking things can only get better?

Something caught her attention. Someone was watching the shop. Her eyes narrowed, then widened in disbelief.

'I'll be back in a moment,' she told Sadie and Dan, getting out her phone before leaving the shop.

Out on the pavement, she put her phone up to eye level and, pretending to take a selfie in front of the shop, took a photo in the opposite direction. She zoomed in and took a few more. As she did so, she realised that the person she was staring at through the lens had looked up from tapping on her phone and had now noticed her. Riley glanced up the street to see no traffic was coming her way, and ran across to the other side.

'Don't you run away from me, Clarissa!' she cried, putting a hand on the woman's shoulder. 'What do you think you were you doing?'

'I don't know what you mean,' said Clarissa, trying to look anywhere but at Riley.

'You were taking photos of the shop. What do you do? Loiter around here to see if any opportunities come up?' Riley snorted. 'You chose the right day yesterday, good for you.'

'I'm only showing the world how devious you are.' Clarissa put away her phone and folded her arms. 'You're seeing some-one else at the same time as Ethan. He deserves to know. He deserves someone better than that.'

'Like you, you mean?'

'Yes, he belongs with me.'

'You're welcome to him.'

The remark threw Clarissa and she frowned.

'Yes, you heard me. You wanted to ruin my relationship with Ethan? Congratulations, you did it. Satisfied?'

Clarissa said nothing.

'Oh, has the cat got your tongue now?' Riley stepped for-ward. 'Leave me alone or I will report you to the police for ha-rassment.'

'You can't do that!'

'No?' Riley turned to leave. 'If you're still here in five min-utes, just watch me.'

Riley marched back to the shop, head held high. She hoped that was the last she'd see of Clarissa. Bullies were nothing when you squared up to them.

'Was that Clarissa you were talking to?' asked Dan, when she went back inside the shop.

'Yes, She was taking photos of the shop.'

'Again? She's bloody mad. What did she say when you con-fronted her?'

'She said she was showing the world how devious I was.'

'The cow!' Dan paced the room. 'Is she gone? Because if not, I've a good mind to go over there and give her a piece of my mind. She can't keep doing this!'

But Riley had her head down. She looked at the photo that she had taken of Clarissa. She could clearly be seen holding her phone up, looking their way. She flicked on to Twitter, to see if

Clarissa had posted anything about her, but the feed was free of her nasty comments.

Before she had time to think of the consequences, Riley typed a tweet.

There are two sides to every story. #Stalkeralert @Clarissapops

Then she uploaded the photo of Clarissa watching the shop, clear for everyone to see. Two could play at Clarissa's silly games.

And then she froze. With horror, she realised she was logged in to the wrong account.

She hadn't sent the tweet from her personal account. She had sent it from Chandler's'. She deleted it quickly, hoping that not too many people had seen it on their feeds.

But knowing that it would have been sent to Clarissa, and what she would do when she saw it, a sense of dread enveloped her.

An hour later, Riley was cursing her impromptu tweet. Clarissa had begun to bombard her with tweets again, tagging Ethan too. She tried to remain calm as more and more came in, hurling abuse at her. If it was left to her, she would have gone home immediately, shut the door on the world and cried her heart out. But she couldn't leave the shop, nor leave Sadie and Dan to deal with the mess.

Mess. That's exactly what it was. She reached for a bag of pound coins and dropped them into the till as she tried to stop the tears from falling. Everything she had done had been out of the goodness of her heart. She'd tried to keep the shop open, keep them all in jobs. How had it all backfired?

'Chin up, Riles,' said Dan, giving her arm a quick squeeze as he served a customer.

'I was wrong, Dan,' she replied. 'I let you all down, and I let myself down.'

'I know it was wrong, but you're only human. Everyone makes mistakes. You know it will be old news tomorrow. There'll be someone else to tweet about for the trolls by then.'

'I wish I had your optimism,' Riley sighed. 'It's made our competition just that little bit harder now. All our work down the pan because of other people.'

'Things are never as bad as they seem,' said a customer.

Riley looked to see an old lady smiling at them. She was buying slippers. Riley fumed inwardly. Slippers weren't going to stop the shop from closing.

'That's what I keep telling her,' said Dan. 'Whatever is done, is done. It's what we do afterwards that counts.'

'I agree,' said the woman, pressing a twenty-pound note into his hand. 'Everything happens for a reason, even if we don't always notice at the time.'

Riley forced a smile before turning back and muttering under her breath. The woman obviously meant well but she was through with people sticking their noses into her affairs. Why was it that everyone else thought they could offer advice, even when you didn't need it?

Then she looked at Sadie, who was staring at her thoughtfully. Sadie smiled, a smile that said she was always on her side, that she would always have her back no matter what.

She looked at Dan. He caught her eye and gave her a wink before turning back to the woman and giving her his charm.

'She'll be okay,' he told the customer. 'Riley is the strongest person I've ever known.'

Riley smiled, but the tears fell.

'Excuse me,' she said, rushing from the shop floor. Dan was wrong. She was weak. She had let herself down by sending that tweet.

Right now she hated herself.

CHAPTER TWENTY-SIX

That afternoon, Riley's heart sank when the shop door opened and she looked up to see Suzanne. She marched up to the till where Riley was standing, her face a mask of dark emotions.

'A word in the back, please,' she said in a clipped tone.

'Stand tall, Riles,' whispered Dan, as he rushed over to her. 'We've got your back.'

'I don't have time for this,' Riley muttered. 'I can't leave the shop floor at the moment, Suzanne,' she shouted at her boss's disappearing figure.

Suzanne stopped abruptly and turned on her heels. 'I can say what I need to right here, so that everyone can hear, or I can say it to you in private. Which is it to be?'

Riley stared at her. She hadn't got anything to lose, and anything Suzanne did say could be said in front of Dan and Sadie.

'What's going on?' Sadie moved over to the counter with a shoe in her hand.

Undeterred, Suzanne took the shoe from Sadie and threw a large smile in the direction of a woman who was waiting to try it on in her size. 'The shop is closing for the rest of the day.'

'But it's not time yet!' the woman protested.

'If you'd like to come back tomorrow, I'm sure we can come up with some kind of discount.'

'Don't worry, I won't be back. If you can treat your customers so badly, I won't be buying anything from you.' The woman picked up her bag and stormed out of the shop.

'Well, that's yet another customer you've lost us, Riley,' Suzanne said as she locked the door and flicked the sign to 'closed'.

Riley still said nothing.

'Just what the hell is going on with you?' Suzanne rounded on her as soon as she got back to the till. 'First, you create a ludicrous campaign that goes viral. Then you bring trouble to the shop.'

'I didn't bring trouble,' said Riley. 'It came looking for me.' Even as she said it, she knew it sounded catty.

'Oh, poor you,' Suzanne hissed.

'If you hadn't threatened us with losing our jobs, none of this would have happened. As it is, I've been subjected to abuse from all sides.' Riley tried to swallow down her emotions. 'All I wanted was to create some well-needed publicity for Chandler's and—'

'You certainly did that!' Suzanne pointed in Riley's face. '*Bad* publicity!'

'There's no such thing as bad publicity,' Dan said, trying to defend Riley, but he was cut down by Suzanne.

'Of course there is, you idiot!' Suzanne waved an arm around the shop. 'There was one customer in here when I came in. One!'

'There were two, actually,' said Sadie. 'One was just leaving.'

Suzanne glared at her.

'It's nearly closing time!' said Riley. 'We were much busier earlier.'

'And I'm not an idiot,' remarked Dan.

'You're right,' Suzanne nodded, taking them all by surprise. 'I'm the idiot for letting this farce continue. Riley,' she folded her arms, 'I'd like you to collect your things and leave.'

'You're firing me?' Riley gasped – after all the effort she had put in lately?

'You can't do that!' said Sadie.

'Riley is the backbone,' Dan stated. 'Without her, there wouldn't be a shop.'

'This is *my* shop! And it *is* going down the pan, whether we like it or not. And now' – Suzanne pointed at Riley – 'because of your little escapades, no one is going to take us seriously. I must admit, I'm surprised at you.' Suzanne didn't address Riley's last comment. 'I would never have you down as a home-wrecker.'

Riley saw red. She pressed her knuckles down on the counter and leaned forward in confrontation. 'You might be my boss, but you do not have any say in my private life. For your information, I have never stolen anyone else's man, and I never will,' Riley pouted. 'As for you and this shop, I think Albert would be turning in his grave. Working for you and the invisible Max has been a nightmare. I've a good mind to tell Dan and Sadie why I think he's missing.'

'Don't you dare!' Suzanne held up her hand.

Riley continued talking, noticing the looks shooting from Sadie to Dan. 'If you're sacking me, then they're going to hear some home truths first. See how you like it when your world comes crashing down around you and you can't control it.'

The air was crackling with tension. Riley's breathing rate ratcheted up at an alarming rate. She could hear her heart beating rapidly, her head fit to burst with the sound. Anger shot through her, but . . . She took a few seconds to regain her composure. There had been enough secret-spilling, enough damage caused.

'This was your idea all along, wasn't it?' she said. 'Get us to sell as much stock as possible and then sell the shop. That's why you were annoyed when I ordered in the sandals.'

'Is this true?' exclaimed Sadie.

'Unbelievable!' cried Dan.

Behind them, the door handle rattled.

'We're closed!' Suzanne shouted without turning her head.

Riley groaned when she saw it was Ethan. Had he turned up to have a go at her too?

Suzanne stood her ground, staring at Riley. 'Please leave my shop immediately.'

'Don't worry, I'm going.' Riley headed downstairs to get her belongings.

'Riley,' said Sadie. 'Wait!'

Riley grabbed her coat and bag and went back upstairs. Ethan was still waiting on the doorstep for her. She walked towards the door with her head held high, unable to look at Dan or Sadie for fear of bursting into tears. She wouldn't cry in front of Suzanne.

'If you lose her, you lose us all,' she heard Dan say.

Riley left them to it. For once, let them fight their own battles. She was through helping everyone else. It was time to put herself first. After all, that's what everyone else seemed to do.

Outside, she threw Ethan an icy look. 'If you've come to have a go at me, it will have to wait until tomorrow. I've had as much as I can take for today.'

'Riley, I—'

She ran down the street, not even looking back as he shouted her name.

Riley had sent Ash a text message after she fled the shop and left Ethan standing in the street. It was only ten minutes until her friend finished work, so she headed to the shopping centre and waited outside Jazz.

Tears pricked her eyes. She bet half of Hedworth knew what she'd done, and if they didn't, they probably would by the end of the day. Clarissa was the type of person who would milk her mistake.

How could she have been so stupid? She'd always prided herself on being fair, seeing both sides to every story, and here she was, just like everyone else. She had been just as bitchy, reacted just as angrily, as Clarissa, Liz and the trolls on Twitter. Ethan probably thought she was a bitch, too. The whole of the internet probably thought she had a screw loose. Nicholas was still trying to get away with things, despite his wife leaving him. How had she allowed that man to get under her skin and continue to ruin her life long after he had disappeared from it?

She noticed a few people staring at her as she waited outside Jazz, so turned to look in the window. But she caught a shop assistant pointing at her. Embarrassed, she turned away and walked a few feet along, keeping her head down. Word had obviously got out about her tweet. What a fool she'd been to overreact, make herself as bad as all the trolls who had been causing her trouble since the competition started.

Someone touched her shoulder gently. 'She can't do this.'

Riley turned to see Ash and found herself in her friend's arms. 'What a mess!'

It was raining when they left the shopping centre. All the way to the bus station, Ash tried to make Riley see sense.

'All this because of that dickhead, Nicholas,' Ash continued, when they were settled on the bus. 'If he hadn't left your photo on his phone – I mean, what kind of arse would have an affair and do that? – his wife wouldn't have seen it, Clarissa wouldn't have spotted you with him and tweeted the photo to get back at Ethan, and then you and Ethan wouldn't have argued because Nicholas, his wife and Clarissa would never have been in the picture.'

'Clarissa would,' said Riley. 'She was watching me as soon as the campaign started.'

'Which you need to finish and pick a winner for.'

Riley balked. 'I'm not doing that now. Not after Suzanne sacked me. She can do her own bloody competition. See how she likes keeping up with all the social media. Although, now the trolling has started again, there might not be as many shoe-ies coming in.'

'Are you kidding? You might be getting trolled by some pathetic people who have latched on to Clarissa's bad behaviour, but the photos of shoes are still coming in, especially as there are only a few days left before the competition closes. If anything, your bad press has increased the number of entries. You started a craze all by yourself.'

'Really?' said Riley. 'I've switched my phone off in case Ethan tries to call.'

'Look.' Ash handed her phone over to Riley, open on the Twitter app.

Riley scrolled through photo after photo of shoes. 'At least I did something right,' she said. 'Even though it won't do much for sales if no more sandals are ordered in, Chandler's will still be well-known for the flash mob.'

'I guess, but it won't be the same without you there, my friend.'

'People will have to get used to it, I'm afraid.' Riley looked at Ash, tears welling in her eyes again. 'What am I going to do, Ash? One minute everything was going fine and now everything has gone so wrong. I shouldn't have overreacted about Clarissa. It makes me look as childish as her.'

'Don't be so melodramatic,' said Ash. 'It was a genuine mistake. Besides, someone ought to give her a taste of her own medicine. She thought she could do anything and get away with it. Now she's been caught out – people are calling her out for what she did.'

Riley gave her a half-smile. The bus came to a halt at a set of traffic lights. She wished it would stay there forever. She wished she could hold back time, go back even. Then neither Clarissa nor Liz would have seen her in the flash mob, and she would still have her job. It had been hard enough to think that Chandler's might close, but to be forced out was too hard to bear.

Then again, if she hadn't called the newspaper to speak to a journalist, she wouldn't have met Ethan. Even though that had gone all wrong, she still couldn't stop thinking of him. He was going to be so mad with her for walking off, as well as for tweeting out about Clarissa. Riley had switched off her phone once she'd texted Ash after leaving Chandler's, but Clarissa was bound to have linked him to a tweet with her response.

Ethan had let her down too. She had trusted him with the Clarissa predicament. If he couldn't stand by her after she'd made a simple mistake, then he wasn't worth her time. She had made an error in judgement. Everyone made them – even him. He wasn't perfect.

One thing was certain: it was about time that Riley started to look after number one. Stop worrying about Dan and his disastrous dates. Stop worrying about how Sadie was getting on without Ross. Stop worrying about what Ethan thought of her.

She needed to think about the consequences of losing her job.

Maybe it was time to move on from Chandler's and make a fresh start somewhere else.

CHAPTER TWENTY-SEVEN

Sadie checked on Esther, found her fast asleep, and then settled down for the night. She sat on the sofa and flicked through the channels until she found her favourite soap. After a few minutes she realised she'd been staring at the screen but hadn't got a clue what was happening. She kept thinking about Riley and what she had said the previous night about losing Ross. She'd wanted to tell her that it wasn't her place to miss him, because he wasn't her husband. But that was selfish. She knew how much Ross had meant to his friends.

Unable to concentrate, she got out her journal. But then an alert popped up on her phone to say there was a message on Grieve Together.

Tanya: *Hey, how are you today?*

Clara: *Having a bad moment, if you must know. I need cheering up!*

Tanya: *Remind me of the time that you met – when he couldn't recall what you looked like the next morning.*

Clara: *Ha ha. Can you imagine him having to ring around his friends to figure out if I was worth meeting again or if I was too ugly? His words not mine. I whacked him one for that, cheeky sod.*

Tanya: *Oh Sadie, that is so funny!*

The hairs on Sadie's neck stood on end as her hands rested on the keyboard.

Tanya had just called her Sadie.

She scrolled back through the conversation thread that had started several months ago. There was no mention of her name being Sadie during the last few months. She flicked back through more messages. There was no mention of it anywhere.

In a panic, she flicked through the messages again. This time round, she was definitely sure she hadn't mentioned it. She slammed the lid down on her laptop, her breathing becoming rapid.

She was logged on to Grieve Together as Clara.

Had she slipped up? Said anything that would let someone know she wasn't really called Clara? And if so, how would they have known that she was called Sadie?

Oh, this was too weird.

She stood up and paced the room, running a hand through her hair. If this wasn't someone named Tanya, who the hell had she been talking to online for the past few months? It had to be someone she knew. Someone close to her.

She reached for her phone to ring Riley, but then decided against it. She had been really upset earlier after losing her job. She couldn't burden her with this. As she was about to call Cooper, she stopped. For all she knew it could be anyone. Was it him?

Calm down, she admonished herself. It couldn't be Cooper. He was her friend. But then who else could know she was Sadie?

Was someone pretending to be Tanya to get to her? And if so, why would anyone do something so low, to try and get information out of someone who was grieving? What on earth could their motive be?

And then it dawned on her. She sat down quickly before her legs gave way. *Was* it Cooper? *Had* he fallen in love with her and she hadn't realised? They had become close since Ross died, and he had been acting quite secretive recently. He'd been calling less than usual too, saying he was busy during the evenings. She supposed it could be true . . .

Had she overstepped the mark? Made him think there was more to their relationship? Then she remembered what he'd said the last time she had been upset. It would be like sleeping with his sister. Was he trying to hide his feelings by joking about it to gauge her reaction? It had been good to feel his arms around her, but had it given him the wrong impression?

She thought back to the last time she had seen him. How had he been? But all she could think of was that he had been Cooper. Her friend, Cooper. There didn't seem to be anything else.

Did there?

Dan was in the middle of a long kiss. It had been instigated by Sarah, but he couldn't stop thinking about Riley. Poor Riley. If it wasn't enough that she had been slandered online all week, for her to lose her job now on top of it all . . . Well, it just wasn't fair.

It wouldn't be the same going to work if she wasn't there. He wondered if they would get through a day without her. Would they be able to do the things she did almost in her sleep, because they were so routine to her?

Maybe Suzanne would come in and see what Riley did. Then she'd realise what a mistake she had made in sacking her. No amount of money would replace Riley and her knowledge. She not only knew how to run the shop – she *was* the shop.

'What's wrong?' asked Sarah, as she felt his reluctance.

'I can't stop thinking about Riley,' said Dan. 'I don't know how Sadie and I will run the shop alone. We barely know how to—'

'I don't want to hear about that shop again.' Sarah silenced him by pressing her lips to his. 'I want to make love.'

But Dan didn't want to. As much as he had wanted this a couple of weeks ago, already he was beginning to regret it. Almost straight away they had fallen into the same routine as they had before they split up.

In some respects, it was as if the last year apart hadn't happened. In others, they were poles apart. And it was this that worried Dan.

'Don't you want to make love?' she asked, staring at him.

'Yes, of course I do, but it's all we've done since we got back together,' Dan sighed, knowing she wouldn't understand what he meant. 'Sex isn't everything.'

'It shows how much I've missed you, surely?'

Dan shrugged. 'Not necessarily.'

'You mean to tell me that you haven't been thinking about me all day? Waiting to see me so that we can be . . . close?'

Dan would have to be careful what he said next. Of course the sex would be great – but he *hadn't* been thinking about it. He'd been worried about Riley. He might have thought about Sarah a few times during the day, but it hadn't been because he couldn't wait to get her clothes off. It was because he still couldn't work out if he was looking forward to meeting her or not. He should be happy that they were back together, and not continually processing their break up. But it still didn't seem right.

He decided to come clean.

'Maybe we're taking things too quickly,' he said finally, after he had told her how he felt.

There was a pregnant pause before Sarah spoke again. 'Do you love me, Dan?' she asked.

Dan faltered. They had only been back together for two weeks. How could she possibly think of being in love again at this stage?

But his silence told Sarah all she needed to know. She sat up and moved away from him. 'I thought you wanted things to go back to how they were.'

'I do,' Dan said, although he couldn't recall a time when they'd had sex twice in a week, never mind twice in one night. 'But you hurt me and I— I need to be certain that this is what I want.'

Sarah gasped. 'How can you sleep with me, if you're not certain that you want to be with me?'

'You sound like a bunny boiler.' Dan began to laugh, although he was being deadly serious. He'd forgotten how clingy she could be.

'That's rich, coming from you,' she remarked.

'What's that supposed to mean?'

'You were the clingy one. Always wanting to know where I was, and who I was with. What time was I going to be back . . .'

'I wasn't like that,' Dan said truthfully. 'I've never been the jealous type.'

'Oh, that's right. You'd never want to fight to keep me, would you?'

Dan frowned.

'I didn't sleep with Philip Carmichael.'

Dan's mouth hung open. 'What do you mean?'

'I just said that to make you jealous,' she confessed. 'And once I had said it, I couldn't take it back. I know it was wrong, but I just wanted you to show some feelings towards me.'

'You're lying.' Dan couldn't speak for a moment. Then his rage grew. '*You* slept with him because you wanted to, and then you told me because you knew it would hurt me to find out.'

'I didn't! I swear to you. I just wanted to make you jealous, because you didn't love me enough!'

Dan's mouth dropped open. How could she say that? She was the one who had messed up. She was the one who had told him they were in a rut and that she had wanted some excitement.

'You're making this up as you go along, aren't you?' he spat back at her. 'If you'd wanted to make me jealous, then why didn't you fight for me afterwards? If you'd tried harder, I might have given in. You know I'm a pushover. I would have come back to you eventually. And now you're acting all strange because I won't say that I love you after a year apart?'

Sarah sat down suddenly. 'I don't know what I'm saying.'

'I've heard enough.' Dan stood up and reached for his coat. 'I'm sorry, but I can't do this. It wasn't working for me the second time round, and now this?'

'Dan, wait!'

Sarah held on to his arm as he left the room, but he shrugged her off. To the sound of her protests he left the flat, almost running down the stairs and outside. How could he have forgotten how possessive she was? He'd put Sarah on a pedestal because she had left him with a broken heart, forgetting all the irritating things she did and said, how she had made him feel inadequate all the time. He'd been clinging on to the past when all he really needed to do was get a grip on his future.

Dan's steps were lighter the further away from Sarah he walked, a huge grin erupting on his face and a feeling of optimism overwhelming him. Sometimes there was no point in going back.

Some things couldn't be mended.

CHAPTER TWENTY-EIGHT

Riley hadn't switched on her phone for a while because she didn't want to see her name spread across her social media accounts. So when she did finally look, the first thing she found was a message from Ethan.

> This is hard for me to write but I think maybe we should cool things. There's too much in the way for us at the moment. Speak soon. Ex

The text message stunned Riley. She read it again as her eyes became blurry. Clarissa had won. But despite thinking she would be better off without him, her heart suddenly broke. Notwithstanding everything, she had really enjoyed getting to know him over these last few weeks. But she had doubted him over Clarissa.

Now it seemed he didn't even want to give her time to explain, talk things through, see if they could move on from it all. Maybe unintentionally she had hurt him more than she thought.

But if he couldn't see it was because of what had happened in *her* past, with Nicholas, then it was probably best that it ended now. Relationships needed sturdy foundations to build on. If they couldn't trust each other at this early stage, then could they ever?

Everything had changed when he'd seen her with Nicholas and jumped to the wrong conclusion, and that really hurt. What the hell was she going to do now? Ethan was the only man she had let close to her since Nicholas. How could he not believe her when she said she hadn't kissed her ex? Had he done it because he was hurting, seeing her with another man? When she'd explained what had happened, he had looked sheepish. Even so, he never should have doubted her.

And now she had been sacked, she had no job, no boyfriend, no rosy future to look forward to. Everything had slipped away since the flash mob had taken place.

Since Tanya had called her by her real name, Sadie's mind had been reeling. She wondered whether to message her and ask her why she had called her Sadie, but for now she didn't want Tanya to know that she knew. Once she'd had time to think things through, see if she could wheedle some information out of Cooper, then she would make up her mind what to do.

She'd arranged to cook him tea that night. Cottage pie was his favourite, but when Christine had dropped Esther off, and had smelled it cooking, Sadie had had no choice but to ask her to stay. Paul was at work until 10:00 p.m. that night.

As they sat around the kitchen table, with Christine and Cooper chatting, Sadie glanced at him surreptitiously. Was this what he wanted? To be part of her family? Not to take Ross's place, but to be with her?

'I can't believe Suzanne would sack Riley,' said Christine, as they ate. 'She's such a hard worker and has the interests of the shop at heart all the time.'

'I'm glad Riley stuck up for herself.' Cooper scooped up another mouthful of mash onto his fork. 'It's about time someone gave that Clarissa woman a taste of her own medicine.'

'Yes, you can't hide behind social media all the time, can you?' said Sadie. 'It's not fair.'

Cooper shook his head. She tried to gauge his reaction, but there didn't seem to be any change in him.

She waited until Christine had gone to help Esther get into her pyjamas before getting Cooper alone in the kitchen. She couldn't wait any longer. All the time she kept thinking of the intimate details she had shared, thinking he was Tanya. How could he have deceived her like that?

She closed the kitchen door and leaned back on it for a moment for support. Cooper was loading dishes into the dishwasher. He was humming an Adele song.

'Why did you do it?' she said.

He turned back to her abruptly. 'Why did I do what?'

'Pretend to be someone else.'

'I don't know what you mean.' He frowned when she didn't elaborate. 'What's going on?'

'I could ask you the same thing, Tanya,' she almost spat.

'I'm sorry, but you've lost me.'

She pointed at him. 'Pretending to be someone else online is a really low trick. Is it because you have feelings for me and you wanted to see if I still loved Ross? Because I can tell you right now, I will always love Ross. He was my rock, and I know I'll never find another man like him. And I'm sure he would have been happy if you and I – well, did get together as a couple. But now I can see that you are just some sneaky, snide creep who was trying to wheedle information out of me. What I can't figure out is why the hell you would want to trick me. You're supposed to be my friend, looking out for me and—'

'Wait!' Cooper held up his hands. 'I haven't been talking to you online. And I certainly haven't set myself up as this Tanya person you've been mentioning over the past few weeks.'

'It *must* be you!' Sadie couldn't stop now. 'No one else would say they were called Tanya and then chat to me about Ross for months on end, almost keeping him alive in my mind.'

'I wouldn't do that! And why just me? All our friends know things about Ross. For all you know, it could have been any of us.'

'They wouldn't trick me to try to get close to me.' She was shaking now. 'I just can't understand why you would do that to me. All you had to do was ask me to my face.'

'I haven't done anything wrong!' Cooper stood staring at her. 'I think you need to find out who's been tricking you, because it certainly wasn't me.'

'You've been asking strange things lately.'

'Like what?'

'Like what's happening on the anniversary of his death? Will I be celebrating it with you guys or just with Esther? Will I be taking her out on my own? Where am I going? How long will I be out? And you've not been visiting as much as you used to.'

Cooper laughed, but it wasn't friendly. 'You are so off the mark that it's unbelievable.'

'Have you any idea how hard it's been for me, with you always trying to keep his memory alive, making me upset by talking about him all the time? I'm never going to move on!'

'It wasn't me!'

'I don't believe you.'

'Cooper's telling the truth.' They both turned to see Christine standing in the doorway. 'It wasn't him. It was me.'

CHAPTER TWENTY-NINE

'You?' Sadie addressed Christine, her voice almost a whisper. A cloak of dread dropped over her shoulders as the situation went from bad to worse. She had just blamed Cooper for everything when he was clearly not at fault. She had accused him of being in love with her! Shame rushed through her. She'd never be able to look him in the eye again.

'But why?' she wanted to know.

'I'm sorry.' Christine stepped into the kitchen. 'It started when I saw your laptop open on the Grieve Together website, when you went to make me a cup of tea. I saw you on there under the name of Clara. And then, when I saw you were chatting to other people, I had the idea to become Tanya. As I chatted to you more, I realised it was a way for me to stay close to Ross, and help you to cope with his loss at the same time.'

'But you spied on me!' Sadie shook her head, turning to look at Cooper. His face was creased with hurt and anger, bringing tears to her eyes. 'And I've just accused someone else of doing it. Cooper, I'm so sorry.'

'Sorry's not enough,' he snapped, pushing past her. Sadie reached for his arm but he shrugged her off. As he levelled with Christine, he stopped. 'What you did . . . That's sick.'

'I—'

'You should leave Sadie alone. Of course she needs to grieve for Ross, but it isn't healthy to hang on to the past. She needs to look to the future.'

'A future with you, you mean?'

'No, that's not what I mean! We're just friends — and that's all we'll ever be.' He laughed harshly. 'Well, at least that's what I thought we were. She needs to make her mind up who she trusts.'

'I didn't know it was her!' Sadie cried.

'But you thought it was me.' His eyes betrayed his hurt. 'And that fucking stinks, Sadie.'

Cooper marched out of the house, slamming the front door. Sadie closed her eyes. The last time she had seen him so angry was when Ross died and he hadn't been able to control his emotions, kicking out at his car and denting the side.

'Mummy, I heard shouting.' Esther came running down the stairs. 'Where has Cooper gone?'

'It's okay, poppet,' Sadie smiled as she went to her. 'Let's get you back to bed. Nanny and I need to have a chat.'

As she settled Esther in bed once more, she half expected the front door to bang again, for Christine to slip out rather than face her wrath. But she didn't. Every minute Sadie was away from her, anger boiled up inside.

When she went back downstairs, Christine stood up as soon as Sadie came into the room. 'I'm so sorry,' she began.

'Have you any idea how stupid I feel?' Sadie cried. 'I've just accused Cooper of spying on me!'

'I never meant for that to happen.' Christine looked up. 'But I'm sure he'll understand. He loved Ross as much as we did.'

'Have you any idea how hurt *I* feel?' She decided to change tack. 'You're the one person I would trust to tell anything you wanted to know about Ross, so why did you feel the need to go behind my back? You could have spoken to me at any time.'

'I couldn't.' Christine shook her head. 'Cooper was right. I was holding you back and I would have felt guilty if you knew it was me. You're young, and you have your whole life ahead of you. I know you need to find someone else, but I wanted to keep Ross alive until you did. For me.' She pointed to her temple. 'All I can remember of him is in here, but I still need to talk about him too. When I was Tanya, you told me things that you wouldn't have shared if we were talking face to face.'

'But we do talk. We talk about him all the time!' Sadie felt exasperated. 'I shared things with you that I would never have shared with *anyone* face to face. Personal, intimate things, too.' She held her breath as she remembered something. 'Did you look in my journal?'

'No!'

'Are you sure? I told you where it was!"

'I would never do that.'

Sadie breathed a sigh of relief. 'Posing as Tanya was still a nasty thing to do.'

'I didn't do it to deceive you.' Christine began to cry. 'Having you to talk to about Ross meant that I could imagine he was still here with us. I miss him so much.'

'I miss him too. But you have to let me move on.' Tears welled in Sadie's eyes. 'And to be jealous of me spending time with Cooper, and my friends? That's just not on.'

'I'm not jealous of the time you spend with him,' Christine said, 'nor anyone else. I'm envious that you have someone to turn to. Since Ross died, Paul and I haven't been coping very well. He's become really withdrawn. By talking to you as Tanya, I got to share your life more and also feel closer to having someone to confide in. I'm so sorry. I never meant to hurt anyone.'

'Sorry might not be enough if I've lost Cooper's friendship.'

'Let me explain to him,' Christine pleaded.

'You've done enough damage.' Sadie shook her head. 'I'm not so sure he'll ever forgive me. And I need his friendship far more than I do yours.'

Sadie left the room, hoping Christine would take this as her cue to get up and leave too. It worked.

Christine went into the hallway, put on her coat and opened the front door. She turned to Sadie with a remorseful expression.

'Will you be bringing Esther round in the morning before school?' she asked. 'We can still look after her for you. Please?'

Her look was so pitiful that Sadie nodded quickly. Christine had her over a barrel where that was concerned, anyway. She wouldn't be able to go to work without her help. And she needed work as much as she needed her friends.

Once the door was closed, Sadie sat down at the kitchen table. She couldn't even cry, she was so angry. Of course she could see that Christine hadn't set out to deliberately hurt her, she could understand her intentions, but it didn't excuse her.

And now she had made things so much worse.

Sadie was up early the next morning after a restless night's sleep. Her mind had stayed in turmoil since Christine left. She was supposed to be one of the people Sadie trusted. Someone she had respected, who had helped her through grief when she had lost her husband, supported her before and after Ross died. And now it hurt so much to find out how deceitful she had been.

Esther had woken early too. Sadie tried to keep in her tears. Esther was sitting on the rug in front of the fire, colouring book open, pen in hand. Sadie wanted to pick her up, hug her fiercely and never let her go. She could see Ross in everything she did. A look every now and then, the way she did everything so meticulously. The way her tongue was sticking out the side of her mouth as she concentrated with dogged determination.

She was also Christine's grandchild. With Christine looking after Esther, taking childcare further than was expected of a grandparent – Sadie had to be grateful for that. She couldn't fall out with her, because she wouldn't have anyone to look after Esther outside school hours. Even though her job was on the line right now, Sadie didn't want to think that she'd have to give it up, perhaps live off benefits. It would drive her mad. She wanted to keep her independence, if she could. So, despite how much she was upset by Christine's actions, Sadie had to make things okay.

She wished she could have confided in Riley, but she couldn't trouble her at the moment. She had enough on her plate.

'What's wrong, Mummy?' Esther asked, her head down as she continued to colour.

'I'm okay, poppet,' Sadie replied.

'You're sad,' Esther acknowledged, this time looking up. 'Are you missing Daddy today?'

'I always miss Daddy.' Sadie gave her daughter a faint smile.

'I miss Daddy too.' Esther held up her drawing book. 'I drew a picture of him for you.'

'Let me look.'

Esther ran across and sat by her mother's side on the settee. The picture was of Ross mowing the lawn in their garden. There was a shed and a line left uncoloured down the middle of a green patch, which Sadie assumed was the garden path. A house was in the background and there were two faces looking through a downstairs window.

'That's you and me, Mummy,' Esther smiled, 'watching Daddy through the window.'

Sadie gave her a hug. For a long time, Esther had drawn pictures of Ross in hospital. Or she'd drawn him in a wheelchair as they'd pushed him around the hospital grounds. Sadie had wondered if it was all she would remember of him. But now it seemed not. Esther could remember a time when her dad was able to do the garden, rather than lie in a bed attached to machines.

For all his bravery, Ross had never once been bothered about showing his weaknesses to her. Sadie recalled the time when he'd got out of the wheelchair, arguing, telling her quite bluntly that he didn't need it. That he didn't need her either, fussing around him like he was a child. He'd walked all of four steps before collapsing, falling to the floor heavily. They'd sat in a corridor, people milling around, as he'd cried in her arms. Several people had come to them, offering to help, but she'd shook her head, a weak smile on her lips, saying 'Thanks, but no thanks.'

They'd stayed there until he'd got his strength back enough to sit in the wheelchair again, and she had pushed him back to his room. She'd come home that night and cried herself to sleep, feeling so lost without him, wondering how she would cope when he wasn't there for them any more.

That had been three weeks before he'd died. And now she had lost Cooper. He would never forgive her for what she had thought. How could she have been so stupid? Cooper, her friend, *their* friend. How could she have thought he was Tanya? And knowing Cooper, he wouldn't even go on to a website like Grieve Together. She had jumped to a terrible conclusion.

Once Esther had returned to the floor to draw another picture, Sadie picked up her phone and rang him. She wasn't surprised when there was no response. Rather than send a text message, she left him a voicemail.

'I'm so sorry. I was wrong. I'll understand if it's too awkward for you to visit me and Esther now, but I— please, if you can forgive me, I need you.'

When she was making Esther's sandwiches, she heard her phone beep. But it was just an email coming in with a twenty per cent discount voucher.

She cried then. She hoped he would forgive her. Esther needed him around too. It would be terrible for her to lose the two men in her life, especially one of them through her mother's stupidity.

Cooper was a true friend, a gentleman, and one day she did want to find someone like him for herself.

What had she done?

CHAPTER THIRTY

When Sadie arrived at the shop after dropping Esther off at Christine's house, she found Dan waiting for her inside the doorway.

'Godzilla's here,' he told her as the shutter went down again.

'That's all we need.' Sadie pulled a face as she shrugged off her jacket. 'Please tell me she isn't staying all day.'

'I'm going home sick with a migraine if she is.' Dan shuddered at the thought.

'I hope she stays. It'll show her how hard Riley works to keep* the shop going. Especially for what they pay her. And us, for that matter.'

'Morning,' Suzanne sing-songed behind them as she came from downstairs to stand behind the till. 'I'm going to be working with you as manager today, so I want everything ship-shape and top-notch.'

'The shop doesn't open for another twenty minutes,' muttered Dan. 'I'm having a coffee first.'

'Me too,' Sadie nodded. 'If she thinks she'll have our undivided attention after what she's done to Riley, she's got another think coming.'

'You look pleased with yourself,' Sadie said, once they were in the staffroom. She narrowed her eyes. 'What were you up to last night? A hot date?'

Dan shook his head. 'But it was a great night. I put a few demons to rest.'

When Sadie frowned Dan decided to come clean. Sadie listened with her mouth wide open.

'Why didn't you tell me you were seeing her?' she asked afterwards.

'I wanted to be sure I was doing the right thing. You never really liked her, did you?'

Sadie shook her head. 'She was okay, but she was a bit too clingy for my liking.' She thought of Cooper then and her shoulders drooped. She hoped she could sort things out with him eventually.

'I guess.'

'But it's what makes you happy that counts.' She smiled at him. 'And now you can get on with finding a new woman without the weight of the old one hanging round your neck.'

'Happy days.' Dan looked at Sadie. 'But you're not happy, are you?'

She shook her head. 'No, but I'll be okay.'

'Is it because Ross's anniversary is getting closer?'

'I wish it was just that.' She paused. 'Oh, Dan. I've made a terrible mistake.' Sadie quickly told him what had happened the night before.

'Wow. I'm shocked,' he said afterwards. 'Although I can understand why Christine did it – grief is a terrible thing and affects people in different ways – but she shouldn't have been so deceitful. How were things this morning when you dropped Esther off?'

'A bit icy, but okay. I don't really have any choice but to visit her.'

'Maybe it will get easier in time. She'll obviously be really embarrassed.'

'It's Cooper I'm worried about.'

Dan sniggered.

Sadie glared at him.

'Well, it *is* funny, when you think about it.'

'It's not! You should have seen his face.'

'I'm sure he'll be fine, once you've spoken to him. Oh, come here, you.' Dan gave her a hug when he saw her shoulders droop again. 'Cooper will understand. It wasn't your fault.'

'But I accused him of having feelings for me!'

'He's a big boy. Besides, he's known you too long. It'd be like sleeping with your sister!'

'That's what he said.' Sadie couldn't help but smile.

'Things will be okay, you'll see.' Dan got out his iPad. 'Have you checked the shop's Twitter feed this morning? Now that the competition is due to close, there have been tons of photos coming in, but I wanted to see how Riley was faring.'

'There's nothing except the same garbage. Although there are a lot of people supporting Riley since she tweeted the photo of Clarissa. Clarissa seems to be putting in her two pennies' worth to keep the hatred going, but it looks to be dying down.'

'She really is an evil bitch.' Dan poured water into two mugs. 'And Ethan seems so nice, I don't know what he saw in her.'

'She made him not trust Riley, though. How could he do that?'

'They were both hurt by other people. I wonder if they'll get back together again after all this has blown over?'

'I don't know.'

'People should be honest with each other from the start, don't you think?'

'I'm a fine one to ask about that!' cried Sadie. 'But these are other people interfering to break Riley and Ethan up.'

'I assume you two have far more to do than chat,' Suzanne interrupted, coming into the staffroom. 'Dan, make me a coffee, please. Two sugars, no milk, and make it strong.'

'Lace it with arsenic, more like,' Dan muttered under his breath so only Sadie could hear. Sadie stifled a giggle.

'Sorry, did you say something?' Suzanne glared at him.

Dan shook his head, an innocent look on his face.

'Well, chop-chop, the two of you.' She turned to leave. 'We have a shop to open!'

Sadie followed behind her, pulling mock-Karate moves with her hands.

'Don't be long,' she said to Dan. 'I won't be held responsible for my actions if I'm left alone with her for too long.'

'Have you seen this?' Riley said as soon as Ash had opened her front door. She marched in, holding up her phone.

'I've only just got up. I worked late last night, so I don't need to be in until eleven.' Ash followed her through into the living room, where she was pacing up and down. 'What is it?'

'A job advert. I've just seen it online on the *Hedworth News*. It's my bloody job.'

'No way!' Ash gasped. 'Let me see.'

Riley handed her phone to her, her hand shaking.

'I knew Suzanne was angry, but I thought she'd calm down after a few days, especially when Sadie told me she was struggling to run the shop. I thought she'd ask me back, but oh no, she's gone and advertised my position!'

Ash moved her to the settee and pushed her down.

'All I wanted was to save our jobs and keep the shop open,' Riley continued. 'I never expected Suzanne to bring in someone else to do my job.'

'She must be pretty pissed off to do that,' Ash said. 'The advert says the closing date is next Friday. You should put an application in under someone else's name and turn up for the interview.'

'What's the use in that?' Riley shook her head. She was never setting foot in Chandler's again.

'Well, I for one would like to see the look on her face when you turn up and tell her where to stick her poxy job.'

'Not funny, Ash.' Riley folded her arms. 'I should have stuck up for myself when Suzanne fired me. Good manners are a sign of weakness – I read that in a magazine a while ago. Well, this is definitely a sign of that. I've done everything I can to save the shop, to help my friends, and what do I get in return? I get fired.'

'It's not your fault all this happened.'

'No, but it is Clarissa's. If she hadn't started all this, it might not have got out of hand and my job wouldn't have been advertised in the paper.'

'Why do you think Clarissa did it?' asked Ash, sitting down next to her. 'She couldn't have done it just to get back at Ethan. And if she was trying to split you up to get him back for herself, then that was pointless too.'

'I don't know, but I wish I had some dirt on her. I'd spread it like wildfire and let her know how much it hurts.'

'No, you wouldn't.'

'Yes, I would.'

'But you're not like that, are you?'

'I did send that stupid tweet, though. I guess that sparked it all up again.'

'You're only human. We can only take so much.'

'More's the pity.' Riley sighed. 'I need to grow some balls.'

'Riley Flynn.' Ash shuffled over and gave her a hug. 'You're perfect as you are. Clarissa's just jealous of everything you represent, and everything you have. Imagine being alone to bring up a baby, consumed by the green-eyed monster, and with no partner to support you. Imagine what that must feel like.'

'I don't want to,' said Riley. 'I'm too busy feeling sorry for myself to even think what she must be going through.'

'Pregnancy hormones – they must be worse than normal ones, right?'

'Oh, yuck. Have we got that to look forward to as well? How I love being a woman!'

'Well, at least we're always right about everything,' Ash grinned.

'Hmm, most of the time,' Riley replied. 'I still don't know what to do about everything,' she added.

'I know, but you still have me to worry about you and take care of you. And we will always have coffee and cake.'

'And wine.'

'And cake.'

'And more wine and more cake.'

'And chocolate.'

'And cake.'

Riley smiled at her friend, who was trying to cheer her up. If only life was that simple. She had given her heart to Ethan. And she wasn't sure how to get it back.

Even though Suzanne was struggling to run the shop, Chandler's had opened on its first day without Riley, and the next one too. Even without Riley being there, Dan and Sadie knew the daily routine. But today they were having a delivery of stock, something that Riley usually took care of. They helped to put it away, but it was Riley who checked it off and made sure nothing was missing.

'Have you counted those trainers?' Sadie pointed to several boxes piled at the back of room.

Dan turned to her with a shrug. 'I can't remember. Have you?'

'Well, according to this list, we should have fifteen pairs and I got twenty-two at the last count.'

'Oh, bloody hell!' Dan pressed a hand to his temple. 'We'll have to start again.'

'We'll be here all day at this rate.'

'How long will it take you to move all these boxes?' Suzanne cried as she stood behind the till twenty minutes later. 'I'm sick of seeing them.'

'A long time, while customers are coming in and out as well,' said Dan, rushing over to someone who had walked in.

'Sadie, can you input these invoices into the computer system?' Suzanne thrust a few papers into her hands.

But Sadie gave them back to her. 'I can help put the stock away, but it was Riley that did all the paperwork. I wouldn't know where to start.'

'It can't be that hard,' Suzanne protested. 'I'll do it myself.' She disappeared downstairs only to return moments later. 'Do you have a password to get into the computer system? I can't seem to find anything on the desk or in the drawers.'

Sadie shook her head. 'Riley is very careful about passwords and doesn't write them down in case we get a break-in and someone hacks into everything.'

Suzanne raised her eyebrows. 'This is a shoe shop, not a government department or a bank.'

'Have you any idea how old that computer is, and how easily someone could swipe all the business's money if they got into it? Riley has done her best with things. She's always thought about what's right for the shop.'

'Ring her and get the password,' insisted Suzanne, 'and then I'll reset it.'

'Sorry, I have a customer to serve.' Sadie walked past Suzanne to a woman who was holding up a shoe. 'Would you like me to see if we have that in your size?'

Suzanne turned on her heel and stormed off down the stairs again.

'Let's hope she stays down there this time,' muttered Dan.

An hour later, after everyone had fallen over the boxes a few times, Dan mentioned to Suzanne that they needed to be moved. 'I'll take them downstairs and put them out of the way until we can deal with them. They're a trip hazard. The last thing we want is for someone to sue you for negligence.'

'Stop being so melodramatic,' Suzanne pooh-poohed. 'But if you want to shift them, be my guest.'

'Oh, I have a customer to serve first.'

Dan went to waltz off but Suzanne grabbed his arm.

'I'll do the serving, you shift those boxes.'

By the time another hour had passed, and Suzanne had been sworn at by a toddler, had a drink thrown over her feet, been harassed by an old man who wanted something for nothing, and had to throw out several teenagers who had come in to shelter from the rain, she sat down on a leather cube. Slipping off her shoes, she groaned as she rubbed at her toes.

'How do you do this every day?' she asked Dan and Sadie. 'My feet are killing me, my back is aching, my head is throbbing from all the stress, and it isn't even the end of my first week.'

'Not to worry,' said Sadie. 'It's lunchtime soon – half an hour break will do you good.'

Before Suzanne could protest, a man came in wheeling a trolley full of cardboard boxes.

'Where do you want this order, love?' the delivery driver asked her.

'I'm the manager,' she retorted. 'Dan, sort this man out.'

'Is it like this every day?' she asked once he'd gone.

'Pretty much,' said Dan. 'We can do our jobs without thinking, but we need Riley to do the rest. She keeps everything running smoothly. You should never have fired her.'

'She lost her job because she was incompetent. And I can't trust you two to run the shop.'

'You mean you're coming to work here full-time?' Dan couldn't keep the horror from his voice.'

'Me?' Suzanne laughed. 'I'm only staying until I get someone else to do it. There's an advert for a manager in the *Hedworth News* today.'

'What?' Sadie glared at Suzanne.

Dan folded his arms. 'I don't want to work here unless Riley is here too.'

'Maybe you'd like to join Riley as she looks for another job,' Suzanne warned.

Dan nodded. 'I think I would. I can't work with you. You're a self-centred underachiever who has been handed this business on a plate. We love Chandler's, but you're going to ruin it.'

'I beg your pardon.'

'Dan!' said Sadie.

'I'm sorry,' Dan said, 'but if Riley isn't here then I'm not staying either. It's not going to be the same.'

'I'm not staying if you two aren't here,' said Sadie.

'You can't threaten me!' cried Suzanne.

'No one is threatening you,' said Dan. He went to fetch his and Sadie's coats. 'Come on, Sadie. Let's go.'

'You can't just leave!' Suzanne shouted after them. 'Wait!'

'We can and we are,' said Dan. 'We're both due an afternoon off anyway, because we both worked Sunday, so consider this the hours in lieu that you owe us. You'll have to run the shop by yourself.'

CHAPTER THIRTY-ONE

Riley had been shocked when Sadie and Dan turned up at her flat. Even more so when they told her that they had walked out of Chandler's.

'It just isn't on, Riley,' said Dan as he flopped down next to her on the sofa.

'But it's your livelihood,' Riley protested. 'You can't just walk out and have no job or no money to fall back on.' She stared at Sadie. 'Nor you!'

'The shop's going to close anyway,' Dan replied. 'It won't stay open if she has anything to do with it.'

But Riley still wasn't happy. 'Look, I get the sentiment, you guys, but honestly, you must go in tomorrow. Don't let Suzanne get the better of you. You don't want her saying you walked out when she needed you most.'

'But she sacked you!' Sadie was outraged. 'I can't be loyal to her.'

'She sacked *me*,' said Riley. 'I can live with that, but not putting you two out of work as well.'

'Can you live with it?' Dan shook his head. 'You shouldn't. It was her fault we had to do all this flash mob, viral, Twitter stuff. If it wasn't for that, you'd still have a job and you'd—'

'Still be lonely and on my own.'

A silence dropped on the room.

'Has Ethan still not been in touch?' Sadie broke in.

'Yes, he's sent me a few messages but I don't want to talk to him. I hurt him, and he hurt me, but it doesn't mean we can start over again. There were too many obstacles in the way. It wasn't all about bad timing. So . . . I'm thinking of moving away from Hedworth and going somewhere like Manchester.'

'Manchester!' Dan and Sadie said in unison.

'Yes, but I really want to finish this competition first,' said Riley, not wanting to be drawn into a discussion. 'Are you two willing to sort out the entries, if I keep it going on social media until the closing date this Friday?'

'Are you sure?' asked Dan.

'Yes. It's no one's fault but my own that I've been sacked. I don't want to let people down.'

Riley let Dan and Sadie out and then flopped back onto the settee again. She needed to keep busy. Someone had to sort out the competition entries. Despite her setback, she couldn't let her colleagues down. Finishing off the competition would give them some great press. Maybe she could email Kim to see if she would run it in the paper. If nothing else, it would be something to put on her CV. She got out her notepad to make a list of things to do.

'Poor Riley,' said Sadie, as she and Dan left the building. 'I can't believe everything has turned out like this. I couldn't bear it if she moved away.'

'Me neither,' Dan agreed. 'She's always been there for us, yet no one seems to look after her. And now everyone knows about the life of Riley.'

Sadie put a hand on his arm and stopped him as they walked across the car park.

'Do you think we should do some sort of social media campaign? Maybe we could get Riley her job back?' she said, all breathless now that she had thought of a way to help.

'She won't want to come back,' Dan said, shaking his head.

'But *we* need her back. We need to show Suzanne just how good Riley is. Then she won't leave for Manchester.'

'I can't think of anything worse than going back to Chandler's, but I know you're right.' Dan shuddered. 'That is, if we still have jobs tomorrow.'

'Riley's right. Suzanne can't close the shop now – not until the competition is over. There would be outrage, after all the entries.'

Dan sighed. 'We're nothing without Riley, are we, Sadie?'

'No, and neither is Chandler's. Do you have Ethan's mobile number?'

'No, but I have his email address on something that Riley forwarded to me.' Dan got out his phone. 'Yes, here it is.'

'I'm going to email him this evening.' Sadie wrote the address down. 'Let's meet at work in the morning, and see what the situation is with our jobs first. We did walk out, after all. Oh!'

'What's up?'

'I've had a text message from Cooper.' Sadie passed her phone to Dan.

Stung a bit, I must admit. Want me to grab a bottle of wine and we can chat about it tonight?

Sadie was back at home after collecting Esther from Christine's. She'd told Christine that she hadn't been feeling too well, so had finished work early. It was easy for the lie to roll off her tongue, and even though she felt guilty when she saw Christine's over-friendly smile drop, she couldn't tell her the real reason.

Christine had obviously assumed that it was because of what had happened the night before, but Sadie couldn't think about that at the moment. Even though Cooper would be calling later, and it would have to be addressed then, her thoughts were with Riley.

While Esther was playing, Sadie got out her laptop and logged on to Twitter. She checked out the tweets that Riley was still getting on Chandler's feed, and the ones that she was able to see on Riley's feed. Some of them were vicious, but many were in support of what she had done. #giveRileyabreak was a hashtag she noticed quite a few times.

Riley had seemed so resigned that afternoon, as if all the fight had gone out of her. Sadie was so used to seeing her with a smile on her face, no matter what, so used to her having an answer to any problem.

She thought about their friendship. How Riley had always been there for her. She had been more than a manager to her for a long time, and yet Sadie had never been there for Riley, not really. Of course she had seen their friendship growing as they'd worked together longer, and had valued every minute of it. But she hadn't seen it as so one-sided until now.

What had she ever done for Riley? Riley hadn't even felt able to confide in her about Nicholas, because she felt too embarrassed. Friends should be able to tell each other anything.

Shame washed over her. After being betrayed by Christine, she tried to put herself in Riley's position. It had happened twice to Riley. Once when Nicholas lied to her, and then with Ethan's ex-girlfriend making trouble because she wanted Ethan for herself.

Ethan had been a fool too. He should have realised that Riley wasn't capable of the things Clarissa accused her of. When she had sent that tweet with the photo of Clarissa attached to it, she had been at breaking point. And now that the competition and the shop were still in the news, Riley had become a target for every weirdo to have a go at. Hopefully they could do something about that now. Ethan had emailed her to say he would call in at the shop tomorrow.

Sadie's phone beeped with the arrival of a message. It was from Cooper, to say he was on his way. Her heart skipped a beat. They'd have to make small talk, as if everything was okay, unless she could get Esther to leave them alone for a few minutes. She didn't feel that was fair. She always seemed to be pushing her out of the room.

She replied to Cooper and then sent Riley a message too.

Hope you're feeling a little better. I just want to say I'm sorry. You've been such a good friend and I haven't. I should have looked after you better. I hope I'll be able to put that right in the future. X

A message came back almost immediately.

Don't be silly. You've had a lot to deal with but you've always been there for me. No need to apologise. Thanks for calling this afternoon. Was good to see you and Dan. X

There was a knock on the front door. Esther came thundering down the stairs.

'Cooper!' she cried, jumping into his outstretched arms. 'I've been practising dancing. Mummy says I can go to Streetwise to learn with Serena!'

Sadie smiled shyly at Cooper. At least there was no awkward silence with Esther at home.

'That's great!' said Cooper, enthusiastically. 'Do you want to show me some moves?'

Esther shimmied down his body, onto the floor. 'I'm practising,' she huffed. 'I'll be down when I'm ready.'

She tore upstairs again.

And there was the awkward silence.

Cooper held out a bottle of wine. 'I had a feeling you'd need this. I bought your favourite.'

'Thanks.' She took it from him and went into the kitchen.

'Have you had a good day?' she asked, trying to fill the silence.

'Yeah, not bad. You?'

'Well, apart from me and Dan walking out halfway through the day, everything has been fine.'

Cooper stared at her in disbelief before pulling out a chair. 'Tell me.'

'I will.' Sadie sat down across from him. 'But we might only have a few minutes until madam has finished her dance routine, so I want to stress how sorry I am about what happened. It was totally unforgivable of me to assume that it was you.'

'It was quite a shock, I must admit,' he said. 'At first I kept thinking that I must have led you on. If I did, it wasn't intentional.'

Sadie felt her skin burn immediately. 'Gawd, don't remind me.'

'Did I, though?'

'No. I just jumped to conclusions. I mean, really jumped to them. I couldn't think of anyone else it could be. You're as close to me as Christine. It just didn't enter my head that she would do anything like that.'

'But I would?'

'No!' She shook her head vehemently. 'I can't even think why I thought it was you now. It was on the spur of the moment.'

Cooper put up his hand. 'Before you go on, I do have a confession. Because I *haven't* been entirely honest with you.'

Sadie paused. Oh no. What was he going to say now?

'I—' Cooper faltered, looking away for a moment.

'What is it?'

'I've been dating Ash.'

Sadie drew her head back and frowned. 'Ash? But you always fool about as if you hate each other! I— oh! Is it serious?'

He nodded. 'I'd like to think so.'

'How long have you been seeing each other?'

'Nearly three months.'

Sadie shook her head. 'Why didn't you tell me?'

'You said you get upset seeing other people together. Plus Ash and I have been friends for so long. I've been wanting to tell you for a while.'

'So no one knows?'

Cooper shook his head. 'What do you think?'

Sadie's chin almost hit the floor. 'It's fantastic news if you're both happy! Why wouldn't you tell anyone?'

'We wanted to be certain first,' Cooper shrugged.

Sadie reached for his hand. 'I'm so pleased for you both.'

'Really?'

'Yes. Why wouldn't I be?'

'Well, with you being in love with me, it might be awkward when we get together for Sunday lunch . . .'

They grinned at each other. Once again, Sadie had been shown that her friends would stick by her through anything. All of a sudden, she didn't feel so lonely.

CHAPTER THIRTY-TWO

Dan and Sadie hadn't expected a welcome when they arrived at work the next morning. But neither of them were expecting Suzanne not to be there.

Dan was waiting for Sadie outside the shop as she crossed the High Street.

'I didn't want to go in on my own,' he told her. 'And I thought Suzanne would be here, didn't you?'

Sadie nodded. 'Do you think she's closed the shop for good? Maybe she thinks we'd given up on it when we walked out yesterday.'

'I hope not.'

'Perhaps we should open up as usual? That might prove how sorry we are.'

'I'm not sorry!'

'Maybe not, but we shouldn't have walked out yesterday. Suzanne might be a cow, but she was struggling and we just left her.'

Dan looked remorseful. 'I suppose. And we can't get Riley back to a shop that's closed. What time did Ethan say he was calling in?'

'He said it would be early, before he started work. I expect he'll be here soon.'

'Right, then.' Dan took out his keys. 'Let's get this show on the road.'

A few minutes before they were due to open, Ethan banged on the shutter. Dan went to let him in.

'Is Suzanne here?' Ethan asked, stepping in cautiously.

'Not yet,' Sadie replied, deciding not to say any more just then. 'We might only have a few minutes. Did you have a think about what I said in my email?'

Ethan nodded.

'Are you able to help in any way?'

'You should, because you're the one who has done the most damage,' Dan said.

'It's not all my fault,' Ethan snapped.

'But it is the fault of that stupid ex of yours. Riley is so thoughtful, always putting everyone else first. She loved Chandler's and is amazing at her job. She—'

'Lets everyone walk all over her.'

Dan froze. 'What do you mean?'

'You're supposed to be her friends,' said Ethan, his hands shooting into his trouser pockets. 'Yet all I've ever heard Riley talk about is keeping Chandler's going. You two have just gone along with whatever she's tried. Grabbing on to her apron strings as if you can't think for yourselves.'

'No, we haven't!' said Dan.

'If anyone has let Riley down,' Ethan continued, 'it's you two, for taking her for granted and putting her under too much pressure.'

'Will you two stop pointing the finger!' Sadie cried. 'Because I think we're as guilty as each other.' She sat down on a leather cube and looked up at them both. 'Riley has been my rock since Ross died, but I haven't been there for her.'

'You've been grieving,' said Dan. 'Everyone takes different amounts of time to get over grief. You can't blame yourself for that.' He sat down too, and sighed loudly. 'If we hadn't done the flash mob, then none of this would have happened.'

'The competition has been successful because of that,' said Sadie.

'I can't believe how cruel people can be online, though.'

'But none of that was true,' said Ethan. 'I've been trying to tell Riley that I can see past it all, but she won't listen to me.'

'That's because you took your time in believing her,' said Dan. 'She's crushed because of you!'

'Okay, okay!' Sadie held up her hands for silence. 'Now that we've established we're all a little bit to blame, maybe we should concentrate on seeing if we can put it right. Without Riley, this shop will be nothing anyway – if there still is a shop after we walked out yesterday.'

Ethan stood wide-eyed. 'You walked out?'

'It's a long story,' said Sadie. 'But it made us realise that we can't let the shop close because of a few thoughtless people – including us. That's why we need to put a plan together.'

'To save the shop?' asked Ethan.

'No. To get Riley back here.'

'Do you think Suzanne will go for that?'

'She might bow down to pressure if we can prove that Riley is popular.' Sadie frowned. 'No one knows she's lost her job over what's happened. We could play on what she did out of the goodness of her heart – for her friends as well as to save the shop.'

'We could get Frank to speak out too,' added Dan, 'and some of the students that have been helping him.'

Sadie nodded. 'You have to agree, since all this started, Riley's followers online have increased a lot. So even if a few idiots have tried to spoil things for her, she's got lots of people behind her. It's these we need to tap into.' She looked up at Ethan. 'What do you think?'

'I think that's a great idea.' Ethan ran a hand over his chin. 'But I might have something else I can offer too. Riley has been a stalwart of the High Street for years. Maybe we could build something around that.'

'You mean think of a good hashtag?' asked Dan. 'On social media?'

Ethan sat down. 'Not exactly . . .'

Sadie was going through her list when Dan nudged her.

'Heads up.' He nodded at the door.

Sadie looked up to see Suzanne coming into the shop. 'Morning,' she said in her brightest voice, even though she was unsure what reaction she would get.

'I came to collect some of my things.' Suzanne walked towards the till. 'I wasn't expecting to see the shop open. I was going to leave it closed until I found new staff.' Her laugh was self-deprecating. 'I couldn't run it by myself, that's been perfectly obvious this week.'

'We weren't sure if we would have jobs this morning, but we both decided to turn up anyway.' Sadie paused. 'Suzanne, we both love Chandler's and we don't want to see it close. We're also both sorry for walking out on you yesterday. Things have been very stressful for us all over the past few weeks.'

'You don't know the half of it.' Suzanne's shoulders drooped. 'If I'm honest, I don't know what to do. I'm not sure I have the heart to keep it open, even if I did find a new manager. I might just call it a day – have a big sale and then close.'

'No!' Sadie and Dan spoke in unison.

'But what about the competition?' said Sadie. 'People will go mad if you don't announce a winner. The closing date is this Friday. Surely you can wait until then to make your mind up?'

'I suppose I could.' Suzanne pointed at the notepad on the counter, with a list of names on it. 'Is that what you're doing now?'

'Yes.' Sadie turned it for her to see. 'Have you seen some of the photos online? We can show you, if you like. Some entries are photos of people wearing their best shoes on a special day, at their wedding for instance. Some people have slung them over their shoulder. Some have just lifted their foot in the air and snapped away.'

'One woman lined some of her shoes against a wall,' said Dan. 'There's even one woman who couldn't decide which shoes she liked best and so has taken a photo of her entire shoe closet!' He smiled at Suzanne shyly. 'Would you like to pick a winner?'

'I suppose I'll have to, now that Riley isn't here to finish what she's started.'

Dan nudged Sadie, although she had been going to speak anyway.

'Speaking of which, we think she should be here to announce the winner.'

'I don't think so,' Suzanne snapped. 'She's caused enough damage. If I choose the competition winner and give out the prize, Chandler's might not be a laughing stock any more.'

'It isn't a laughing stock,' cried Dan.

'It's too late. You know I've advertised for a new manager. If I can get someone to run the shop, Chandler's will stay open. If not, it will close in a month's time.'

CHAPTER THIRTY-THREE

It had been a few days since Riley had been fired, but she desperately wanted to see the competition through to the end. Online she was still the bright and bubbly Riley Flynn, manager of Chandler's Shoe Shop and a judge in a competition. Offline she was miserable, weepy Riley Flynn, with a broken heart and no job.

She'd decided that she was going to go into Hedworth the next day. She'd text Sadie in the morning, ask her to let her know when Suzanne wasn't in the shop, and then she'd gather the rest of her belongings. There wasn't much that she had left behind, but she also wanted to take one last look around the place where she had been so happy. Then she would walk out with her head held high.

She would find another job, even if she had to temp and work her way up from the bottom. Taking part in the flash mob had given her the confidence she needed to realise she could do so much more if she wanted to.

As well as a new job, she would find a new Ethan. It had been a week since she'd seen him, spoken to him, or had any kind of communication with him. Still, her heart ached for him, her arms wanted to drape themselves around him.

Really, she didn't want to find any new things. She was happy with the old things. Or rather, she had been until recently. Even Sadie and Dan had been quieter since they'd gone back to Chandler's. Riley was glad, in a way. They had got their priorities straight, and maybe they thought it would be awkward for her to hear about the shop now.

'Riley Flynn, will you listen to yourself,' she scolded, out loud. 'You're not about to give up that easily.'

She was dozing on the settee when the buzzer to the door woke her. She glanced at the clock. It was 10:15 p.m. Riley frowned. It was late for anyone to be calling unless it was bad news. She rushed across to the intercom.

'Hello?'

'Riley, it's Suzanne. I . . . could I talk to you?'

Riley stood still for a moment, shocked. Then she buzzed Suzanne into the building.

'I'm on the first floor, flat 4,' Riley said into the intercom.

Checking her face to see that she didn't look too much of a mess, she quickly changed out of her pyjamas and into a pair of skinny jeans and an oversized jumper. A brush through her hair would have to suffice, as a knock came at her door.

Suzanne stood there, looking every bit as nervous as Riley felt.

Riley made a sweeping gesture to beckon her in. 'Would you like a coffee?'

'No thanks.' Suzanne shook her head. 'I won't be staying long. But thank you for taking the time to talk to me.'

Riley pointed to the settee as she sunk into the armchair, drawing her feet up at her side. Unsure what this was all about, she waited for Suzanne to speak.

'Beautiful place you have here,' Suzanne said, looking around the room. 'It looks like a lovely place to live.'

'It is.' Riley's tone was snippy. She wanted to know what Suzanne had called for, and wished she'd stop acting all nicey-nicey. 'Is there something that you want?' she asked.

'I think it's best if I come clean straight away.' Suzanne swallowed, wringing her hands as they rested in her lap. 'I'm sorry for being so angry with you all the time. I thought I was acting for the best, and I now realise I wasn't. But, as you said on that tweet, there are two sides to every story.'

Riley didn't understand what Suzanne was referring to.

'You had every right to be angry that Max was taking money from the till.' Suzanne glanced at Riley fleetingly before her head dipped again. 'I hadn't realised until it was too late. I'm broke. Max has gambled everything away, our credit cards are up to their limits and I have no favours to call in.

'Soon after Dad died, I made Max a joint partner in the business. I thought he wanted to make a success of the shop and then maybe we'd buy a few more around Hedworth. I didn't know that he had a gambling addiction. Before he left, he told me that he'd only stayed married to me for so long because he wanted the money when Dad died. I gave him thousands, only now realising he had lost his job and had no income.'

'I thought he was away, working in Italy?' said Riley.

Suzanne shook her head. 'I threw him out.'

'Oh!' Riley decided that Suzanne did have some balls after all.

'Max bled me dry. That's why I was so desperate for the shop to do well. I needed it for an income. I don't have anything else. And I couldn't let my father down. He worked so hard to keep Chandler's going over the years and here I was, coming along and making a hash of everything and running the shop into the ground. You were the one who was keeping it going, Riley, and I wanted it to be me. I . . . I was jealous of your rapport with people, your business knowledge. You knew how to run the shop better than I ever would. And never has that been clearer than when I sacked you.'

Riley cringed. It had been the lowest moment of her life.

'Since I sacked you, I've tried to run the shop single-handedly. I wanted to make it work all by myself, but I've realised how much you did. Dan and Sadie pull their weight and keep the shop floor running, smoothly I might add. But it's the day-to-day running of the business that you do so well. I couldn't do that without you. I made enough of a hash of it that Dan and Sadie wanted to leave too! I assume you know they walked out?'

'They were only protecting me,' said Riley. 'I told them to go back. I don't want them to lose their jobs too.'

'They won't.' Suzanne shook her head. 'I must admit, I hadn't the heart to go in the day after it happened. So it was quite a surprise when I arrived to see that Sadie and Dan had not only returned that morning but had opened the shop. I thought they'd both walked out for good. I was sure that they wouldn't come back after how terrible I'd been.' Suzanne looked at Riley then. 'I don't want Chandler's to close,' she admitted. 'And if I run it, it will. So I was . . . I was wondering if you would come back?'

'To Chandler's?' Riley said the first stupid thing to come into her head because she was so shocked. She knew that it must have taken a lot for Suzanne to ask.

Suzanne nodded. 'I want to help out more – don't worry, I promise not to get in the way. I'll learn the business alongside you, and you could even become a partner.'

Riley's mouth dropped open. A year ago she would have gladly welcomed those words – but now? The business was failing, one of the partners had run up debt and, most probably, ill will. The prospect wasn't entirely thrilling, to think that she would be walking into such a mess.

'I . . . I'm shocked, if I'm honest,' she said finally.

'I can imagine.' Suzanne nodded. 'I should have trusted you more. Why mend what isn't broken? And if I hadn't tried to drum up trade with that stupid competition, then you wouldn't have thought about doing the flash mob, which was a genius idea really. And then it wouldn't have brought those two women into the shop and aired all your dirty laundry. I was just desperate to bring some money into Chandler's. I was also envious of you running things so smoothly. People were flocking around the shop, talking about Chandler's because of you.'

'Me?'

'Yes. It seemed the more promotional things you came up with, the more confidence it gave you. I half expected you to resign once you'd finished the campaign and go off and do something different anyway. It just seemed to change you.'

'No, I don't think it did. Well, apart from me being rude to you.'

'That was warranted.'

'No, it wasn't.' Riley shook her head. 'I should have known better, and I'm sorry. But maybe you're right. It did make me realise that I could do more, push myself further.'

'So would you like to go into partnership with me?'

'No. But I will take my old job back, if it's on offer?'

Suzanne nodded eagerly.

'And we'll definitely need to buy in new stock. The marketing campaign on Twitter – all the photos coming in of shoes – I've been scrolling through them, making notes of what's in fashion and where to buy them. Those sandals I bought in went down a storm. I reckon if we get a few more in different colours, and then one or two different designs, with Frank's tote bags bringing in lots of the local college students it might work out well.' She got out her notepad. 'I can come up with some strategies, perhaps visit a few fashion shows, source some new things, and make Chandler's what you always wanted it to be – *the* shop to go to for shoes. It wouldn't cost much to implement, provided that the bank will help you with an overdraft if you're stuck for cash. And most things are on sale or return. We can try a few lines and see what's most popular. We could also start up a website, like I mentioned, sell things online and—'

'You're thinking way too far ahead for me.' Suzanne held up her hand and Riley stopped talking. 'I do like your thinking, though, and the way that you are planning more long-term. I had thought that Chandler's wouldn't be around come autumn, and that made me sad. When would you like to come back to the shop?'

'Whenever you'd like me to.'

'How about you take the rest of the week off and come in on Friday when we're ready to announce the winner of the competition? It's going to take a lot of work to sort out all the entries. I don't think I'd know where to start. You can do it here with minimal chance of interruptions. I can keep an eye on the shop until then . . . I think!'

'I've been working on the competition already, actually,' said Riley, smiling.

Suzanne smiled too. 'Thanks. I can drop off everything you need, if you let me know what you want. Perhaps you can keep the entries coming in until the closing date, if you go all-out on social media?'

Riley nodded. This was perfect. Time away from the shop would give her what she needed to get the competition sorted and get back in the game. Social media ate up time, so it would be brilliant to concentrate on it fully until Friday. Then she could go back to Chandler's. And her head would definitely be held high.

CHAPTER THIRTY-FOUR

Riley leant her head back in the seat of the bus as it made its way into the centre of Hedworth. Although she was excited about the competition that morning, and about returning to Chandler's, she still hadn't heard anything from Ethan. Now, as she had her job back, she'd found herself wanting to call him and tell him about it. No, she wanted to *see* him and tell him all her news. The shop was going to stay open, and there was only one thing missing from her life now.

Him.

She had been a fool to be so stubborn and not try to contact him, but she didn't much care about that right now.

'Do you think I should ring Ethan?' she asked Ash, who was sitting next to her. 'I bet he'd like to see the competition winner being announced. After all, he did get Urban Angels involved, and give me some great photos to use on social media.'

When there was no reply from Ash, she tapped her on the shoulder, waited for her to remove her earphones and repeated the question.

'No.' Ash shook her head. 'He was in the wrong. Let him crawl back to you.'

'But what if he doesn't?' Riley wasn't sure she wanted to chance it. 'Don't you think I messed up as much as he did?'

'No, I don't! The man's a loser if he can't see what's right under his nose.'

Riley frowned. It wasn't like Ash to be so nasty about Ethan. But then again, Ash was her best friend. She was only sticking up for her. Maybe she was right. Riley couldn't be sure how he would react anyway.

Suddenly, she sat up in her seat, turned her head and strained to see out of the window as the bus sped along. There was a piece of white card fastened to a lamppost.

'Did you see that?' she turned back to Ash, nudging her sharply.

Ash sighed, removing her earphones again. 'Did I see what?'

'I'm sure I saw my name on a sign.'

'I doubt that very much.'

Riley sat back in her seat. 'You're right. Ignore me, I must be seeing things.'

She rested her head against the window, not bothering with the condensation that was wetting her hair.

At the next set of lights, the bus stopped again. There was another sign, and this time she could clearly see the words.

#BeMineRileyFlynn

Suddenly her phone started to beep. She took it out of her pocket and looked at the screen. There were over 60 notifications waiting for her. She sighed. The competition had closed the night before. She hoped people weren't still tweeting images, thinking it was still running today.

But then she gasped. Her hand covered her mouth as she scrolled through the tweets.

Do it @RileyFlynn! #BeMineRileyFlynn

@RileyFlynn Go for it #BeMineRileyFlynn

She scrolled down further.

We're with you @RileyFlynn. #BeMineRileyFlynn

'Ash,' she nudged her friend again. Noticing the Twitter handle of the *Hedworth News* included in one of the tweets, she clicked onto their feed. There was an article attached. With her heart in her mouth, she clicked on the link:

LIVING THE LIFE OF RILEY

Sometimes no matter what you do, no matter how good your intentions, things will turn out wrong. That's what happened to Riley Flynn, manager of Chandler's Shoe Shop. When faced with the potential closure of the place where she has worked for the past eight years, she decided to come up with some whacky PR stunts to bring customers back into Chandler's and reinvigorate sales.

Chandler's has been in Hedworth High Street for over eighty years, first opened by Albert Chandler, senior, before being passed down to Albert Chandler, junior. I expect at one time or another every one of us in the town has visited the shop. Albert Chandler was a gentleman and the business was a credit to him.

'When Albert died, we were all worried that the shop would close,' said sales assistant Dan Charles, who has worked there for six years. 'We're a very close-knit bunch of colleagues and the thought of losing that, alone, was horrible, even more so than the thought of losing our jobs.'

But Albert's daughter, Suzanne, had other ideas. She was determined to make a go of things. As shops on high streets across the nation began to close, Suzanne was determined to keep the legacy her father had started alive.

'I went the wrong way about it, though,' admits Suzanne. 'I tried to make the staff work harder to bring in sales, when all the time they were the backbone of the shop and it was the products that were letting them down. Riley's brilliant idea to come up with a competition that showcased everyone's favourite shoes has given me insight into what is popular and,' she laughs, 'what is not. So, the shop window of Chandler's will be changing in the near future. I shall be sourcing new stock, with Riley's help. There will be some exciting things on the horizon.'

None of this would be possible without the determination and grit shown by Riley Flynn. By thinking outside the box, she instigated a flash mob, choreographed by Serena Erikson, dancer, instructor and owner of Streetwise Dance Studio. Joining in the dance, Riley and the staff became an internet success almost overnight. Even local girls Roxy Madeley and Sally Tunstall, two members of the sensational girl band Urban Angels, joined in by posting photos of their shoes all across social media platforms, encouraging others to do the same.

However, the publicity came with its downside. Even though everyone now knew about Chandler's, some people used its success to attack Riley. A slander campaign was started, and she became subject to vile abuse on social media.

But still she kept going.

The competition winner is to be announced later this morning.

'Riley has been a great friend,' added sales assistant Sadie Stewart, who has worked with Riley for five years. 'It just wouldn't be the same at Chandler's without her. My husband died last year and my friends in the shop got me through it and held me together. Without Riley to guide me, help me and support me, I don't know where I would be.'

If you're in Hedworth this morning at 8:45 a.m., you just might want to go and show Riley your support. I can't say more than that, for fear of spoiling the surprise. But suffice it to say, there's going to be some fun on the High Street.

Riley looked at the byline, to see who had written the feature. It was Ethan.

'What the . . . ?' She turned to her friend with a look of bewilderment, showing her the screen. 'Have you seen this, Ash?'

Ash flipped through the article before handing it back.

'That will be good for the competition,' she said.

'But Ethan has written about something happening this morning on the High Street. Do you think he's coming to take photos of the competition winners? I'd—'

Riley stopped as the bus pulled into the station. There was another sign attached to a waste bin a few feet in front of them.

#BeMineRileyFlynn

She turned back to Ash, and caught her trying not to smirk.

'You *do* know,' she cried. 'Tell me.'

Ash stood up quickly. 'I haven't got the faintest idea.'

'Ash! Ash!' Riley grabbed her arm but her friend marched ahead. Just then, her phone began to ring. It was Ethan.

'Ethan, do you have any idea what's going on?' she said, as people began to look at her.

'Yes, come to the shop and I'll let you in on a secret.'

The line went dead before she had time to say anything else.

'Ethan?' Riley cursed under her breath. 'This is embarrassing.'

'It isn't.' Ash shook her head. 'It's romantic!'

Riley disagreed. Even though minutes earlier she had wanted to see Ethan, she had hoped to do it a little less publicly. But her smile was huge.

'Is everyone in on this?' she asked. 'Dan? Sadie?'

Ash nodded her head. 'Come on.'

They jogged up the stairs and drew level with the High Street. Riley couldn't wait to get to Chandler's now. Ethan had obviously gone to a lot of trouble to arrange all this. She couldn't wait to see him.

Just before they drew level with the shop, Ash stopped. She held out a pink envelope. 'I have to give you this,' she said, thrusting it into Riley's hands.

Riley tore the envelope open. Inside was a white greetings card with a hashtag printed on it in gold lettering: #missyou

Riley opened the card.

Riley,

I've been a fool. You are the nicest, kindest, funniest, most hardworking and, yes, most beautiful, woman I have ever met. I'm so sorry. Please say we can start again.

Ethan x

P.S. Jimmy misses you too.

At the mention of Jimmy, Riley felt hot tears pour down her face, and she wiped at them furiously. Could she trust Ethan again? Could this be the chance she needed to rid herself of the demons left behind by Nicholas and find true love, someone to settle down and be happy with?

'I'm not sure I can bear to have my heart broken again, Ash,' she said quietly.

She looked up, to see that Ash had disappeared. But every shop window on the High Street was emblazoned with a sign:

#BeMineRileyFlynn

Her eyes widened. Did everyone know what was going on? She headed towards the shop, to catch up with Dan and Sadie. But then she heard the familiar notes of a tune. Ryan, her dancing partner from the flash mob, appeared and took her hand. He led her down to the shop. Three more dancers appeared and she grinned, although still embarrassed, when she realised what was about to happen.

She was in the middle of her own flash mob.

Through the people who were stopping to watch, she spied Serena in a doorway. But her eyes didn't stop there, because she was searching for Ethan.

Dan shimmied along the pavement to the sounds of Pharrell Williams' 'Happy'.

Then she spotted Ethan.

As Riley's gaze met his, she didn't know whether to laugh or cry. This was too embarrassing, but she was completely enjoying the sentiment. As the music continued, she laughed as Dan, Sadie, Ash and Serena sashayed in a line and came to a halt in front of her. Ethan walked in front of them all. He was carrying a large bouquet of red roses.

When the music stopped, Riley stood still and silent. She half expected the whole High Street to pause while everyone listened to what he had to say. Luckily, the applause that followed hid their embarrassment.

Ethan stepped towards her, taking her shyly by the hand.

Riley didn't know whether to burst into tears or to burst out laughing at the whole thing. She looked up into Ethan's eyes, which were clearly telling her how excited he was to be back by her side.

'I'm so sorry, Riley,' he said, drawing her into his arms.

'If this ends up going viral on YouTube again,' she told him, 'then it's over. But if you can keep this between you and me . . .'

Dan and Sadie came rushing over to her. So did Ash, and Cooper, who had appeared too. Suzanne followed behind them a little more slowly, standing on the periphery of the group.

'That was so much fun,' said Sadie. 'I think I might take up dancing lessons too,' she said to Dan.

'Not possible, I'm afraid,' Serena informed her, as she too joined the group. 'Streetwise Dance Studio has a waiting list now.'

Riley beamed. It seemed that her campaign had worked extremely well in some respects. She smiled at Suzanne, a smile that said 'things are going to work out just fine'.

'I hate to break up the fun, but we have a competition to judge,' Suzanne laughed before she added her last few words. 'Come on, chop-chop!'

As Riley headed back into Chandler's, with Ethan's hand covering hers, and her friends and the people she knew surrounding her, she began to feel positive about the future. Life would never be perfect, and people would no doubt disappoint her again, but for now she was back where she belonged.

ONE MONTH LATER

Sadie woke up to the sounds of someone in her kitchen. She jumped up and threw back the duvet, glancing at the clock as she pulled on her dressing gown. It was 6:30 a.m., barely light.

'Esther!' she said, as she flew downstairs to see a light on in the kitchen and her daughter standing on a stool at the side of the sink.

'Morning, Mummy!' Esther said. 'It's Daddy's special day today, so I wanted to make you breakfast in bed.'

Sadie glanced around the room. It looked as if a bomb had been dropped on it. There was a tray on top of the table, with a plate and a knife. She could smell toast burning in the toaster, and tried not to laugh – like mother, like daughter! But the situation could have been much more serious if she hadn't woken up when she did.

'I wanted to surprise you,' Esther said, as she filled a glass with juice. 'I know I can't make you a cup of tea, because I'm not allowed to touch the kettle, but I can pour you a drink of orange and make a piece of toast.'

'You're not supposed to use the toaster either, missy,' said Sadie in as stern a voice as she could muster, 'as you well know.'

'Don't worry, Mummy. Nanny had been showing me how to do it. She said that I needed to be a big girl now, and that I could learn how to make toast. I was going to surprise you.'

'You certainly did that,' said Sadie. When she saw Esther's face drop, she relented a little. 'Come on, then,' she said. 'I'll make us both a nice cup of tea and we can share your toast together. Does that sound good to you?'

Esther nodded and Sadie came up behind her and gave her a hug. Seeing her daughter preparing breakfast had made her realise that her little girl was growing up, and her daddy wasn't here to see it. She held back the tears threatening to fall. It was going to be a tough day to get through.

'Don't be sad, Mummy.' Esther looked up at her. 'We have lots of things to do today, don't we?'

'We most certainly do, poppet.'

'I have a card from Nanny to give to you,' Esther said, tearing out of the room. She thundered up the stairs and came back down moments later with a pink envelope. 'She says I need to leave you to open it on your own, because it might make you cry and that you wouldn't want to cry in front of me because you try so very hard not to.' She looked up in earnest. 'You can cry in front of me any time, Mummy. I can make you happy then.'

Sadie wanted to ask her if she could mend broken hearts too. Instead, she thanked her and took the card. Esther, true to her word, ran into the living room.

'I'll be back in a minute!' she shouted before closing the door. Sadie took out the card.

Sadie, I deeply regret what I did. It was a selfish thing to do but, please, I lost my son a year ago, and I don't want to lose my daughter-in-law too.

Sadie read the words twice, the second time through tears as they welled in her eyes and then fell down her face. Christine was right. Pretending to be someone else had been a terrible thing to do, but in a way she could understand why. It wasn't for selfish reasons, it was because of grief. And Sadie needed her too. More than she would ever tell her.

Maybe Sadie wouldn't forget what Christine had done for a long time. But it was time to forgive her.

It was shortly after one o'clock that Riley's phone beeped. She read the message. 'She's on her way,' she told everyone.

They were sitting on the wall surrounding Sadie's front garden. To Riley's right, Dan and Ethan were chatting away. Ash and Cooper were sitting to her left. She smiled at Ash when she caught her eye. It had been a shock to find out the truth about her and Cooper, but she couldn't be more delighted for them. Ash had ribbed her for days about having conned her into thinking that she was dating a twenty-three-year-old.

Sadie pulled up in her car. Esther got out first and ran to Cooper.

'What are you all doing sitting on my wall?' asked Sadie, checking her watch. 'We said two o'clock, not one, didn't we?'

'How was it?' asked Riley.

'It was okay,' said Sadie. 'I had a lovely morning with Christine and Paul. Well, perhaps lovely isn't the right word. But I did manage to scatter Ross's ashes in the garden of remembrance in Hedworth Crematorium.'

The thought brought tears to Riley's eyes.

'I never really liked them in the house,' Sadie said, her voice faltering. 'Afterwards we sat quietly, all lost in our thoughts while Esther chatted away to Ross as if he was still with us. And then I realised that he *is* still with us.'

'He'll always be in our memories and our hearts,' Riley said.

'We won't forget him, will we?'

Sadie looked in so much pain. Riley drew her into her arms. 'Never.'

Cooper tapped Sadie on the shoulder. 'We have something to show you before we go inside, but you need to close your eyes.'

Sadie frowned.

'Close your eyes, Mummy!' said Esther, 'or you'll spoil the surprise!'

'Do you know what it is?' Sadie stared at her daughter.

'Yes, I kept it secret too!' Esther clapped her hands.

Cooper pulled a woollen scarf from his jacket pocket. 'Put this around your eyes and no peeking!'

'I'll just keep my eyes closed,' said Sadie, pushing his hand away.

'Not a chance. I know you.' Cooper put it in place and tied a huge knot at the back of Sadie's head. 'Are they closed?'

'Yes, but I couldn't see anything even if they were open. What are you up to, Cooper?'

Cooper led her down the side of the house and into the back garden.

'I can't see a thing!' Sadie protested, feeling the way with her toes as she held out her hands in front of her.

'That's the idea,' said Riley, coming to her side. 'Here, let me take your hand.'

'Mind the step,' shouted Dan, taking up the rear.

Out in the garden, everyone started to speak in whispers.

'What are you lot planning?' Sadie's shoulders drooped. 'I hope you didn't get a trampoline, Cooper, or else!'

Cooper undid the scarf.

At the far end of the garden was a wooden bench. There was a small plaque in the middle.

'Come and see what it says, Mummy,' said Esther, grabbing her hand.

Sadie walked with her and read the words: 'Look up to the stars and you will see me.'

Sadie's hand covered her mouth. 'Who did this?' She looked at them all in turn.

'We all did,' said Riley. 'Ross was such a big part of our lives that we wanted to buy you something special. We could have bought a bench to be placed in the crematorium but, this way, we thought it would be more personal.'

'And,' said Dan, coming to her other side, 'as we all hang around in your garden, because none of us have one of our own, we thought what better way to remember him when we come over to see you, than to sit on his bench.'

'We all know how much he loved the garden,' said Cooper.

Sadie's eyes filled with tears as she ran a finger over the plaque.

'Cooper, was this what you were planning?' Her skin began to flush. 'I'm so sorry!'

Cooper put up a hand. 'No need for that. Do you like it? You don't think it's too morbid, do you?'

'We can take it away, if you do,' said Ash, coming to stand next to Cooper.

Sadie shook her head. 'It's perfect. Thank you.' She looked up at them. 'Thank you all.'

Sadie still couldn't get used to Cooper and Ash being an item. But it was the best pairing she could think of. Perfect in all ways. Ash wouldn't feel threatened in any way if Cooper helped Sadie out, and if they ever did have their own family Sadie probably wouldn't need him so much by then anyway. Maybe she might even have met her own man by then.

Behind her, she heard a cork popping and glasses chinking. Ethan filled the glasses and everyone stood for a moment.

'To Ross,' said Cooper and raised his glass in the air.

'To the bench,' said Dan, following suit.

'To the best husband ever.' Sadie tipped her glass upside down and poured the drink over the bench. 'No one can love me like you.'

She looked up at everyone as they stared at her in dismay. 'I'm toasting the bench, you idiots,' she laughed.

Riley moved closer to Ethan and he wrapped an arm around her shoulders, drawing her close. Looking around at her friends, even though Ross was no longer with them, she felt so lucky to have so many.

Things had started to look up for them all. She had Ethan. Ash and Cooper had taken a bit of getting used to, but now it seemed as if they had been together for ages. Dan was happier in himself now and, with all of their support, Sadie and Esther would be fine.

But the best thing to happen was that Riley had found a new confidence in herself. She'd always thought herself weak, but to get through everything life had thrown at her over the past few months she was obviously strong. With a great bunch of friends to watch her back, she was ready to bring Chandler's into a new era.

As well as that, over the past couple of weeks she'd been head-hunted by several larger companies. After seeing the social media campaign, the success of the competition and the way Riley had showcased the Designed by Frank tote bags (which had got him a lot of attention too), some had asked if she was interested in working in PR. It was something she had thought of, but for now she had declined.

From September, she was going back to college. Ethan had put the idea in her head. And, having recently got to know a lot of students through Marsha and Frank, it didn't matter that she was older than them. She would fit right in.

A couple of nights a week would get her a Fashion and Design diploma, and she had enrolled on a short OU social media and PR course too. Afterwards she could decide what she wanted to do next. Whether that would be staying in Hedworth or going further afield, she wasn't sure, but it would definitely be a move from Chandler's. Working there over the past few months had shown her what she was capable of, and what else might be out there for her if she took a chance. And hopefully, by then, the shop would be thriving.

But one thing was certain – her plans certainly involved the man standing beside her. She smiled at Ethan, who squeezed her hand in return.

Who knew where her shoes would take her next?

A LETTER FROM MARCIE

First of all, I want to say a huge thank you for choosing to read *The Second Chance Shoe Shop*. I hope you enjoyed my third outing to my fictional town of Hedworth, and getting to know Riley, Sadie and Dan as much as I did. This was a dream book to write – friendship, love and shoes, my favourite things!

If you did enjoy *The Second Chance Shoe Shop*, I would be forever grateful if you'd write a review. I'd love to hear what you think, and it can also help other readers discover one of my books for the first time. Or maybe you can recommend it to your friends and family…

Many thanks to anyone who has emailed me, messaged me, chatted to me on Facebook or Twitter and told me how much they have enjoyed reading my books. I've been genuinely blown away with all kinds of niceness and support from you all. A writer's job is often a lonely one but I feel I truly have friends everywhere.

You can sign up to receive an email whenever I have a new book out here:

www.bookouture.com/marcie-steele

Love, Mel Sherratt (Marcie) x

Keep in touch!

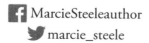

MarcieSteeleauthor

marcie_steele

A LETTER FROM THE AUTHOR

Ever since I can remember, I've been a meddler of words. Born and raised in Stoke-on-Trent, Staffordshire, I used the city as a backdrop for my first novel, *Taunting the Dead*, and it went on to be a Kindle number one bestseller. I couldn't believe my eyes when it became the overall number eight UK Kindle bestselling book of 2012.

Since then, my writing has come under a few different headings – grit-lit, sexy crime, whydunnit, police procedural, emotional thriller to name a few. I like writing about fear and emotion – the cause and effect of crime – what makes a character do something. Working as a housing officer for eight years gave me the background to create a fictional estate full of good and bad characters.

But I'm a romantic at heart and have always wanted to write about characters that are not necessarily involved in the darker side of life. Coffee, cakes and friends are three of my favourite things, hence writing under the name of Marcie Steele too. I can often be found sitting in my favourite coffee shop, sipping a cappuccino and eating a chocolate chip cookie, either catching up with friends or writing on my laptop.

Mel Sherratt (Marcie) x